SATAN'S REACH

Also by Eric Brown

NOVELS
The Serene Invasion
Helix Wars
Murder by the Book
The Devil's Nebula
The Kings of Eternity
Guardians of the Phoenix
Cosmopath
Xenopath
Necropath
Kéthani
Helix
New York Dreams
New York Blues
New York Nights
Penumbra
Engineman
Meridian Days

NOVELLAS
Starship Spring
Starship Winter
Gilbert and Edgar on Mars
Starship Fall
Revenge
Starship Summer
The Extraordinary Voyage of Jules Verne
Approaching Omega
A Writer's Life

COLLECTIONS
The Angels of Life and Death
Ghostwriting
Threshold Shift
The Fall of Tartarus
Deep Future
Parallax View (with Keith Brooke)
Blue Shifting
The Time-Lapsed Man

Eric
Brown

WEIRD SPACE

SATAN'S REACH

ABADDON
BOOKS

WWW.ABADDONBOOKS.COM

An Abaddon Books™ Publication
www.abaddonbooks.com
abaddon@rebellion.co.uk

First published in 2013 by Abaddon Books™,
Rebellion Intellectual Property Limited,
Riverside House, Osney Mead, Oxford, OX2 0ES, UK.

10 9 8 7 6 5 4 3 2

Editors: Jonathan Oliver & David Moore
Cover Art: Adam Tredowski
Design: Simon Parr & Sam Gretton
Marketing and PR: Michael Molcher
Creative Director and CEO: Jason Kingsley
Chief Technical Officer: Chris Kingsley
Weird Space™ created by Eric Brown

ISBN: 978-1-78108-131-0

Printed in the US

To Nick Throup and Kate Ryan

CHAPTER ONE

DEN HARPER HAD never before visited the world of Ajanta in the star cluster known as Satan's Reach – he'd heard so many horror stories that he'd decided to keep well away – but a commission to deliver a steamboat engine had proved too lucrative to turn down. He just hoped he wouldn't regret his decision.

He instructed his ship, the *Judi Hearne*, to phase from void-space and sat before the viewscreen as the grey swirl of the void was replaced by a resplendent starscape. At its centre rolled the jade-banded planet of Ajanta attended by its seven moons. 'By the Seven Moons of Ajanta' was a well-known space shanty. It told of how the colony ship *Forlorn Hope* crash-landed on the planet five centuries earlier, and how the colonists survived inimical conditions in the equatorial jungles only to fall victim to the planet's inhabitants. Now the two races lived alongside each other in macabre symbiosis.

Harper lay back in his sling and said, "The last verse again."

A soothing female voice sang, "*It's a harsh life 'neath the seven moons, in thrall to Ajantans and dhoor alike. / Visitors beware of their basilisk stare and the threat of the dhoorish spike...*"

The 'basilisk stare' referred to the gaze of the reptilian aliens, the Ajantans, who resembled tree frogs the size of ten year-old children. A 'dhoorish spike' was the drug to which the human population was addicted.

Harper had once met a star captain in a bar on Murchison's Landfall, with a terrifying tale to tell of a close shave on Ajanta. He'd come to trade machine parts for Ajantan fruits which were a delicacy across the Reach. "But a double-dealing merchant spiked my mash and that was me, bound for a tree-frog brothel."

"What saved you?"

"Only the fast thinking of my engineer. He slit the throat of the merchant and dragged me from the bar." The captain had shaken his head with retrospective dread. "If not for his actions I'd've been meat, and then dead meat, in an alien orgy."

"Dead meat...?" Harper echoed.

"The Ajantans take their pleasure with you when you're living, and then when you succumb to the poisons in their... secretions, let's say... you go into painful paralysis. This lasts a week, during which you still suffer the indignity of the aliens' lust. Then, mercifully, you expire. But, you see, there's a preservative in the Ajantan's jism that keeps you fresh for a month while they continue to take their pleasure. After that... well, the heat and humidity of the hell-hole has its way, and the Ajantans feed you to the bellyfish."

Harper had finished his drink and thanked the captain. "In which case I'll heed your words and steer well clear, sir."

Yet here he was, a year later, commanding his ship to spiraldown to the planet's only spaceport. It would be a quick transaction, he told himself – deliver the engine to the spaceport warehouse, fill in the requisite chits, receive his fee and take off. Six hours at most – and he'd never even leave the 'port.

And he'd be eight thousand units the richer, his average wage for six months. He'd reward his enterprise with a few weeks off, maybe even visit the sequestered atolls of Amahla.

He enjoyed the view as Ajanta swelled in the screen. It was a magnificent sight, with its ripped chiffon cloud cover ranging through varied shades of green. He tried not to dwell on the depravity concealed by the clouds and the plight of the human colonists enslaved by the Ajantans.

"Have you found images of the aliens yet?" he asked.

Judi replied, "The Ajantans proscribe the taking of images of themselves, Den. It is, they say, against their religion."

"They're religious?"

"Well, they hold certain primitive beliefs. They worships an apocryphal giant bellyfish – the Destroyer of Everything, they call it, which will consume their world and the entire universe at the end of time."

"And their morality, or lack of?"

"They are solipsistic. According to their beliefs, all living beings in the universe were created their inferior. Therefore, they can do as they wish with those they meet. If they dwelled within the jurisdiction of the Expansion, then the human authorities would decree their world out of bounds. But as they're in the core of Satan's Reach..."

The Expansion had no authority here, which made the Reach a haven for all manner of reprobates, ne'er-do-wells and free thinkers – and Den Harper himself, for that matter.

"But to answer your original question. I have managed to locate a single low quality 3D of an Ajantan. Here it is."

Harper leaned forward as the bottom quadrant of the screen showed a squat, bulbous creature with spindly limbs. He had expected the aliens to facially resemble terrestrial frogs or toads, but their faces were flattened and fish-like at the same time, with great glaucous eyes and mouths revealing two rows of spiked teeth.

"I've seen enough."

The image vanished. "The chances are," *Judi* said, "that you won't come across the natives. They do not frequent the 'port, but stay hidden in their underground jungle lairs."

"But they're a space-faring race?"

"Correct. They have inhabited three of their moons, and centuries ago made hostile forays on the neighbouring world of Pharray, where they subjugated the inhabitants and plundered the planet's minimal riches. They withdrew after a couple of decades, leaving a dead world behind them, and haven't ventured forth since."

"Let's hope it stays that way," Harper said. "Very well, I think a little music while we descend, and if you would care to sing..."

"An aria from Grenville's Fourth, perhaps?"

"Perfect."

He leaned back in his sling and closed his eyes. "And if I fall asleep, wake me when we land."

The music swelled around him, followed by the singer's sweet contralto.

He drifted off. He had only vague memories of his mother, singing in the house where they lived on the world of Denby. She had sold him to the Expansion shortly after he'd tested psi-positive at the age of four. Sixteen years later, when he'd graduated from college as a certified Grade I telepath, he'd taken the leave due to him and gone in search of his mother. He harboured little resentment towards her for selling him into what was effectively a life of servitude to the state – she'd no doubt had her pressing reasons, but he'd wanted to know those reasons.

He'd returned to Denby to find that she'd moved on. Following rumours and scant leads, he'd traced her last known whereabouts to the world of Ixxeria. For a month he trawled the records of the planet's major city and discovered that she'd worked as a singer in a bar in the sea port of Nova Cadiz. He'd found the bar and sat nervously in the shadows as three singers entertained the drinkers one by one. He'd left his ferronnière – the device that would amplify his tele-ability – back at the hotel, not wanting to intrude upon his mother's mind... if he should have the good fortune to find her. He would reserve the right to read her later, if she proved unforthcoming with her reasons for giving him up.

He reckoned she'd be in her fifties now, but the singers were all in their twenties. Later, drunk and downhearted, he'd approached one of the singers, introduced himself and asked her if she knew the whereabouts of one Salina Sanchez.

The look in the woman's eyes prepared him for disappointment – but not for the tragic tale that ensued. Salina, she reported, had passed away just one month earlier, beaten to death by a drunken punter.

Harper had kept his emotions in check – something he'd been well taught to do during his telepath's training – and did not enquire too closely about his mother's last profession. The reference to a 'punter' was ominous, and he preferred to think of his mother as a singer, an entertainer.

He'd asked the singer about his mother, and perhaps out of kindness the singer had painted a glowing picture of a kind-hearted soul, the life of the party, who would help anyone in times of trouble. She added, with a smile, that she had never forgotten about the son she'd sold to the Expansion.

"And she had other children?" Harper asked, thinking of possible brothers and sisters...

She shook her head. "You were her only child." And he had been unable to work out whether he should be thankful for that, or not.

She had excused herself, slipped through a door behind the stage, and emerged a minute later bearing a data-pin. She passed him the pin and said, "You might like this. A few years ago we recorded a jazz duo. Your mother is the contralto..."

"Do you have any pix?"

"I'm sorry, no. Only her voice..."

Harper had listened to the three songs on the pin, over and over, the pin becoming his most treasured possession. Five years ago, at the age of twenty-five, Harper absconded from his duties as a Grade I telepath. He would have fled anyway: the work had become too much, the pressure mentally crushing – privy to the private thoughts, the psychoses and neuroses, of criminals and psychopaths day after day – but then he'd been pushed into fleeing by an incident that still pained him, and which proved the barbarity of the ruling regime.

He'd snapped, plotted his escape, and a month later stole a small starship and lit out for the closest sector of space not under Expansion authority, Satan's Reach.

He'd had his ship's computer nexus synthesise the data-pin and create new songs – jazz, opera, and popular ballads, from his mother's voice. He even reprogrammed the ship's neutral male voice to sound like his mother's sweet, soothing contralto.

And it was this that lulled Harper to sleep as the ship spiralled down to the surface of Ajanta.

"WAKE UP, DEN. We're coming in to land."

He awoke from the usual dream: a bounty hunter had caught up with him, was raising a laser to his forehead and pressing the firing stud – dispensing the summary justice meted out to all absconding telepaths.

He awoke with a cry, sat up and worked to calm himself.

The ship was coming in low over darkened jungle. Ahead, a cluster of lights denoted the spaceport.

Beyond was a further sprawl of lights, the city of Kuper's End.

"Local time?" he asked.

"Just after seven in the evening."

"How long's a day last here?"

"Ajanta spins fast, Den. A day is a little under eighteen hours, with just ten hours of daylight, though daylight is a misnomer as the level of light rarely reaches that of terrestrial twilight. We're a long way from the sun."

Through the viewscreen Harper made out the red dwarf sun balanced just above the jungle horizon. It dropped like a red-hot coin as he watched, and minutes later was lost to sight.

Judi hovered above the 'port, its apron pocked with docking rings and cradle berths. He counted a dozen ships, small traders like his own and much larger transport liners. It was a quiet 'port, compared to many, which all things considered was not that surprising.

They landed with a cannonade of multiple concussions as the docking ring took hold and a dozen grabs made the ship stable.

"If you could establish a link with whoever's in charge of trade here, send them our details and request the transfer."

"Will do."

Six hours, at most, and then plain sailing all the way to Amahla...

He climbed from pilot's sling and stood before the viewscreen, staring out across the 'port. He made out a line of ornate buildings, constructed from what looked like timber. The terminal buildings had an ancient, down-at-heel appearance, and he wondered if this was indicative of the city beyond the perimeter.

Minutes later *Judi* said, "There is a problem, Den."

"Go on."

"The 'port has warehousing facilities, but the purchaser of the engine does not have an office in the terminal. So although we can authorise the unloading of the goods, the transaction can only be ratified – and the goods paid for – at his workplace."

"Don't tell me," Harper said. "That's in the city, right?"

"Correct."

Harper swore, then said, "Okay. Contact the merchant and see if he'll meet me at the terminal. I'm sure we can conduct business there."

"I will try, Den."

The minutes elapsed. A sliding scale at the foot of the viewscreen indicated that the temperature outside was in the nineties, with a humidity rating of fifty-nine. The old star captain's description of Ajanta as a sweltering hell-hole was no exaggeration.

"Den, the merchant refuses to come to the terminal building. He insists that all business must be conducted at his premises."

He had little option but to concede to the merchant's demands. "Very well then. If he's there now, I'll leave immediately."

"Krier Rasnic informs me that he will be at his desk until midnight."

"Inform the good Rasnic that I'll meet him at his office, but don't release the engine until you hear from me. I'll want his address and the directions."

He moved to his bed-chamber behind the bridge and slipped a velveteen case from a drawer. He withdrew the loop of his ferronnière, placing it around his head, and ducked to check the result in the mirror. The silver filament of the ferronnière showed through his curls. It might arouse comment, which he could do without. He opened a storage unit, selected a hat – a navy blue tricorne – and set it on his head at a jaunty angle, concealing the ferronnière.

He would only activate the amplification device in the company of the merchant, he decided, to ensure Rasnic's probity. The idea of opening his mind to the thoughts of the locals for a prolonged period did not appeal.

Two minutes later *Judi* relayed Rasnic's address and Harper stepped out into the sweltering heat of the Ajantan evening.

THE CITY OF Kuper's End was laid out on a grid pattern of narrow canals. He was surprised to find that not the slightest hint of modernity informed the architecture of the city. He'd seen pictures of cities on mediaeval Earth, of crooked timber buildings crowding over narrow streets like a convocation of ruffians up to no good, but he'd never expected to experience their like in reality. He felt as if he were walking through a museum, and this in turn gave him the idea that the people bustling through the many night-markets and over the humpback bridges that spanned the canals were no more than hired extras. This impression was heightened by the bizarre nature of their attire. The men wore dour blousons and puffed leggings, the women long skirts and layered top-coats. They spoke the *lingua franca* of the Reach – a corrupted form of Anglais – with broad, rustic accents. He listened to the cries of street-hawkers and stall-holders, and wondered at first if the language was indeed his own. Only when his hearing accustomed itself to the extended, fruity vowels did he make sense of the sounds: "Fine bellyfish fresh from the drink!" sang one ancient crone, while another waved a fistful of black berries at him and cried, "Nightfruit, ten francs a dozen!"

He was further surprised by the nature of the illumination above the market stalls. At first he thought the balls of light floating above his head were ingeniously lighted balloons, until he stopped directly beneath one and looked up. It was tethered by a length of string to the awning of a stall, but that was its only similarity to a balloon. The light was a living creature, a bloated insect whose abdomen pulsed a steady sulphurous glow.

He walked on, his way lighted by these bizarre entomological illuminations.

The claustrophobic nature of the city, with its crowded streets, narrow alleys and squashed bridges, was exaggerated by the proximity of the crowding jungle which pressed in on all sides. The animal calls that issued from the surrounding darkness only served to befuddle his already confused senses; it didn't help that he was unable to identify the nature of the beasts responsible for the cacophony of shrill howls, moans and guttural roars that competed with the more mercantile cries of the stallholders.

At least, he thought as he hurried over an arched bridge, he had yet to bump into a native of the planet.

He followed *Judi's* directions and found himself on a broad boulevard that ran between a canal and a higgledy-piggledy line of timber dwellings behind which loomed the inky jungle. This was Spinner's Way, and in the third building along the street was housed the venerable company of Rasnic, Rasnic and Gotfried, General Merchants.

And yet the third house along the row appeared to be a public hostelry, not a merchant's shop. The carousing clientele had spilled from the building and stood in noisy knots, enjoying flagons of ale in the humid evening air. Harper looked right and left, thinking he'd mistaken *Judi's* directions, but the premises on either side of the inn were shuttered and in darkness.

There was little else for it but to enquire within.

Enduring the curious stares of the locals, he pushed through the crowd and stepped into the warped timber interior of the inn which was named – he read on a sign above the door –The Rat and Corpse.

He had expected the interior to be a facsimile of the scene outside – rowdy quaffing accompanied by much noise. He was surprised to find himself in a plush, timber-panelled public bar occupied by sedate, seated drinkers, of both sexes, intent on a small stage situated at the far end of the long room.

He approached the bar and asked a small, dumpling-shaped woman the whereabouts of the premises of Rasnic, Rasnic and Gotfried. The barmaid screwed her face into an expression of mystification and made him repeat his request. His words, enunciated this time with exaggerated care, elicited a look of enlightenment. She pointed over his shoulder and said something incomprehensible.

He looked behind him, expecting to see an exit leading to an alley or some such, but instead saw only a wall of timber drinking booths.

"I'm sorry," he said to the woman.

"Krier Rasnic, yes! There be 'is office. Here till midnight, every night he be. Take a seat."

"Ah..." Harper said, staring at the indicated booth. "But I don't see Rasnic..."

"He'll be makin' room for more," said the woman. "Take a seat, and no doubt it's a jar you'll be wantin'?"

She pulled him a flagon of foul-smelling ale, and when he proffered his data-pin she stared at it with disgust. "Cash here. None of your fancy pins, m'boy. But fret not, I'll put it on Rasnic's slate and he'll add the cost to his bill."

Nodding his thanks, Harper carried his flagon to the booth and sat down.

The ale tasted as noxious as its odour promised. He glanced at an open door marked 'Gents', but of Rasnic there was no sign.

At the far end of the room, four members of a pipe band stepped onto the stage, and a murmur of appreciation passed around the room. Seconds later a slim, dark-skinned woman of uncommon beauty took centre stage to a patter of muted applause.

She stood upright, her face downcast, and remained like this while the pipers began a sad refrain. The reedy notes twisted and twined, producing a tune that suggested melancholy and grief. The tempo increased, became upbeat, and the woman began ever so slightly to tap her foot, then to sway sinuously to the rhythm.

Harper watched, quite captivated.

He judged that the woman was perhaps ten years younger than himself, perhaps twenty, with a midnight cataract of jet black hair, a thin black face and huge obsidian eyes. Her face appeared so singular as to be almost alien, and Harper did indeed wonder if she were human. She swayed back and forth, lost in a transport of identification with the mellifluous strains, and a minute later began to sing.

Her voice was high and fluid, and trilled a tale of loss and lament, though Harper was quite unable to make out a single word. If she were singing in Anglais, then it was in a dialect so corrupted as to be incomprehensible. Then again it might have been a foreign language.

Her song came to an end, but the music continued; the audience applauded, and Harper clapped in appreciation. The woman's dark eyes scanned the drinkers, saw him and seemed to linger before passing on, and he wondered if his off-worlder's apparel had caught her attention.

Perhaps, many years ago, his mother had enjoyed appreciative audiences like this one.

"Eye not the bitch, for she be promised."

Startled, Harper looked up. "Excuse me?"

The fat stranger belched. "The bitch be promised and she's as good as meat already," he said.

Harper shrank back, hoping that the drunkard would pass by, but to his surprise the man slumped into the opposite seat and said, "You be 'Arper, no doubt?" He frowned at the untouched flagon and went on, "And Aggy foisted a jar of wash on you, for shame. Aggy!" he yelled to the bar. "Two jars of Finest and no scant measures!"

"Why, thank you," Harper said. He reached out a hand. "I take it I have the pleasure of addressing Krier Rasnic?"

They shook. "And no other," Rasnic said with a belch. He was in his fifties, squat and exceedingly ugly, with a bald bullet of a head, his face a playground of pustules and warts. His eyes, however, belied his general air of drunken dishevelment. They were brilliant blue and piercing.

Harper looked around him. "Rather unique office, if I may say?"

"You may. Been said before by off-worlders, but what do they know? Papers?"

"Ah..." Harper held up his data-pin, and Rasnic almost spat at the sight of it.

"No, no, no... At the warehouse, when you off-loaded the goods. They should've given you the papers for me to..." He waved a hand, interrupted by Aggy bearing two flagons of ale which smelled as unpleasant as the first.

Harper sipped. The pungent brew tasted only marginally less vile than the first. He smiled politely and said, "The engine is still aboard my ship. I intend to release it only when I've been paid."

"But how do I know that the goods are in order? Answer me that." Rasnic pointed at Harper's pin. "That might contain nothing but lies. For all I know your engine might be no more than an empty box!"

Harper smiled again and began to reassure Rasnic, but the other waved his reassurances away.

Harper reached under his tricorne, ostensibly to scratch his head, and activated his ferronnière. A brief scan of Rasnic's addled sensorium would ensure him that the merchant was attempting no duplicity.

He slid the switch and suddenly the room around him blazed with the actinic flare of mind-noise. He read murder in the mind of a nearby man, grief and despair in another. A thousand emotions swirled in an incoherent maelstrom that Harper struggled, with depressing familiarity, to modulate. He concentrated, focussed, and directed a probe across the table.

But where Rasnic's mind should have blazed there was nothing but an opaque blankness, an emptiness. Harper's probe slid off and around the lacuna where the merchant's mind should have been... and his alarm intensified.

It could only mean one thing. Krier Rasnic was shielded, and if Harper had learned one thing in his years as a star trader, it was not to trust a shielded merchant.

He attempted to present an unruffled exterior while his mind raced with a dozen malign possibilities.

"Nothing for it," Rasnic said, "but I'll have to go to the 'port and check myself." His shrewd gaze pierced Harper. "Put me to a lot of trouble, young man."

"On that score, my apologies. But the 'port is only five minutes away. I'll come with you and we can conclude business there, and then I'll be away."

Harper made to stand, but Rasnic reached across the table and laid a meaty hand on his shoulder. "Stay put. Finish your Finest. I'll be back before you know it, and anyway I have to collect some paperwork on the way. And the ten thousand – I don't carry that amount around with me, of course."

"It's no trouble, I assure you." Harper had no desire to spend a minute more in the bar than was absolutely necessary.

But again Rasnic pressed down with his weightlifter's hand, halting Harper's ascent.

"Stay, I say, and I'll be back. Finish the Finest, it's on my tab, and be grateful."

"In that case I will notify my ship to allow you to enter the hold."

Rasnic pushed himself to his feet and staggered towards the exit. Harper thought of the ten thousand, and the holiday he would spend on the atoll. He'd brought the engine for less than two thousand units a month ago... If only all his transactions were this profitable.

He reached under his hat and deactivated the ferronnière, and the mind-noise that swelled in his head was no more. The sudden silence was a balm.

He activated his wrist-com and seconds later got through to *Judi*. "There have been developments," he said, and reported his meeting with Rasnic. "The merchant is on his way. Open the hold and monitor him while he inspects the engine."

"You suspect the motives of this Krier Rasnic?"

"I'm not sure. But it's best to proceed with extreme caution."

"Understood," *Judi* said, and cut the connection.

Harper lifted his flagon and took a sip. He decided that the brew was a taste one could come to acquire – and the singer on the stage was a sight to please the finest sensibility.

She was giving voice to another soulful lament, and Harper fell to wondering if he'd heard Krier Rasnic correctly. The woman was promised, and was good as meat? Given what he knew of this planet and its natives, Harper feared the worst.

The woman finished her song to a patter of polite applause. Harper raised his hands, clapped in appreciation, and hoped to catch her eye again. She murmured something to the audience, which he didn't catch, and the band filed off for what he guessed would be a short intermission.

The woman stepped from the stage and, to Harper's surprise, made her way across the room towards where he was sitting.

He took another, longer swallow of ale, realised that he'd consumed half the flagon, and watched the woman as she paused before him and gave a shy half-smile.

He considered activating his ferronnière again, but elected not to. He would wait until she had declared her interest, and only then would he consider reading her to learn whether her words matched her intent.

"If I might be seated, sir," she murmured, indicating the bench just vacated by Rasnic.

"Please, be my guest."

He watched her lower herself to the seat with sinuous grace, and he revised his estimate of her age. He had judged her to be ten years his junior – but realised now that he was mistaken. She was much younger than twenty. He had taken her stage presence, her elegance, as denoting maturity, but seated timidly before him, eyes downcast, she could not have been more than sixteen standard years old.

He took another swig of ale. Unaccustomed to alcohol, he felt light-headed and tipsy.

"I take it you're not local," he said.

Her eyes lifted quickly to regard him. "You are observant," she said with playful sarcasm. "Ajantans are as white as canal whelks." She laid a hand on the table-top beside his. Next to his coppery skin, hers was almost black. "My parents came to Ajanta a dozen years ago, when I was a child, and I *hate* it here," she said with venom.

"Then why don't you leave?"

"If actions were as easy as words! You are an off-worlder. You don't understand Ajanta and its ways."

"The man I met here tonight, one Krier Rasnic, he told me that you were... promised. What did he mean by that?"

She regarded him, and said at last, "My parents died five years ago, succumbing to the dhoor. As off-worlders, they did not have the locals' resistance to the drug."

"Then why did they take it?" he asked, realising as he did so that it was probably a silly question. Her expression confirmed this.

"It was not a choice they could make, sir. Everyone on Ajanta takes dhoor, in one form or another. It's in the water, in the very air we breathe. It makes us... compliant."

"Compliant... to the Ajantans?"

Her eyes downcast, she went on, "My parents were poor refugees from Kallasta. They had funds to take them only so far, and it was bad luck indeed that they fetched up here. And bad luck again that in their penury they found themselves beholden to an Ajantan hive-master. They were given board and lodging in return for their... services."

Harper murmured, "I'm sorry."

The girl looked up and said bravely, "And when they finally succumbed to dhoor, they still had not paid off their debt. And so I became, in effect, a chattel of the Ajantan hive-master."

She is promised... Krier Rasnic had said.

It was on the tip of his tongue to say, "I'm sorry," again, but stopped himself just in time.

"The Ajantan hive owns me. I am their property, by all the laws of the planet."

He could not meet her eyes. His senses swam with the effect of the ale and her tragic story. He found himself saying, "You sing beautifully."

She gave a quick laugh, more of a snort. "It is my only relief, sir. I sing in Kallastanian, and fortunately the Ajantans do not understand a word. I sing of my plight, my fate, the evil of the green men, the stupor of the humans here. The fools who come to listen to me applaud and throw me coins, but little do they know that I am mocking them."

She is promised, Rasnic had said, *and she's as good as meat already...*

"Once," she went on, "a stranger came to the bar, an off-worlder. He understood Kallastanian, understood my songs and my plight. I begged him to take me away from here..."

"But?"

"But he was too fearful of Ajantan reprisals. The natives are a bellicose lot, and very possessive. They do not take lightly to having their goods stolen. Also, he claimed that it would be impossible to get me through customs."

"He was probably right."

"At the time, yes," she said, "but not so now."

"And why is that?"

"Because," she said, "I have obtained the necessary data, a new identity, bought at great cost from a star trader whose valour stretched only so far as to furnish me with the pin. He refused adamantly to take me off-world, citing the wrath of the green men."

"You find yourself in an intolerable position," Harper said.

"I am promised to the hive, but there is another term for my kind: Living Meat. Within the year – which is short here on Ajanta – the green men will take me to their subterranean lair and... use me."

He laid a quick hand on hers to stop her words.

"Within the year," he murmured. Six standard months...

She smiled sadly. "So do you comprehend my plight, sir? Do you understand my need to be away from here?"

He stared at her. A thought had occurred to him. Krier Rasnic's sudden going, the girl's approach and sad story... Might they be in collusion, working not only to rob him of his ship and all it contained, but to sell his body to the green men too?

As she stared at the table top, idly tracing patterns in the condensation with a graceful forefinger, Harper slid his hand under his tricorne and scratched his head, at the same time activating his ferronnière.

The content of her mind leapt at him and he reeled back in his seat, stunned. He quickly deactivated the ferronnière and slumped, breathing with relief.

"Sir?" the girl enquired, touching his hand.

"The drink," he said. "I'm not used to such strong ale."

"Be wary of drinking too much, sir. If you were to stagger from here and fall into the canal, you would end up as a meal for the bellyfish, or worse."

He stared at her, pained by the emotional tsunami of her young mind; her fear at her fate, her hatred of the green men – and her desperate hope.

Her name was Zeela Antarivo, and she was barely eighteen and would not live to see her next birthday, and she yearned to live, to see the stars, to be away from this putrid world.

At the far end of the room the musicians were returning to the stage. One of them called out to Zeela, and she stared at Harper with a look of desperation.

She made to rise. "I am sorry if I have disturbed your evening, sir. I will trouble you no more."

He grabbed her wrist, halting her departure. "I will be finished with my business here before midnight. When I leave, follow me back to the 'port. Do you have possessions?"

Her eyes were wide, filled with desperate hope. "Nothing that I couldn't live without, sir."

"But you have your identity pin?"

"With me all the time!"

"Then follow me to the 'port. We will meet outside and pass through customs together."

"I... I don't know what to say."

"Say nothing. Go, Zeela, complete your final session on Ajanta and I'll see you at the 'port."

Her eyes widened still further as he said her name, and then she turned quickly and hurried to the stage.

Was it Harper's imagination, or did the songs she sang for the next half hour seem less melancholy than those he'd heard earlier? Certainly she smiled from time to time, and when her glance lighted on him her eyes seemed to glow with gratitude.

He drained his ale and wondered whether it was the drink that had encouraged his decision to save the girl. Undoubtedly he felt inebriated, but he hoped he would have acted as he had without the Dutch courage of alcohol.

He was so intent on Zeela that he failed to notice the approach of Krier Rasnic until the merchant clapped him on the shoulder. "And just in time, I see," Rasnic cried, slamming down a further two flagons and sliding onto the bench opposite Harper.

"All in order?" he asked.

Rasnic took a long pull on his ale, belched, and declared, "A fine engine, 'Arper, and no doubting that. And you have a wily woman aboard the ship, though she wasn't showing herself."

Harper tried not to smile. "Wily?"

"The sweet-tongued bitch wouldn't let me take the engine from the hold... and me just wanting to warehouse it at the 'port!"

"You have the papers, and the money?"

"Now curb your impatience, young sir. First we drink to the deal, in the age old Ajantan tradition. No agreements can be sealed without the consumption of Finest!"

Reluctantly Harper raised his flagon and drank. The ale slipped down, not at all unpleasantly, and he found himself in good cheer. Soon he would be eight thousand units richer and the saviour of a beautiful girl...

His mother, he thought, would be proud.

Rasnic pulled a scroll of crumpled parchment from his jacket and slapped it down before Harper. The merchant provided a stylus, too, and Harper found himself appending his signature to a dozen official forms, smiling at the novelty of this old-fashioned custom.

Five minutes later, with all the forms completed, Rasnic drew a bulging wallet from an inside pocket and slapped down a wad of notes on the tabletop.

Harper said, "Local scrip? You have no Reach currency?"

"The agreement was ten thousand units, 'Arper, and no mention of what scrip!" Rasnic growled.

Sighing, Harper made a great show of counting through the notes. He would get the currency changed before he left the planet, no doubt at a punitive rate of exchange.

"And now drink up," Rasnic cried, "and I'll stand another round!"

Harper regarded the dregs of his flagon. The idea of downing the last muddy inch of ale did not appeal, still less of drinking another full measure. He was beginning to feel ill, and when he looked around the room – attempting to focus on Zeela, a tiny distant figure on the stage – the images swirled like the tesserae in a kaleidoscope.

He spluttered a protest and attempted to stand up. His legs were suddenly imbued with the property of over-cooked spaghetti. He sat back down quickly and the motion forced bile into his throat.

Rasnic's vast face, hideous with its population of warts, swirled grinning before him.

"I think I should be going," Harper managed, swaying in his seat.

Rasnic reached a massive hand across the table and cupped Harper's cheek with mock solemnity. "Taken against Ajanta's Finest, have we?" he chuckled. "Or perhaps it was the dhoor?"

Harper groaned, tried to protest, then slumped head first across the table, unconscious.

CHAPTER TWO

HE WOKE TO darkness.

No – not absolute darkness. He lay on his back and stared up at a light, the distended, glowing abdomen of a tethered insect. He tried to move, and groaned in pain. His head throbbed, either from the ale or the dhoor, and he seemed to be paralysed into the bargain.

He managed to move his head back and forth, enough to take in his surroundings. He was aboard a barge puttering along a canal. They had left the city in their wake and dark jungle loomed on either side. The illuminated insect, tied to the barge's gunwale, cast an eerie glow across the vessel and its cargo. The only sound was the rhythmic popping of the boat's engine.

He was in a cage, a rectangular construction made from what looked like bamboo bars, and he was not alone. He was packed tight between two other prisoners, and made out perhaps twenty further unconscious humans piled across the deck. They had evidently been tossed on top of each other with scant concern for their welfare. He was fortunate indeed that he was not buried at the bottom of the pile. He tried to squirm into a more comfortable position, and in doing so felt a body beneath him. The man swore softly, like someone disturbed in their sleep.

Harper felt a stab of panic. He cursed himself for a fool, and Rasnic for a bloody, conscienceless murderer. Not that he would gain anything by blaming the merchant. He should have suspected something when he discovered that Rasnic was shielded, and left the inn then – or refused all offers of ale, at least.

He moved his right arm and found that the Ajantan scrip was no longer in his jacket pocket. Also his data-pin was missing. He reached up to find his tricorne gone, but his ferronnière, thankfully, was still lodged in his tangled curls. He dragged the band from his head and stuffed it into his trouser pocket. He tried to move his left arm, only to find that it was gripped by paralysis. He reached over with his right hand to check that he still had his wrist-com, and then discovered why his left arm seemed to be paralysed. It was trapped painfully between his neighbour – a foul-smelling old woman – and the body beneath her. He tried to tug it free but lacked the energy. He collapsed back onto the body beneath him and tried not to give in to despair.

He turned his head and squinted along the length of the barge. A squat figure sat cross-legged on the point of the prow, and he realised with a jolt of shock that the creature was a native alien. It sat with its bowed back to him, its head hidden from sight, and appeared to be staring down into the water cleaved by the barge's prow.

Harper looked to the rear of the boat, expecting to see further aliens. There was no sign of any more green men, as Zeela had called them... and he felt a sudden surge of hope. If he could free himself, summon the energy to make his way forward and attack the Ajantan...

But with what? The aliens were fleet and lithe, according to the starship captain he'd spoken to on Murchison's Landfall, and possessed a fearsome set of barbed teeth which they used to good effect.

He wondered where the barge was heading, and how long it might take to reach its destination. What had Zeela said about the Ajantans' subterranean lair?

Zeela... he wondered if she were at the spaceport now, waiting for him. Or... had she seen his collapse in The Rat and Corpse, and Rasnic carry him from the premises?

On any civilised world he might have expected Zeela to have summoned the judiciary, but he was on Ajanta now. No human police force kept order here; it was a lawless world governed by the inscrutable edicts of the green men. Humans were here on penance, the descendants of the starship crash five centuries ago, and as such knew no better.

He tried again to tug his arm from under the obese crone, and gave up seconds later when the cartilage of his shoulder threatened to snap.

Unbidden he recalled the images he'd gleaned from Zeela when he'd briefly accessed her thoughts. He vicariously shared her horror of what, one day, would happen to her. He could not shut out her fear, or the attendant images: a slithering mass of green Ajantans taking their pleasure with comatose humans. The vision made him retch.

He recalled the words of the old space captain. *"The Ajantans take their pleasure with you when you're living, and then when you succumb to the poisons in their... secretions, let's say... you go into painful paralysis. This lasts up to a week, during which you still suffer the indignity of the aliens' lust. Then, mercifully, you expire. But, you see, there's a preservative in the Ajantan's jism that keeps you fresh for a month while they continue to take their pleasure..."*

A hot wave of nausea rose from his midriff. He tried to vomit but evidently he'd emptied his stomach earlier. He closed his eyes and drifted into unconsciousness, smiling at the thought of the atolls of Amahla.

A sound brought him to his senses.

He turned his head with difficulty and stared through the bars behind him. Something splashed in the water. A bellyfish, perhaps, anticipating an early feast of human corpses.

The canal appeared calm, but he made out a slim shape just beneath the surface, swimming towards the gunwale. It rose from the water beside the boat in a sleek cascade.

He almost cried out in alarmed surprise, but Zeela gripped the bars beside his head and, with her free hand, pressed a finger to her lips. "Shhh!" she whispered. "We are one kilometre from the caves where the Ajantans will unload you. We must work fast."

"Fine, but..."

She gripped the bars with both hands, her pointed chin just above the surface of the water. "Under no circumstances," she warned, "attempt to overcome the green man. They are ferocious and he would kill you in seconds."

"I had no intention of attacking it," he said.

"Are you still drugged? Can you move?"

"A little," he hissed. "But I feel..." It seemed weak to admit to feeling sick, so he held his tongue.

Zeela removed a hand from the bar, slipping it beneath the material of her dress. "Chew this," she said.

She passed what looked like a twig into the cage. He took it with his free hand. "Chew?"

"It will counter the effects of the dhoor and give you energy."

He took a bite and tasted liquorice, or something similar. He chewed, then swallowed the resultant saliva, and within seconds his nausea abated.

Zeela said, "The bars are flimsy. They can easily be prised apart. The Ajantans expect none of their drugged cargo to try to escape."

"There is just one slight problem," he whispered. "My left arm is lodged tight beneath..." He indicated the bloated human to his left. He tugged on his arm to illustrate his plight.

Zeela twisted her mouth in a frown, assessing the situation, then quickly reached through the bars.

Her hand found the woman's face and covered her nose and mouth. Seconds later the crone spluttered, thrashing as she fought for breath.

Zeela flashed him an imperative look. He took the hint and, as the woman struggled, he reached out with his free hand and attempted to push at the doughy bulk, at the same time pulling his left arm.

It came free suddenly, robbed of all feeling from being crushed for hours. Seconds later he felt the painful, tingling sensation of pins and needles. He rubbed his arm vigorously, attempting to massage life back into the useless limb.

Zeela lost no time and set to forcing the bars apart. Ahead, the Ajantan's attention was still on the water. Harper slipped his shoulders through the gap, and Zeela took his arm and eased him head first into the tepid water. He slipped the rest of the way with a splash, submerged, and came up seconds later trying not to splutter.

He trod water and glanced at the barge. It was sailing slowly away, engine puttering. He made for the bank, swimming in Zeela's wake.

He was allowing himself to feel the first flutterings of relief when, as he pulled himself from the water, he heard a cry from the boat.

He turned in time to see the Ajantan leap to its feet and aim a weapon. A bolus of fire leapt from the rifle's splayed muzzle and burst against a tree beside Harper's head.

Zeela gripped his wrist. "Run!"

Then he was stumbling at speed through the jungle, the night rent with the fluting cries of the alien and the accompanying blast of its incendiary weapon. Behind them the jungle blazed.

There were no incandescent insects here to light their way, just the glow of the fire which grew fainter as they ran. Soon they were crashing through pitch black jungle. He felt vines and tendrils whip and slash at his face and arms and found his ankles clutched by barbed undergrowth.

"Do you know..." he panted, "exactly where we're heading?"

"Approximately," she shouted, "to the spaceport."

"How far?"

"Again, approximately, ten kilometres."

He ran on, considering their plight. A minute later he glanced over his shoulder. There was no sign of the pursuing Ajantan. The fire was faint, a distant glow in the darkness.

"Okay," he gasped, "slow down. I have an idea."

She came to a sudden halt, still gripping his wrist, and he almost barrelled into her. He heard her breathing a matter of inches from his face. "Yes?" she asked.

"A better... better idea than trying to make for the 'port through... through all this," he panted. "I can summon the ship to me."

"You can? Then do it!"

He slumped to the jungle floor and heard Zeela squat beside him. He fingered his wrist-com in the absolute darkness and cursed the jungle canopy. Where was the light of just one of the planet's seven moons when it was needed?

He activated his com and got through to *Judi*.

"A slight change of plan," he said. "Get a bearing on my current position."

"You are eleven point two kilometres south west of the 'port. I judge that you are in the jungle, but surely that is incorrect?"

"Think again, *Judi*. That's just where I am. I'll fill you in later. Now, I want you to leave the 'port and make for my position, understood?"

"Affirmative."

"The landing might be rough, but no matter. And come down twenty metres north of where I am, or you'll fry us."

"Understood. I'm on my way."

He cut the connection. Zeela's gripped tightened on his wrist. "Your co-pilot?"

"Something like that."

"And now?"

"We sit tight until she gets here."

Her fingers bit into his arm as if she were afraid of letting him go.

He said, "Thank you for saving my life."

"And thank you for agreeing to take me away from here."

He smiled in the darkness. "That makes us even, doesn't it? Always assuming we *do* get away from here."

He listened for sounds of pursuit, but heard only anonymous animal noises near and far: low moans and high piccolo notes, then something booming deafeningly not too far away.

"How long will your ship take to reach us?" Zeela asked.

"There are various procedures to go through with the 'port authorities. They should take five minutes, no more. After that... *Judi* should take only a matter of minutes to find us. So perhaps in another ten, fifteen minutes at most."

She leaned against him in the darkness. He was aware of her odour, a sweet scent combined with sweat. She murmured, "I still find it impossible to imagine a life away from Ajanta. I fear a last minute tragedy, the green men finding us or your ship not being allowed to leave."

He smiled. "There is no risk of the latter. I booked the 'port berth for a temporary stopover. The ship's leaving now will arouse no comment."

"And then?"

"And then we will phase into the void and never look back."

"Bound for...?"

"I had been thinking of a holiday on the atolls of Amahla, before Rasnic robbed me."

"Maybe you will be able to go there, after all," she said.

He stared at where he thought her face should be. His vision had adjusted to the darkness, but even so he could make out only the vague outline of her oval face. "Meaning?"

She gripped his arm suddenly. "Shhh! Listen. I thought I heard..."

He tensed, listening.

"There!" she hissed. "That long, high note. There are more than just one of them. They are combing the jungle, and heading this way. Oh, I knew it was too good to be true!"

Among the cacophony of other animal noises – which sounded like an undisciplined orchestra tuning up – he made out long fluting sounds coming from the direction they had fled.

Zeela bounded to her feet, dragging Harper with her. "This way!" she cried, and was off.

They ran side by side, Zeela still clutching his wrist. The heat was oppressive, the humidity murderous.

Harper dragged in lungfuls of fetid air. He wondered if the Ajantans' hearing was acute. Certainly he and Zeela were making enough noise, as they thrashed through the undergrowth, to alert any but the most stone deaf of pursuers.

As if to abet their chances of capture the canopy high overhead became patchy and two sailing moons sent long silver searchlights probing down into the jungle. Harper saw grotesque shapes to right and left, growths more like tumours or goitres than anything arboreal. It was a nightmare landscape, and it seemed entirely appropriate that they were fleeing for their lives from aliens bent on eventual murder – once they had had their fun.

He shut out that thought and concentrated on running.

At least *Judi* would be monitoring his progress and would intervene in due course – but how long might that be? He'd lost all sense of time. He seemed to have been running for ten minutes or more, or did it just seem that long because the aliens were giving chase?

He heard a roar, and his heart leapt with elation. The braking jets of his ship's auxiliary engines... He must have exclaimed aloud, as Zeela hissed at him, "What?"

"I heard my ship. It can't be far away now."

"Your ship?" Zeela cried. "No – the green men's fire-guns, more like."

The sound came again, and he knew that the girl was right. He looked over his shoulder. The jungle bloomed as the goitrous growths burned like phantasmagorical candles. He saw a dozen tiny figures swarming in pursuit, perhaps a hundred metres away. One fired again, and a couple of metres to Zeela's right a tree trunk exploded like a defective firework. Sparks and timber shrapnel peppered his head and chest.

Zeela yelped and dragged him around the burning tree. She pulled him to the right, and he saw her reasoning. Behind them the tree was billowing smoke which concealed their flight from the chasing aliens.

He wondered whether it was too soon to hope that they might escape with their lives.

Zeela jinked again, using the cover of the smoke to take off on a trajectory almost at right angles to their original flight. Harper looked over his shoulder but saw no sign of the Ajantans or evidence of their fire-guns.

He activated his wrist-com and yelled, "Where the hell are you, *Judi*?"

"Five hundred metres from your current position, Den. Veer to your left and keep going. I estimate landing within thirty seconds."

His heart kicked. Zeela was pulling him to the left, through whipping vines. She had relaxed her grip on his arm now that salvation was almost in sight.

Brightness bloomed before them, and Zeela stopped suddenly with a scream. From the jungle ahead, three squat Ajantans appeared and levelled their weapons. Harper turned in panic and saw a further six aliens step from the jungle.

Zeela was in his arms now, sobbing. Over her shoulder he saw a small Ajantan step forward and raise a weapon, this one unlike the other fire-guns. The tree frog depressed the firing stud, and Zeela spasmed in pain and screamed. Harper looked down and saw the flight of a dart embedded in the small of her back.

He felt something stab his right bicep and seconds later released his hold on Zeela and slumped to the jungle floor.

HE CAME AWAKE suddenly, and his first thought was for Zeela. He must have murmured her name. She replied, "I'm here."

He turned sluggishly, the alien drug retarding his movements. The girl was lying a metre away. He reached out a hand and she gripped it.

"Where are we?"

She smiled at him with infinite sadness. "In the Ajantans' underground lair."

"Ah..."

He blinked and his eyes adjusted to the gloom. Ten metres away was a glowing insect, its light illuminating a small cavern. Here and there in the concave rock wall were dark patches which he guessed must be exits. As his vision adjusted to the half-light he made out perhaps twenty human figures lying around the cavern. Immediately to his left was his old friend, the adipose crone.

He sat up, massaging his shoulder where the dart had impacted. "We've got to–"

Zeela said, "They have armed guards on all the tunnels leading from here. Earlier I tried to find a way out."

He touched his left arm, alarmed. His wrist-com was missing.

"What?" Zeela asked.

He told her.

She squeezed his hand. "I knew it would end like this."

He shook her. "It hasn't ended, just yet. The Ajantans' are small. I could easily overcome..."

"They guard the tunnels in groups of three. And they are armed. You wouldn't stand a chance."

They fell silent, each staring at the mossy floor. At least there was no sign, yet, of their tormentors. That horror was to come.

A few minutes later Zeela said in a small voice, "And I thought I was doing the right thing when I followed Rasnic from The Rat and Corpse."

He smiled. "You were. You were very brave."

She smiled in return. "I kept to the shadows and followed him to the Ajantan quarter. He had you on his back. Your hat fell off... I considered stopping to pick it up, but feared he'd get away. From a distance I saw him bartering with the Ajantan bargee. Money changed hands, but not before Rasnic went through your pockets and stole the notes he had given you, and something else."

"My data-pin."

"Then he dumped you in the barge and walked away, whistling at a job well done."

"I wonder if that was his motive all along? He lured me to Ajanta with the spurious order of a steamboat engine, but meant to sell me to the green men?"

"Of course. And once you were as good as dead he'd steal your starship and whatever goods he'd ordered. It is a well known fact that Rasnic bribes the 'port officials."

"Oh, how I'd like to get even with him, one day."

"That's what I thought," Zeela said, "so I followed him."

He stared at her. "You what?"

"I followed him. The barge was not due to set off until midnight, and anyway it travels so slowly that I'd catch it up in no time. I followed him to his house on Pie-Maker Row. He was still drunk, weaving this way and that, and as he passed into the shadows between glowbugs I seized my opportunity. I tripped the ape and he fell like a dead man, and before he could stop me I went through his pockets."

She reached into a pouch in her dress and came out with a bundle of soggy notes. She passed them to Harper, and he took them with a smile. "I applaud your resourcefulness, Zeela. I don't know what to say."

"They're a little wet, but I thought they'd dry out. Oh, and this..." she went on, withdrawing his data-pin and passing it to him. "Not that it will be of any use, now."

He held the pin up before his eyes, then smiled at the girl. "You are," he said, "a marvel."

She blinked. "I am?"

"Look at it," he said. "An effective weapon, no? A sharp needle as long as my hand... I'm sure I could surprise an Ajantan or two when they show themselves."

She smiled, and he thought her expression was almost one of pity.

He looked up as something moved at the far end of the chamber. Three bobbing Ajantans entered and crossed to the closest comatose human. Two of the creatures stooped and gripped an old man's arms and legs while the third, weapon poised, passed a gaze around the cavern.

If I acted now, Harper thought... But the trio was too far away. The armed guard would fire long before Harper closed the distance. But perhaps if he positioned himself closer to the exit, beside the humans, and played dead until the aliens returned for their next victim...

"They're taking them to what they call their pleasure chamber," Zeela whispered, "a vast cavern many times the size of this one, further underground. Perhaps if we move to the back of the chamber..."

"I was thinking the exact opposite," he said, and explained his reasoning. "Stay here while I..."

Her eyes flared with anger. "I will come with you!"

He climbed unsteadily to his feet. He was aware of the beating of his heart as he crossed the chamber to where half a dozen men and women, in various stages of torpor, lay side by side.

He positioned himself next to the opening and sat down against the rock, Zeela folding herself beside him.

Minutes passed. Harper willed the green men to show themselves. He wanted to be active, anything but this passive dwelling on what might happen if his plan of action failed.

"One thing..." Zeela said.

"Yes?"

She looked at him. "In The Rat and Corpse, you knew my name. But I had not told you it."

He considered lying to her, saying that he'd overheard a member of the audience mention her name in appreciation. Instead he said, "It's a long story, Zeela, but I am telepathic. Don't worry," he said quickly, "I can't read you now. My ability needs to be..." Instinctively he reached into his pocket, and smiled as his hand encountered the cold metal band of his ferronnière. He explained about the amplification device.

Her eyes were wide. "And you read my mind?"

"Only briefly. I suspected you – I'm sorry to say – of being in league with Rasnic. I would never normally have invaded your mental privacy."

"I'm very glad to hear that." She cocked her head and said, "And you can't read me now, not a thing?"

He smiled. "Not a thing."

"It must be strange," she mused, "to be able to read the thoughts of your fellow man."

"It's a terrible thing, Zeela. A torture. You cannot begin to imagine... One day, perhaps, I'll tell you all about it."

She smiled. "That would be nice." She paused, then said, "And your name?"

He laughed as he realised that introductions, in all the excitement, had been overlooked. "Harper, Den Harper."

She reached out a solemn hand and shook his. "It's good to meet you Harper Den Harper."

He was about to correct her, before realising from her cockeyed smile that the mistake had been intentional.

"If you don't mind me asking, Den, what is a telepath doing in Satan's Reach, working as a star trader? Shouldn't you be catching villains for the Expansion?"

He nodded. "That's right. I should. And I was, once upon a time."

"Oh, and what happened?"

"That's another long story, for another time. Let's just say that I had to get away."

He was about to change the subject when he heard footsteps issuing from the exit to his left.

Zeela stiffened, regarding him with wide eyes.

He placed a finger to his lips, then gestured for her to lie down. He sat back against the rock and half-closed his eyes. He gripped the data-pin in his right hand, readying himself to attack.

As before, three Ajantans stepped into the chamber. They halted and looked around at the scattered humans as if deciding which one to take. The armed guard was just too far away, Harper judged, to attack without the risk of being shot. Perhaps if it moved closer...

To his alarm, the two unarmed aliens stepped towards him, exchanging comments in their fluting tongue. The first one gestured to Zeela and, as Harper watched mutely, bent to pick her up.

He thought fast. He would allow them to lift her – hoping that Zeela wouldn't give the game away and struggle – and then he'd follow and attack.

He watched through slitted eyes as the Ajantans gripped the girl's shoulders and ankles, braced themselves, and lifted. He had expected them to struggle under her weight, but they proved to be surprisingly strong as they hefted Zeela between them and moved towards the exit. The armed alien, ever watchful, scanned the cavern and then followed his compatriots through the exit.

Just as the alien was passing from sight, Harper saw something attached to its skinny arm – his wrist-com...

He counted to three, sprang to his feet, and gave chase.

The corridor was low, designed for Ajantans, and he had to crouch as he loped along after them. The guard was a couple of metres ahead, and strategically positioned glowbugs cast dancing shadows across the rocky floor.

He had to act sooner rather than later. The guard was carrying his rifle casually now, its muzzle pointing at the ground. As the trio rounded a bend in the corridor, Harper took his opportunity. He leapt forward, grabbed the alien beneath its oleaginous chin, and drove the data-pin into the centre of its back with all the force he could muster. He felt the pin slide through muscle and hit bone.

He withdrew the pin as the alien squealed and fell. He grabbed its rifle, pulled his wrist-com from its arm, and ran around the corner. He came upon the remaining pair so suddenly that he had no time to find the rifle's trigger – so he used the weapon as a club and slammed its butt against the head of the closest alien. Its skull crunched with surprising ease and its brains, pale and gelatinous, slopped against the tunnel wall.

Zeela fell to the ground with a cry, then struggled upright and kicked out at the remaining alien. She missed, and the Ajantan fell into a crouch and leapt at her. Harper found the firing stud and levelled the weapon, but Zeela was between himself and the alien and he couldn't get a clean shot. The Ajantan hit Zeela and they rolled, a spray of red blood – human blood – jetting into the air.

Zeela screamed in terror. She and the alien rolled apart as they hit the ground. Harper swung the rifle and fired. At least a dozen darts slammed into the alien's narrow chest. At such close range the darts crunched bone. The alien squealed, spasmed, and lay still.

He ran to Zeela and pulled her upright. Her dress was slashed across her left shoulder, and with it the flesh beneath. She pressed a hand against the wound, then raised bloody fingers to her incredulous eyes.

She looked over his shoulder and screamed.

Harper turned in time to see the alien he'd stabbed – the same alien he thought he'd killed – dive at him. He lifted the rifle and thrust, and impaled the Ajantan on the barrel. Behind him Zeela gagged. Harper pulled his rifle free and grabbed her hand.

Before them, the corridor forked.

"Do you have any idea," he asked, "which way is up?"

She was too shocked to respond. Blood trickled from the wound in her shoulder. He made a snap decision and took the tunnel to the left. He ran, pulling Zeela after him. To his dismay he realised, seconds later, that the ground was sloping downwards. To make matters worse he heard fluting sounds from up ahead. Before he could turn and retrace his steps a dozen Ajantans rounded a corner, stopped in surprise, and then came at him.

He fired a dozen darts, wondering how many the rifle held. The aliens screamed, three fell and the others came after him. He fired again, spraying darts right and left. Beyond the first group of aliens, another dozen Ajantans appeared – some of them armed. They pushed past their compatriots and fired at Harper and Zeela.

He pulled her to the ground and returned fire, hitting the armed aliens as darts whistled over his head. He heard the fluting calls of even more

Ajantans further ahead, leapt to his feet and dragged Zeela back the way they had come. At the end of the tunnel he made a sharp u-turn where the initial tunnel forked. He rounded the bend and sprinted along the second corridor, expecting this one to rise...

He should have known, given his recent run of luck, that it would do no such thing. The tunnel was descending further into the hellish bowels of the planet.

He heard scuffling sounds behind him. A posse of aliens was giving chase, but the fact that they hadn't fired yet suggested they weren't armed. He turned and fired as he ran, slowing them down. Glowbugs were positioned at more regular intervals now, which suggested they were approaching a more populous area of the lair.

Seconds later, hard on this thought, yet more aliens appeared up ahead. This delegation, he saw with sapping dread, was armed – and armed not with dart guns, but with the wide-muzzled incendiary rifles.

He slid to a halt, Zeela panting beside him. Behind them, he was aware of the following aliens edging closer.

He raised his rifle and fired – or rather tried to. The rifle clicked, spent. Crying out, he turned it quickly and gripped its barrel, intending to use it, in the last resort, as a club.

The three leading aliens halted and raised their weapons – something almost human in their arrogant postures of triumph.

Then another alien moved around the trio, this one bearing a dart gun. It halted and raised its weapon...

So he and Zeela would be tranquilised again, and no doubt monitored so that they could not attempt another escape... and then they would be carried to the pleasure cavern and...

He pulled Zeela to him. "I'm sorry," he said.

He would launch himself at the alien armed with the tranquiliser in one last, desperate effort. Even if it failed to effect their escape, he would go down fighting.

Harper raised his makeshift club and was about to attack when a great roaring sound, the rushing, pounding cacophony of a tsunami, filled the tunnel. A second later the noise was accompanied by a staggering typhoon – like the back-blast of a starship's maindrive – which skittled the aliens and pushed Harper and Zeela backwards. The howl raged, hot and inexorable and laced with excoriating particles of grit and dust. Harper covered his eyes and battled forward against the raging storm, laughing out loud in manic delight.

He could smell expended solid fuel and charged particles and the unmistakable reek of displaced, ionised air... and it was the finest perfume in the universe.

They stepped on the bodies of prostate Ajantans, crunching bones, stumbling once or twice but keeping their feet. He dragged an insensate Zeela after him. The headwind was abating, and with it the howling roar, and it could only be a matter of seconds before the tumbled aliens regained their feet and gave chase.

"What...?" Zeela cried, in response to his laughter.

"Salvation is what!" he yelled in return. "We're saved, girl! Saved!"

The tunnel widened and a minute later they staggered into what had obviously been the Ajantans' pleasure cavern, a vast chamber the size of a starship hangar... which was not that crazy a description.

Around the perimeter of the dome were the grisly remains of the aliens' depravity, dozens of human corpses in varying stages of decomposition. Among them, startled *in flagrante* by what had happened, several aliens lay staring about in a stunned stupor.

Not that Harper had eyes for the aliens...

Zeela came to sudden, shocked halt and stared at what filled the chamber. "What...?" she began.

"Welcome to the my ship," he said.

He dragged her across the chamber towards the hatch of his ship, which slid open at their approach. He heard a cry behind him and turned. A lone Ajantan appeared in the mouth of the tunnel, raised its incendiary weapon and fired. Harper ducked, pulling Zeela with him, and the bolus of flame hurtled overhead and exploded against the ship's carapace.

He pounded up the ramp, Zeela at his side, and seconds later threw himself into the ship. He commanded the hatch to shut and *Judi* to phase back into the void.

He held Zeela to him. It seemed oddly wrong to be static now, after so much hectic flight – but he told himself that they were safe at last, that they had survived, and seconds later he felt a vibration pass through the ship as they made the transition into the void.

He led Zeela to the recovery-room and had *Judi* prepare the med-pod. He laid her on the slide-bed, then removed the tattered dress from her torso to reveal a long, deep wound.

Zeela stared up at him.

"Don't be alarmed," he soothed. "You'll be unconscious for up to a day, and the med-pod will do its work. By the time you wake up, we'll be far away from here."

The med-pod snaked an analgesic probe towards Zeela's torso and eased itself into her flesh. Harper squeezed her hand.

"We're *really* safe?" she said in wonderment.

"We're really safe," he said. "*Judi* scanned our approximate position – thanks to my wrist-com – located the chamber and phased into the void. Then it phased back into reality in the pleasure cavern."

"Your co-pilot..." she said sleepily, "deserves a medal. I'm looking forward to... to thanking her."

Harper smiled. "All in good time," he said. "Now, sleep."

She closed her eyes, and Harper eased the slide bed into the med-pod and shut the hatch.

He climbed wearily to the flight-deck and slumped into the pilot's sling.

Through the viewscreen he watched the depthless, marmoreal swirl of the void.

"Good work, *Judi*," he said, dog tired. He felt like laughing, or crying – he couldn't decide which.

"Den," *Judi* said, "I detect that the Ajantans sent a vessel into the void a matter of minutes after our departure. Judging by its course and velocity, I think it is following us."

"Very well," he said. It was not the easiest of tasks to chase a ship through the void, and he was confident his ship would lose the Ajantans. "Take evasive action and keep me posted."

He closed his eyes and minutes later he was asleep.

CHAPTER THREE

SHARL JANAKER OFTEN said, when drunk, that she hated the Expansion authorities but took their filthy lucre in order to make ends meet. She spent a lot of time drunk these days, between missions, and her big mouth got her into a lot of trouble. The Expansion was seething with spies and petty informers, and only the fact that she was good at her job had kept her out of jail.

She left her two-person scout ship at the port on Hennessy's World and took the monorail to the towering needle of the Expansion headquarters.

She was in a pretty foul mood on two counts. Her lover of three months, a slight blonde as physically unlike her as it was possible to imagine, had ditched her – and, while trying to get over the girl with a holiday on the resort world of Khios, she'd had word from her contact in the Expansion, Commander Gorley, to get back to Hennessy pretty damned quick. She'd felt like telling Gorley to go fuck himself, but that would only have resulted in him sending a team of militia to rough her up and drag her back, kicking and screaming.

She wondered what he wanted this time. It had to be pretty important for him to contact her personally. Usually he delegated the task to one of his crawling minions.

She rode the upchute on the outside of the needle, staring out over the multiple waterfalls that made the planet a prime tourist destination. A dozen stepped lagoons tipped perfect arcs of water from one level to the next; rainbows and snowbirds played in the spume. Normally Janaker might have enjoyed the view, but not today.

When she reached Gorley's penthouse office, the bastard kept her waiting for thirty minutes.

She strode back and forth in reception, fuming, and was about to hammer on Gorley's door when his PA smiled sweetly and said, "Commander Gorley will see you now, Ms Janaker."

She paced into his office and towered over his desk, staring down at the thin, rat-like man. In her experience he was typical of Expansion high-ups, physically puny specimens – and often psychologically pathetic, too – who compensated for their inadequacies by wielding cruel and indiscriminate power.

Gorley sat back in his mock-leather recliner and steepled his fingers before his pinched mouth. "Sit down, Janaker," he said, indicating a chair with a limp hand. "You know how your constant pacing irritates me."

Or rather, she thought, *when I stand over him he feels intimidated.*

She sat on the edge of the chair and snapped, "Must be important, Gorley, to drag me all the way back from Khios. What's happened? A jail break? Some assassin's after your blood?"

He smiled, and it wasn't a pleasant sight on a face so rodent-like. "I have militia trained for that eventuality, Janaker. They wouldn't get within a light year of here."

I could give them some pointers, she thought.

She wondered if her dislike of Gorley was merely a sublimation of her guilt at taking the coin of the Expansion. He represented everything she hated about the repressive, totalitarian regime, the regime she had colluded with for the past ten years.

"So who is it this time?"

"First, some background... You've heard the rumours?"

She sat back, staring at him. Massive troop movements across the Expansion to the planets of Rocastle and Woczjar, a sudden increase in the budget in the area of weaponry development – and, from a contact in the marines, word that the colony world of Cassandra had been evacuated.

She nodded. "Sure I've heard the rumours. The Vetch are sharpening their claws again."

Gorley laughed. "How misinformed you are, Janaker. In fact, relations between ourselves and the Vetch have never been better, as you will soon find out. No... this is a threat altogether more serious than any that might be posed by the Vetch."

She stared at him. "A threat? So where do I come in?" A threat that serious could only mean extraterrestrials other than the Vetch.

He tapped his pursed lips, considering. "I want to impress upon you the seriousness of this matter. Thus informed, you will realise the importance of your mission." He paused, then went on, "The Expansion is being invaded."

She looked past Gorley's head, through the plate glass, to where thin clouds like silver ribbons drifted. "I've heard there's been trouble on Rocastle and Woczjar," she said.

"And on other planets, though we're trying to keep that under wraps."

"So who's invading us?"

He reached out and touched a sensor on his desk. A screen rose from its surface and he flicked it around so that she could see the images.

She sat forward, squinting. "What the hell are they?"

"We call them after the name given them by the first humans to come into contact with these... these creatures. The Weird."

She grunted a laugh. "Suits them."

The screen showed a succession of creatures: some were humanoid, empurpled and featureless – like unfinished clay models of the human form – while others were vast, bloated, and vaguely whale-like. Some were thin and gargoylish, and others as squat and repulsive as giant toads.

"And they're *all* the Weird?" she asked.

"All," he said. "They go through stages, change from one form to the next as they... individually evolve."

She looked at him. "So where are they from? Which planet? As I see it, we go in, bomb the fuck out of their world, and job done."

"That's just the problem, Janaker. They're from no single planet."

"I don't get it. They have to be. Where the hell else can they be from?"

"They're from the realm, the dimension, that underpins our reality..."

"The void? You're saying that these ugly bastards inhabit the *void*?"

She was about to ask why humanity had never come across them before, but Gorley forestalled her.

"Not the void," he said. "They're from *beyond* the void."

She sat back and stared at him. "This all sounds kind of screwy to me, Gorley. How do you know all this?"

"Because, six months ago I ventured with a team of marines through Vetch space to the Devil's Nebula. We discovered the world where these creatures first manifested themselves. They... they erupted into our reality through a manufactured portal and enslaved a human colony there."

"I didn't know there was a human colony in the Devil's Nebula."

"Well, you learn something every day, Janaker. I saw these creatures at first hand. I saw their portal... and I saw the human beings they'd enslaved."

"But if the portal is all the way across Vetch territory..." she began.

"Janaker," he said, "it appears that they now have the ability, the wherewithal, to open portals at random across the Expansion."

"So we find where they've opened these portals and blast the holy shit out of them."

His steely stare was all the more intimidating because it was accompanied by a withering silence.

"What the fuck, to employ your favoured vernacular, do you think we've been trying to do on Rocastle, Woczjar and Cassandra?"

She opened her mouth to say something, but no words came to mind.

"We've thrown everything at these portals – neutron bombs, hydrogen missiles... Between you and me, we've reduced Rocastle to rubble – it's nothing more than an asteroid a tenth the size of what it was, and the portal is still functioning."

"And the... Weird?"

"They are still sending through their... creatures, which have the ability to exist perfectly well in the vacuum of deep space. We're hard pressed to destroy these as they emerge."

She thought about it. "So... these Weird... what is it exactly they want from us? Territory, presumably?"

"They want *us*, Janaker. They want to absorb us, our knowledge, our culture. They aren't an enemy in the accepted sense of the world. They aren't... evil, exactly, because to be evil they must have some understanding of us as creatures in our own right."

Her throat was dry. "And they don't?"

"The Weird are... *is*... a hive mind. They do not see us as sentient individuals. Rather, they see the human race – and the Vetch race, too – as the sum total of our intellectual culture. It's this that they want to assimilate, absorb, understand. And to do this they ingest us as individuals and see no wrong in doing so."

"You paint," she said, "a charming picture of these creatures."

"I can assure you my words are nothing compared to the reality of the Weird I witnessed in the Devil's Nebula."

She was about to ask where she featured in all of this, but Gorley went on, "However, their portals are not the immediate danger."

"They're not?"

He told her that a century ago the Weird enslaved an alien race in the Devil's Nebula – it was from this race that they learned how to manufacture machines, starships and the like – and sent a fleet of ships into Vetch- and human-space.

"These ship were loaded, for want of a better word, with Weird mind-parasites, which could infect humans and the Vetch, lying dormant until they decided to take control of the individual. We have no idea how many humans in the Expansion have been infected over the decades. We assumed a worst case scenario of tens of thousands – and of course we have no idea who or where these people are. You see, they don't even know they are infected themselves. We assume that by now the parasites have infiltrated their hosts into positions of power in the Expansion..." He fell silent.

She stared at him. "Holy. Fucking. Shit."

"Quite," he said.

"So..." she said at last, "there's absolutely fuck all we can do."

He shook his head. "That's where you're wrong, thankfully. You see, these mind-parasites are detectable... by telepaths. There is no hiding from the probe of a telepath, and already we have a psionic team working to root out the infected. We're recruiting more individuals who test psi-positive, and fast-tracking their operations. We are also tracking down rogue teleheads, those individuals who have absconded, for whatever reasons, down the years."

"Ah... so this is where I come in, right?"

He nodded. "Five years ago a Grade I operative absconded from the Expansion, stealing a starship and heading for the Reach."

"Satan's Reach?" she said.

"Do you know any other Reach? Of course Satan's Reach. We sent an operative after him, but word came out a little later that he'd killed the operative in a shoot-out on the border planet of Rhapsody."

"So you want me to go in after this killer telepath and bring the fucker back?"

"That's about the size of it, yes."

Satan's Reach, the lawless, ungoverned drift of tightly packed stars beyond the jurisdiction of the Expansion... She had never ventured anywhere near the Reach before, never even met anyone who'd been there. She'd heard rumours, of course, that the Reach consisted of peaceable worlds just like any you might find in the Expansion, and also planets run by criminals, hell-holes settled by fleeing cults, and worlds inhabited by monstrous alien races.

"Who is he?"

Gorley touched the sensor again and the images of the Weird were replaced by the head-and-shoulders shot of a man she guessed to be in his early thirties. Dark, thin faced, with suspicious slit eyes and a wide mouth.

"He goes under the name of Den Harper these days, according to word that's reached us, and he works as a star trader with the ship he purloined from an Expansion Commander."

She grunted. "The bastard has chutzpah in bundles," she said, "and then you sent someone after him and he killed the poor fucker? So it'll be a walk in the park for me, right? A holiday in Satan's

Reach going after a homicidal telepath... Anything else you haven't told me?"

Gorley went on, "Word has reached us that he works out of a planet in the core of the Reach called Tarrasay. I suggest you check out the spaceport there, initially. We'll give you all the data we have on Harper, as well as the spec on the ship he stole."

She sat back and smiled. "You talk as if all this is a *fait accompli*, Gorley. You assume I'm all for this escapade like a kid at the circus."

He smiled, thinly. "You have no choice, Janaker. Or rather you do. You trace Harper in the Reach, and bring him back, or face the firing squad."

She pointed a blaster made out of fingers at him. "That's what I like about the Expansion, Gorley. Its humanity."

He opened a drawer in his desk and passed her a small, flat silver oval, which fitted snugly into the palm of her hand. She raised her eyebrows at him.

"A shield," he explained. "So that the telepath cannot read your mind."

She nodded, and slipped the device into her jacket pocket.

"Oh – and you're right," Gorley went on. "There is one thing that I haven't yet told you."

From his tone, she knew she wasn't going to like this one bit.

"Which is?"

"You're not going alone."

She sat forward, belligerently. "You know I always work alone, Gorley! I don't need an Expansion chaperone!"

"You'll have a partner this time, Janaker, and it's no Expansion chaperone."

She sighed, "Okay, but only if she's cute and puts out."

Gorley smiled, but she didn't like the sly look on his face.

"What?" she said.

"Your partner is a Vetch."

She stared at him. "A Vetch! A fucking Vetch? You're kidding? This is a joke, right?"

"Calm down, Janaker. Put your xenophobic prejudices to one side for a while and face the facts. We have recently entered into a pact with the Vetch. All our old hostilities have been set aside in the face of the threat our races jointly face. We will work together with the Vetch to defeat the Weird. To this end, Helsh Kreller is accompanying you to the Reach in order to bring the telepath back to the Expansion."

A Vetch... She had never actually met a Vetch in the flesh – images of them had been enough to put her off the idea of ever encountering one. They were big and hairy and dog-like – and rumour had it that they stank – and they had faces that looked like rectal haemorrhoids sliced into bloody strips... and they had been at war with the human race for god knew how long, and were responsible for atrocities on the human-settled border territories fifty years ago...

And she was going to share her starship with one of these bastards?

"You've overstepped the limits of your authority here, Gorley."

"You could, Janaker, always take your place before a firing squad, if you don't like the idea of working with an alien."

"Fuck you."

He smiled. "I take that as an agreement to work in inter-species harmony to aid our joint efforts to thwart the Weird." He glanced at his watch. "You will meet Helsh Kreller in one hour. Before that, you might like to take a meal with me in the restaurant."

JANAKER PUSHED ASIDE her plate, the food untouched, and stared past Commander Gorley at the... *thing*... that had entered the restaurant.

Heads turned, and a ripple of comment passed through the gathered diners as the Vetch strode towards their table.

Janaker closed her mouth and tried not to show her revulsion.

She guessed the alien was three metres tall, and very broad. It wore a black flight-suit that emphasised its military aspect, and had arms and legs that seemed disproportionately long in relation to its torso, and when it walked its legs flexed in a way that was not normal. But it was its face that she found repulsive, and at the same time fascinating. There was something of the hound about it, especially around the bulging eyes, but the pendent, blood-coloured tentacles that hung from the centre of its face – and acted, so she'd read, as both a nose and a mouth – were like something from a nightmare.

She stood, and Gorley made the introductions. The Vetch held out a claw, six-fingered and covered in hair, and Janaker found herself responding. The creature's grip was surprisingly slack.

"I do not take orders," it said in a gruff, muffled baritone which seemed to issue from somewhere amongst its tentacles. "We work in unison, as equals, sharing knowledge, debating scenarios. You agree?"

"I have no objections to that," she said. "And it's refreshing that you don't beat around the bush."

"Which means?"

"Ms Janaker means," Gorley said, "that she likes the way you forthrightly articulate your thoughts."

The Vetch regarded her with its bloodhound eyes. "In my experience there is no other way. Perhaps you humans practise verbal deceit, yes?"

Gorley smiled and defused the situation. "Would you care for a drink, Mr Kreller?"

"Water, while I speak with Sharl Janaker."

Gorley ordered a glass of water, then excused himself. "I'll leave you to discuss the mission," he said with a smile at Janaker, "and get to know each other a little better."

The Vetch sat down at the table. "So that you know, I would rather be embarking upon this mission alone."

She smiled, though she was sure the expression was lost on the alien. "So that *you* know, Kreller, I too would rather go it alone. But as I've been saddled with you, I'll make the best of a bad situation. We'll bring this bastard back to the Expansion in double quick time, Kreller, and then go our separate ways."

"I see that you too speak forthrightly."

She nodded and drank her beer. "Your Anglais is excellent."

"I perfected your tongue while interrogating human prisoners during the Territories War."

She stared at the monster. "But that was fifty years ago..."

"Your knowledge of recent history is excellent," Kreller said, and she thought she detected humour in his tone. A Vetch who cracks jokes, she thought; whatever next?

"I am over one hundred human years old," he said.

She smiled to herself. At thirty-five she felt like a mere child.

"Vetch have faster eye-to-hand reactions than humans," Kreller went on. "Also, we process reality faster than you do. This is an established scientific fact."

"Why are you telling me this?"

Its bloody eyes regarded her. "In my dealings with humans, Janaker, I have found that your ignorance of my people is vast. You will no doubt find out much more about my people over the course of the next few weeks."

"I can't wait," she said, and smiled sweetly at the Vetch.

"We are due to phase out *en route* for the Reach at midnight tonight," Kreller said. "I suggest that before then we share our information on the intended subject."

"Why not?" she said. "But first, perhaps I could introduce you to the delights of human beer?"

"I have tasted the liquid," he said, "and found it objectionable. I will take another water."

Janaker ordered a second beer, and a glass of water, and decided that the mission to the Reach with the Vetch was going to be... interesting, to say the least.

On the plus side, her informants had been wrong on one count about the Vetch... Thankfully, they *didn't* stink.

CHAPTER FOUR

THE *JUDI HEARNE* was Harper's home. It had
everything he required by the way of accommodation
and amenities, with the bonus of being supremely
mobile. He had equipped the ship to his own
tastes, buying old rugs, tapestries and furnishings
in markets far and wide across the Reach. He
liked to call himself a star rover, with no particular
allegiance to one planet or star system. If, however,
he were pressed on the matter and asked to state
his favourite world from the many hundreds he had
visited, he would always answer Tarrasay. It was the
planet to which he returned again and again, the
place where he felt safest. Situated on the far side
of the Reach from the human Expansion, Tarrasay
was the oldest planet settled by humans. Some said
that the first settlers had made their home among the
wooded vales and pastures over a thousand years
ago, but certainly the majority had fled here five

hundred years ago when the draconian rise of the authoritarian Expansion had pushed radicals, free-thinkers and persecuted minorities to seek refuge elsewhere. Over the centuries others had made the star cluster their home, criminals and religious cults and bizarre political factions, though Tarrasay itself – being a sleepy backwater with no great cities and little wealth – harboured none of these.

The planet boasted one small spaceport, situated next to the capital city on the coast, though Harper rarely availed himself of its facilities. He preferred instead to come down on the headland of a bay twenty kilometres north of DeVries, the capital city. Here was a small town tucked into the crook of the bay – Port Morris, by name – with a number of convivial inns and pleasant restaurants.

He had given his destination considerable thought on the voyage through the void. He would have continued on past Tarrasay to Amahla, but for the fact that he was carrying a passenger. Amahla was a series of sparsely populated atolls and islands, perfect for the holiday-maker but no place to make a home. Tarrasay, by contrast, would suit Zeela down to the ground. The capital city favoured artists, musicians and singers: she would find work there without much difficulty.

When he'd set the girl up with a place to live, and put her in touch with his contacts in the city, he would continue on to Amahla. He still had the steamboat engine in the hold, which he hoped to sell, *again*, on the water world.

Three days after leaving Ajanta the ship phased from the void above Tarrasay and dropped through a cloudless sky to the planet's sprawling equatorial continent. Harper sat in the command sling and admired the view: it was a sight that never failed to stir an appreciation of the planet's beauty and a sense of grateful homecoming.

"*Judi*," he said, "what of the Ajantan ship?"

"I can confirm that it was following us from Ajanta," *Judi* said. "A fast vessel of alien design, but lacking in manoeuvrability – that, or its pilots were unskilled."

"You managed to lose it?"

"Affirmative. There is a chance that it might pick up our ion signature, in which case we had better beware. I would advise only the briefest stopover on Tarrasay, before heading off again."

"Good. I'll do that."

"One other thing. The Ajantans are a tenacious, persistent race. They have had little contact with the outside Reach, and consider all other life-forms inferior. They also have a ferocious code of honour. They see the human race on Ajanta as little more than chattels, their souls ceded to them through what they call *kleesh*, the edict that in return for a ready supply of dhoor, every human on the planet belongs, in effect, to them. They claim that the agreement was made between themselves and the captain of the starship which crashed on their world over five hundred years ago."

"Go on."

"All of which is explanatory to this: that the Ajantans do not give up their possessions easily, or without a fight. We need to be ever vigilant of their continued pursuit."

"Understood."

He stared through the viewscreen. His life, for years, had consisted of nothing but being on the run, of constantly looking over his shoulder. He exaggerated, of course: in the early days that had been so – certainly for the first few years. Then, when he had dealt with the bounty hunter, he had worked to cover his trail, assumed new identities with obsessive regularity, and over the past year or two had gradually allowed himself to relax. Recently, in fact, he'd had hardly given a thought to the possibility that the Expansion might still be trying to track him down. Surely, he reasoned, they had more fish to fry than the capture of an errant telepath?

But now he had the pursuit of the aliens to exercise his thoughts.

He ordered *Judi* to come in low from the north, as always, so that his first sight of Port Morris would be from the sea, a merry jumble of colourful weatherboard buildings clustering around the harbour, with emerald pastures rising beyond. He tried to forget about vengeful aliens and concentrate on the beauty of the view.

He heard a sigh behind him and turned to see Zeela standing at his shoulder. He had withdrawn her from the med-pod two days ago, and she had expressed wonder at her rapid recovery and the fact that her shoulder and chest were unscarred.

Harper had found a few old clothes to cover her nakedness, a shirt two sizes too big for her and a pair of baggy trews, cinched at the waist by a thick belt. She had lost her shoes in the flight from the green men, and went barefoot now.

"But it's beautiful," she exclaimed.

"Port Morris," he said, "on the world of Tarrasay. I've made this place my base for the past two years."

He indicated the co-pilot's sling, and she eased herself into its embrace. "And you live here with your co-pilot?"

Harper smiled to himself. "You could say that, yes."

"I would like to meet her, to thank her for our timely rescue."

He nodded. "Very well," he said. "*Judi*, meet Zeela Antarivo. Zeela, I'm pleased to introduce you to *Judi*."

Judi said, "I am delighted to make your acquaintance, Zeela Antarivo."

Zeela looked around, her pretty features pulled into an expression of perplexity. She glanced at Harper. "Is she *hiding*?" she whispered.

He laughed. "'She' is not quite the right word to describe *Judi*," he said.

Zeela's frown deepened. "Then is she... *alien*?"

"*Judi*," Harper said, "please tell Zeela who you are."

"I am a Mark III smartware logic cortex with an integrated self-awareness paradigm," *Judi* said.

Zeela shook her head. "I'm sorry, I don't understand."

Harper explained. "*Judi* is an artificial intelligence, housed in the starship's computer nexus system."

"So... so she doesn't possess a body?"

"Of course not. Or rather, perhaps, the ship is her body."

Zeela shivered. "Oh, but that must be terrible! To be locked inside one's head! To not have a physical body... It sounds like my worst nightmare!"

Harper smiled. "Why not ask *Judi* how she feels about it?"

Zeela looked around, as if attempting to find a focus for her attention while addressing the ship. "*Judi*," she said tentatively, "what is it like to be... to not have a body, to be just... *brain*?"

"To answer that question," *Judi* replied, "I would first have to have experienced what it was like to possess a body, so that I could make a comparison. All I can say is that I find my existence infinitely rewarding."

"But... but don't you get just a *little* bored, merely running the ship day after day?"

Judi trilled a very human laugh. "But that accounts for a tiny fraction of what I do, Zeela! For the most part I study the many philosophies, human and alien, that have accrued across space over the millennia, and in my spare time I access and integrate the various happenings in the Expansion and the Reach."

"Den is very lucky to have you," Zeela said.

"I owe my existence to Den," *Judi* said. "When he... acquired me, I had no logic cortex. Indeed I could hardly be said to be self-aware. I was like a small animal, no more. But over the years Den has added to my smartware cortex, allowed me to grow, to flourish."

Harper said, "I've tried make *Judi* the very best I could afford." He did not add that the reason for this was due, in large part, to self-interest.

"Anyway," Zeela said, "I'd like to thank you for saving our lives. If not for your timely arrival, Den and I would now be dead, or dying."

"It was a simple matter," the ship said, "and the correction of a terrible injustice."

Judi banked, sailing in slowly over the bay.

Buildings passed below, tiny as seen from this altitude. Harper made out citizens in the streets, and cars beetling back and forth along the coast road.

The ship approached the headland and came in to land on an emerald greensward overlooking the sea.

Zeela had been silent for a time as she stared through the viewscreen, and now she said, "How old are you, Den?"

"Thirty, by standard reckoning. That would be..." He calculated, "in Ajantan years, almost sixty. And you're almost eighteen, standard."

She looked surprised, then said, "Ah, you read that in my mind, yes?"

He smiled, then pushed himself from the sling and ordered *Judi* to open the hatch of hold number one and prepare the ground-effect vehicle.

"Have you ever been married?" Zeela asked.

"Only to my work..." He clapped his hands. "Now, we have things to do. I'm taking you down to the capital, DeVries, where a talented singer like yourself..."

He reached into his jacket and produced the sheaf of Ajantan units. He passed them to her and went on, "Keep them. You'll be needing funds to set you up, initially."

She regarded the notes forlornly, then looked up at Den. He glanced away quickly, ill-at-ease with her pleading expression.

"I was rather hoping," she said in a small voice, "that the money might pay my way across the Reach to Kallasta."

He kept his gaze on the sea beyond the viewscreen. "A liner fare all the way across the Reach would be almost double that," he said.

She was silent for a time. Then, "I was rather hoping," she said, "that you might see your way to taking me back to Kallasta, if I returned the money – and if I cooked and cleaned for you all the way."

"*Judi* does all that," he said, "and anyway I'm heading in the opposite direction. Zeela..." He turned and looked down at her, where she slumped in the co-pilot's sling with a forlorn expression, "I'm sorry, but Kallasta is way off the beaten track. I'm a trader. I have work to do, markets to trawl..."

She nodded. "No, I'm sorry. I understand. I owe you my life, you and the ship, I should be grateful for that." Unspoken, but weighing heavily between them, was the fact that he owed her his life, too.

But hadn't they agreed, back on Ajanta, that on that score they were even?

"Come on, you'll like DeVries. It's a thriving city, with a lot to do. A young girl like you..."

He hurried from the flight-deck, and presently Zeela followed.

HE DROVE THE ground-effect vehicle from the hold, Zeela silent in the passenger seat, and took the coast road south. He elected not to stop off at Port Morris and catch up with events there – he would establish Zeela in DeVries, head straight back, and phase out immediately. The Ajantans might not have traced his ship to Tarrasay, but he was taking no chances.

The road hugged a scalloped coastline like a series of bites taken by some vast and voracious creature. To their left was the silver-blue expanse of the ocean, dotted with boats and ferries, and to their right a series of rolling vales with the odd farmhouse or village. A greater, more pacific contrast to Ajanta he could not imagine.

"Den," Zeela said a while later. The silence until then had been uncomfortable, but Harper had been unable to come up with an opening line that did not seem trite. "Can I ask you a question?"

"Of course?"

"Have you killed before?"

He gripped the wheel at its apex and stared at her, surprised. "What a strange question. Why do you ask?"

She looked at him, her head tipped to one side. "You're an odd person, Den. A telepath, yet a star trader. An educated man – I saw the old books aboard the ship, and your music files and all the artwork... And yet the way you handled yourself in the Ajantans' lair, the way you killed the creatures without turning a hair..."

"It was a case of kill or be killed, Zeela. In those situations, it doesn't pay to consider the morality of one's actions. The Ajantans were attempting to kill us, eventually – a state of affairs I did not view with delight."

"You acted like a practised fighter. You must have had training?"

He frowned. They were straying into territory he would rather leave untrod. "Many years ago," he said in a tone of finality.

"With the Expansion authorities?"

He sighed and remained tight-lipped.

"Come on, Den. Open up. You told me you're a telepath. I'm not a complete idiot – I know you must have worked for the Expansion, and received combat training."

"It's a time of my life I'd rather not talk about, if it's all the same to you, Zeela."

She asked quietly, solicitously, "Why not, Den?"

"Hell... because it's painful, okay? It hurts. What happened back then, how it happened."

"How *what* happened?"

He turned to look at her. "You're persistent, aren't you? Okay, if you must know... when I was four my mother sold me to the Expansion authorities. I'd tested psi-positive – that is, I was potentially telepathic. I underwent an operation to release that potential, fitted with software up here." He stopped, then went on, "I never saw my mother again. Years later I tried to trace her... I found where she'd last lived, that she'd been a singer, but she'd died a month or so earlier. Can you begin to imagine what it was like, to be brought up by a loving mother... or so I thought at the time... and then sold to the militaristic Expansion?"

She stared at him. "I'm sorry. No, I can't imagine."

"I wanted to know why my mother sold me, why she felt she had to. I've since found out that they paid her fifty thousand units for me... so it might have been that she was desperately poor and needed the cash – but we never seemed that poor back then." He shrugged. "But what do kids know about things like that?"

"Nothing," she whispered. "The adult world is a mystery to children, isn't it?" She was quiet for a time, then said, "It's a pity you didn't find her before she died, Den. Things might have... I don't know, turned out differently."

"Maybe," he said. "Who knows? Maybe I wouldn't have liked the women she was. Maybe I would have discovered that she'd sold me because she was greedy and didn't really want a snivelling brat holding her back."

He stared straight ahead, wishing that the girl had not made him dredge up all the memories, the bitterness.

"You said your mother was a singer."

"I'll tell you something else, too, while you're so intent on psychoanalysing me–"

"Hey, who said anything about–?"

"*Judi*'s voice is copied from my mother's." He told her about the recording of her singing, and how he'd had the ship synthesize his mother's voice. He went on, "It's all I have of my mother, other than a few memories. I find it... comforting."

"I'm sorry," she said. "And you said that working for the Expansion was hell..."

"They work you hard, make you do things you'd rather not do. And all the time they're indoctrinating you, so that you believe that the terrible things they do are done for a cause, for the right reason." He laughed without humour. "But as a telepath, Zeela, you can see right through all their lies and propaganda, even though all the trainers and high-ups are shielded. You read the minds of the underlings, the desk-jockeys and hangers-on... and you see what a vast organ of repression the Expansion is."

"So how did you get away, if you don't mind me asking?"

"And there I was, saying that I'd rather not talk about what happened... How do you do it, girl?"

She shrugged. "Maybe it's not me. Maybe it's you. Maybe it's just the right time to talk, to tell someone all about it."

He slid a quick look at her as she stared ahead at the road. He'd underestimated her, patronised her. She might be young and pretty, but she was also as sharp as hell.

"One day," he said, "something happened which was the final straw, as much as I could take. It pushed me over the edge. Let's just say that it was painful, and afterwards I considered killing myself. Death seemed preferable to what I'd gone through. But I was too much of a coward to kill myself – so I did the next best thing. I took some leave and stole a starship – *Judi*, here – and took off across the Gulf to Satan's Reach. It was the only thing in my life up to that point that I was proud of doing, and it wouldn't matter if they caught me and killed me. I'd defied them, made a stand."

"And they sent someone after you?"

"You bet they did. They sent a trained killer. A rogue telepath is a dangerous person in the eyes of the authorities. They know too much, and can get to know much more. They're a liability, and rather than just capture them, have them retrained or jailed... it's quicker just to summarily execute the rogues. I knew this when I got out, and it didn't give me a second's hesitation."

Zeela opened her mouth with sudden understanding. "Ah... now I get it. The Expansion sent a killer. He found you, right – and you killed him?"

He gripped the wheel. "*Her*," he said.

"Oh."

The silence stretched. "Like I said," he went on, "it was a case of kill or be killed. Me or her. I didn't like what I did back then. I'm not proud of it... But there was no other way. She came after me, made a mistake, and I took advantage of her slip and..." He shrugged. "It's strange, but for months, maybe even years afterwards, a part of me even wished she'd succeeded and killed me. I know, I don't even understand it myself."

"Life is mysterious," Zeela said. "I'm sorry. That's a platitude, but it's something that my parents said all the time. They were pacifists, and they brought me up to be the same."

He stared at her. He considered her questions about his past, the killing; it didn't seem mere prurient curiosity on her part now, but genuinely interested enquiry from someone to whom killing was anathema.

"That's something I've never really understood," he said. "Pacifism. It seems to me the idealism of people who have never faced the dilemma of having to fight for their lives."

She regarded him and smiled, it seemed, sadly. "But that's just it, Den. My parents did face that dilemma, and they held by their creed. It happened long after they left Kallasta and settled on Ajanta. They had very little money and certainly not the means to leave the planet, once they found out how things worked with the Ajantans."

"What happened?"

"They became addicted to dhoor. Every human does, given time. The Ajantans supply the drug, and it has a magical effect on humans, gives us a euphoric, perpetual high for many years. My father worked as a carpenter, and a third of his earnings went to paying for his and my mother's, and then my own, addiction."

He said, "You? But..."

"I took my last dose of dhoor five days ago. I should be suffering the effects of withdrawal pretty soon, now. It can kill people, if they're not strong." She stared at him. "But I am strong, Den. I'll survive."

He nodded, but said nothing.

Zeela went on, "Anyway, my parents... When I became addicted – I was only around ten standard years old at the time – my father decided that we had to leave Ajanta, irrespective of how dangerous that might be for him and my mother. They were not healthy people, and further weakened by their addiction. They had no way of affording passage from the planet, so they approached someone, I don't know who exactly, a criminal... someone who might help them. This crook made my father an offer; he would finance their passage off-planet if my father would do something for him."

"Ah," Harper said.

"The crook wanted a business associate killed, without being incriminated himself. The man he wanted dead was a notorious criminal, a despicable human being the world would be well rid of... But my father refused. He clung to his pacifist ideals, even if by doing so he was consigning himself, his wife and his daughter, to eventual death."

Harper nodded. "That must have taken a lot of... courage," he said at last.

Zeela sighed. "I'm just glad that I never had to face that dilemma. You know, in the Ajantan lair... if I had not been with you, then I doubt whether I could have overturned a lifetime's indoctrination and fought for my life." She laughed. "'Life is mysterious'," she said. "Anyway, that's one reason I want to go back to Kallasta. My parents never told me why they left the planet. I recall it as a paradise. I was very young at the time, and no doubt my parents shielded me from the reality, but it seemed idyllic. We lived in a small town on a rain-forested plateau... and yet my parents felt compelled to leave."

"Did you never ask them why?"

"No, but I recall asking them why they chose Ajanta. The fact was that they had little choice. They had sufficient funds to get them so far, and 'so far' was the spaceport of Ajanta."

"So you want to go to Kallasta and see what your parents left behind?"

"That's about the size of it," she said.

He was silent for a time, going over what she had told him as he negotiated the sweeping bends of the coast road and approached the city of DeVries.

She had ten thousand Ajantan units to her name, which would probably last her a month at most. It would take her years, working as a singer in the sea port bars, to save enough for the trip across the Reach.

And soon she would be suffering the withdrawal symptoms of her addiction to dhoor.

He said, "These withdrawals... how bad are they? I mean, is there anything I can do?"

"Thanks, but I'll survive. I'll just... lock myself away, take plenty of sugar and water and think of Kallasta."

He nodded and said nothing as they drove through the plush residential suburbs of the city, ultra-modern domes and silver needles contrasting with ancient timber terraces and A-frames. It was this mixture of the old and the new, this acknowledgement that the planet's rich history mattered to people, that made DeVries one of his favourite cities of the Reach.

"Den," Zeela asked a little later, "What is life like for the average citizen beyond the Reach?"

He glanced at her. "What have you heard about life in the Expansion?"

"Not much. A few stories from travellers I met in The Rat and Corpse."

"And what did they say? No, don't tell me. They were in the Reach, which means that they'd left the Expansion for some reason. I suspect their views were pretty much like mine."

"Which are?"

"The Expansion is a closed system, ruled by a totalitarian regime which will tolerate no opposition. Military rule exists in all but name on every planet in the Expansion – some two thousand in all. Over the centuries this draconian rule has cowed the populace, along with ethnic repatriation and selected breeding."

Zeela shook her head. "Meaning?"

"In the early days of expansion from Earth, citizens were free to live where they wished. They could settle any planet they liked, just so long as they could afford to do so. Over the last few hundred years the authorities have not only proscribed free movement, but 'consolidated' planets – that is, moved great swathes of the populace, often by racial groupings, from one world to another in order to make governing them that much easier. And selective breeding... or eugenics... this is a program to wipe out certain races and make 'pure' others." He looked across at her. "Now you've got to understand that

I was brought up like any other ignorant youth to think that the authorities were always right; their way was the only way I knew. Then much later, when I had the cut, and could read the minds of others, dissidents, freethinkers, radicals... I came to see that the Expansion hadn't always been so totalitarian, that at one time diversity was the norm. It wasn't perfect back then, but at least people were free to make their own choices, their own mistakes."

He took a flyover into the city centre. "So... the average citizen of the Expansion knows nothing other than what the party tells them. They know nothing of difference, of diversity; they live homogenised lives on their identical planets, eating the same standardised food, watching the same 3V shows, reading the same books and newsies...

"Now, contrast that to the Reach... Tarrasay, for instance. Here democracy rules; there is accountability. People vote for political parties which offer widely divergent views, and vote them out again if they don't deliver on their promises. There is crime, and corruption, but there is also freedom. Of course, the Reach has planets like Ajanta, and worse... but at least people are free to travel, for the most part."

Zeela stared at the silver scimitar shapes of the high-rises lining the coast, and the cantilevered domes pendent over the narrow alleys of the ancient parts of town. "I have so much to experience," she murmured to herself, "so much to learn."

"I can't begin to imagine what your life must have been like back there..." Which was not quite true: he'd had that brief glimpse into her mind back at The Rat and Corpse, which had been enough to show him the fear she experienced daily...

"It was hell... but do you know something? I'm amazed now what people can put up with. You learn to live with foul conditions, don't you? You accept. It never occurred to me, when I was growing up on Ajanta, that things might be any different. Only later, when I began to sing at The Rat and met people from other worlds... only then did I realise that I might have a life that was very different to the one I was living."

"And the dhoor obviously helped to pacify the populace."

She nodded. "Oh, I think that made things tolerable. It created a... a haze between you and reality." She smiled. "I think back and feel the rapture I experienced every three days when I drank my dhoor."

"You're missing it?"

In reply she held out her hand, which was shaking. "I'm beginning to feel the effects of not having had any for days, Den."

"You'll be fine. A few rough days, then you'll be back on your feet and enjoying all the new things that life on Tarrasay has to offer."

She hugged herself and murmured, "Yes, I'm looking forward to that."

They left the flyover and Harper steered the car into a cradle on the outskirts of the old town. They took an elevator down to ground level, then stepped into a narrow street between two rows of timber buildings. The place was bustling with citizens in a variety of fashions. Zeela stared about her in wonder.

"So many people," she gasped, "and..." She pointed to a shop window. "And why do people display their clothing like that?"

Harper looked from Zeela to the window of the boutique. "It's a shop," he explained. "Those dresses aren't owned by one person – they're for sale. You can go in and buy them."

She shook her head at the idea. "I see... just as on Ajanta you can go into The Rat and buy Finest or wash? I made my own clothes, and we bought food from night markets. So this is like a big night market, but the goods are kept in buildings, and they're open in daytime."

"It's cool enough during the day to do so," he said.

She laughed. "To think of it... buying things from buildings during the day!"

He smiled at her naivety. "Later I'll buy you a dress..." He almost added 'as a going away present', but stopped himself.

The crowd jostled, and Zeela reached out to take his hand. Harper contrived to scratch his head, then pointed down a narrow street at right angles to the main thoroughfare. "Down here."

"Where are we going?"

"I know someone who runs a bar, the Endolon on Phreak Street. In my early days on Tarrasay I almost lived in the place, and every time I'm in DeVries I drop by for old times' sake."

"I see. So you think they might give me a job?" She sounded less than enthusiastic at the prospect.

"They hire singers, and as I recall not many of them are as talented as you."

She was silent as she skipped to keep up with him.

Phreak Street was one of the oldest in DeVries – named after Jeremy Phreak, a pirate of the spaceways – a row of three storey timber buildings whose great age was emphasised by the silver spires of the spaceport's terminal buildings in the background. The Endolon was a narrow mock-Tudor establishment with a painted sign swinging above the iron-banded timber door. The sign showed a bloated grey alien clutching a foaming tankard of ale.

Zeela looked up at the sign and exclaimed, "What a strange picture!"

Harper laughed. "The inn's owner, and a good friend of mine."

She stared at him as he invited her to step through the warped timber door.

The inn's interior was low and dark. A bar stretched the length of the room on the left, propped up by drinkers. The lighting was minimal, a series of imitation candles strategically positioned not so much to afford illumination but to provide anonymity to the drinkers who inhabited shadowy booths opposite the bar. In olden times, so the story went, the Endolon had been the haunt of criminals and cut-throats.

At the far end of the narrow room sat the Endolon itself.

Zeela looked around uncertainly. "They have singers *here*?"

"In the evenings in the upstairs room," he said. "Come on, I'll introduce you."

He led the way to the throne at the far end of the bar, aware that Zeela was hanging back.

He understood why. The Endolon was grotesque. The creature was a great grey mass, not dissimilar to a bloated walrus if that animal had been positioned upright and wedged into a timber seat. Its fat spread in folds two metres wide, bulging through the gaps between the throne's arms. It was without legs, but possessed four stubby arms just long enough to be able to lift a flagon of ale to the slit of its mouth in its domed head.

Two moist eyes, like oysters swimming in engine oil, peered out from an otherwise featureless face.

Legend had it that the Endolon had been *in situ* for three hundred years – some stories even claimed that the building had been built around the alien five hundred years ago. At any rate, the creature had not moved from its seat in living memory.

"Denphrey Harper!" the alien burbled. "And who is this?"

Harper drew up two stools and positioned them before the Endolon. Zeela climbed onto hers and stared at the alien. Harper signalled to the barman for two beetroot beers, his favoured tipple when in town, and said, "Zeela Antarivo, meet the Endolon. Endolon, meet Zeela."

"The pleasure is mine entirely," said the alien. "You appear young. Is Zeela your daughter, Denphrey, or your wife?"

"Neither. A friend. She hails from Kallasta, and sings like a songbird. I was hoping that she might find work here."

The Endolon gestured with a wave of one of its tiny hands. "I will audition you myself, Zeela."

"We're here *en route* from the world of Ajanta..." Harper went on, and recounted their escape from that planet, pursued by the aliens.

Zeela took her pot of beetroot beer and sipped, glancing at Harper and smiling her appreciation.

"Ah, Kallasta," said the Endolon. "Clement world, fourth planet from its primary. Agricultural, settled in 1246 by members of the Universal Church of Peace. Approximately two hundred light years from Tarrasay..." the Endolon went on in this vein for some time, regurgitating all the facts in its possession regarding the world of Kallasta. It closed its eyes, as if in bliss at being able to perform the service.

Zeela caught Harper's eye and pulled a quizzical face. He leaned towards her and murmured, "The Endolon never forgets a fact, and delights in recounting them at any opportunity."

The Endolon had once told Harper that there were few of its race left in this sector of space, and for all it knew anywhere else across the face of the galaxy. Once its kind had been a proud star-faring people, with life-spans of thousands of years standard, and a peaceful philosophy. Over the millennia they had spread far and wide, settling on quiet worlds and acting as sages and repositories of knowledge for races both alien and human. Someone had once told Harper that the Endolon had fled the Expansion five hundred years ago – its creed not in accord with the militaristic bent of the human authorities – settled on Tarrasay and established the eponymous drinking establishment. The Endolon, however, was reluctant to speak of its own past.

Its oleaginous eyes opened and shuttled from Harper to Zeela. It called out a name, and seconds later a serving boy scurried across and knelt before the throne. He opened a cupboard in the throne's base and pulled out a bulbous container. Harper averted his gaze and tried not to inhale as the boy slipped a towel over the chamber pot and staggered away with it.

"Will you eat?" asked the Endolon.

"Thank you, but no," Harper said. He glanced at Zeela who was staring aghast at the serving boy, who had returned with the empty pot and was inserting it beneath the throne.

She shook her head. "Nor me, either, thank you."

"But you do not mind my taking sustenance?" the alien asked, then told the boy to fetch a baguette from the kitchen.

A minute later the Endolon held a great truncheon of bread in one of its four hands and proceeded to alternate between taking noisy bites of baguette and slurps of ale.

"But Denphrey," the alien said, chewing, "I understand that congratulations are in order? The lady has found you, I take it?"

Harper was thrown. "The lady?"

"Yesterday a large human woman – one Sharl Janaker, she called herself – came to the inn and enquired after you. I assumed she had found you, and that you were here to celebrate."

Harper sipped his drink, quelling the first stirrings of alarm. "Celebrate what?" he asked.

"Ah," said the alien, "then your paths have not crossed, and you are in ignorance of your good fortune! It falls to me to relay the good tidings. The woman said that she was seeking one Den Harper, as enquiries at the port had led her to this very establishment. Apparently your uncle on Nova Rodriguez passed away five years ago, leaving you a legacy of some half a million units. The woman, Janaker, is a representative of your uncle's solicitors, come to bestow the bequest."

Zeela was looking at him with wide eyes, smiling in anticipation of his own delight.

Harper, however, felt anything but delight. True, he had had an uncle on Nova Rodriguez and, according to his mother, he had possessed wealth... but that a 'large woman' should be sent into the Reach to inform him of his legacy was unlikely to say the least.

"Can you describe the woman?" he asked.

The Endolon closed its eyes. "Tall, broad, white-skinned, thick dark hair. Masculine in appearance, and muscular. I should guess given to combat, as she was armed with a side laser. She wore the dark raiment of the Expansion, and spoke in clipped Anglais."

Harper drained his flagon, a sick feeling curdling in his gut. The Endolon had described no individual of his direct acquaintance, but the type he knew well: she fitted the description, down to the laser side-arm, of a bounty hunter the Expansion would send after him.

He kept his tone even. "What did you tell her?"

"I said that you came to DeVries from time to time, and always dropped by for a flagon. I said that I had not seen you for a good three months, but that all things being even you would show yourself before long. She gave me an address where you might find her – the Old Rose hotel beside the spaceport."

"In which case," Harper said, setting his empty pot on the bar, "I had better go in search of my fortune. It's been a pleasure, as always."

"The pleasure has been mine entirely, and I look forward to hearing you sing, Zeela Antarivo."

Harper slipped from the stool and, as he hurried from the bar, he took Zeela's hand and tugged her along after him.

"Something tells me that all is not as it seems," she said as they emerged into the sunlit street.

He paused under the overhang of the inn. "I think the woman was lying. She would not come all the way to the Reach just to inform me of a bequest."

"Then?"

"A bounty hunter..."

Her big eyes expanded. "So... what now?"

Harper considered his options. He was torn by conflicting impulses. A small, rational voice in his head told him to flee, to get out while the going was good; another voice – prompted by the insatiably curious side of his nature – suggested that it was always wise to know one's enemy.

"Now we go to the Old Rose."

She looked alarmed. "But you said that she might be a bounty hunter!"

"Don't worry, I'm not so foolish as to go up to her and introduce myself. I just... need to know for certain. We'll go to the hotel and keep a safe distance, and with my ferronnière..." He tapped his jacket pocket.

"Ah," she said. "And then, when you have established whether or not this woman is pursuing you?"

He set off along the busy street, Zeela trotting after him. "Then I will either flee, or accept my Uncle's largesse, unlikely though that scenario is."

"And what of me?" she asked, hurrying after him.

He turned and regarded her, slowing down. "I don't know."

She called out, "Please, don't leave me here. If you flee, take me with you. But if the woman is not who you fear she is... then, might I stay with you also?"

He steadfastly refused to meet her gaze. He said, "There would be no sense in either scenario. If she did turn out to be a bounty hunter, and if you came with me, your life too would be in danger. And if she was who she said she was, and I came into a fortune... then you would be better off taking a ship directly to Kallasta, which I would gladly pay for."

Zeela said nothing but ran along at his side as he turned down alley after alley towards the spaceport. Her silence burned like an accusation.

The boulevard that approached the spaceport was a hotchpotch of architectural styles, from the latest soaring towerpiles to old brick-and-timber buildings, the later occupying narrow niches between the former. A kilometre away, at the far end of the boulevard, starships came and went like bees at a hive.

The Old Rose was the grandest hotel in DeVries, a palatial stone-built pile in its own lawned grounds. Across the thronged street was a restaurant with a second floor balcony at which afternoon teas might be enjoyed. Harper gestured to the elevated tea room and told Zeela, "From there we will have a safe view of everyone who comes and goes from the hotel."

Minutes later they were established on the balcony with china cups of green tea and dainty sandwiches.

Harper removed his headgear – a dun beret this time – and pulled the ferronnière from his pocket. He placed the device inside his beret and sat with it on his lap, ready to don the hat should anyone fitting the woman's description show herself.

He sipped his tea and stared across the thoroughfare towards the long lawn of the hotel. Guests came and went, humans and aliens. The street below was busy with pedestrians, and from time to time an air-car passed slowly by on level with where they sat.

Zeela glanced at his ferronnière and said, "And will you read my thoughts when you put that thing on?"

"The woman's thoughts only, Zeela."

"You can be so selective?"

"Of course. My talent is directional, if you like. I can filter out much of the mind-noise around me, after a few seconds, and concentrate on the subject. Anyway, I promise not to pry into your mind."

"It's okay if you did," she said. "I have nothing to hide."

He glanced at her and smiled. "Nothing? Are you absolutely sure about that? Everyone has something to hide."

She looked away and said quietly, "Not from people they trust."

He did not deign to reply to that, and concentrated on the entrance of the Old Rose hotel.

A little later Zeela said, "This is amazing..."

He glanced at her. "Your cucumber sandwich?"

"No." She gestured all around her. "This. The city. The spaceport. All these different people. I mean... all the aliens. I never knew so many different kinds existed!" She leaned forward, placed a hand on the balcony and propped her chin on her closed fist, staring at the boulevard in wonder.

She pointed. "That one, for instance... Do you know what it is, Den?"

She was indicating a being like a puce octopus garbed in diaphanous robes; it flowed along the street on a dozen tentacles, trailed by half a dozen smaller versions of itself.

"That one is… if I'm not mistaken… a Zuban from a planet in the Procyon star system. The smaller ones in its wake are clones, which accompany it everywhere in case of an accident. They share one mind, though, and are unique amongst extraterrestrials."

"And that one?"

"The incredibly tall, stick-thin blue man?" he said. "That's a Glaydian from Glay in the Lesser Magellanic Cloud. They're traders, and drive a hard bargain as I've found out to my cost. And see that one there, in the yellow rolling bubble? That's an Ooom from Betelgeuse III – I forget the name of its homeworld. It doesn't breathe our air, so must go everywhere accompanied by its own sulphurous atmosphere. You don't see many of them abroad, so it's probably someone important like an ambassador."

"So many aliens…" she said in awe.

"They tend to frequent the Reach in preference to the Expansion," he explained. "The authorities there impose stringent trade restrictions, which don't maintain here."

"And can you mind-read them all?"

He smiled. "In theory, yes. That is, I can access their minds, though often their thoughts are sometimes just too *alien* for me to make any sense of. And with some extraterrestrials I'd get a raging migraine just trying to achieve mental contact."

She looked at him. "Your ability has obviously made you what you are."

"What do you mean by that?"

She frowned. "Superficially friendly," she said, "but in actual fact reserved, distant. But that's understandable, I think."

He was about to defend himself and say that if *she* had read the minds he had, if *she* had had to protect herself from the machinations of others... then she would be reserved, distant – but he supposed that that was exactly her point. He said nothing, and returned his attention to the long path leading up to the hotel.

Ten minutes later a figure emerged from the foyer of the Old Rose hotel and strolled down the path. Harper sat forward, his heart racing. The woman was human, tall – strapping, he would have said – with a hank of jet black hair, handsome in a severe, masculine kind of way, and armed with a laser side-arm.

Something about her poise and swagger, the way she held her head erect and forever on the look-out, suggested she was an Expansion bounty hunter.

"Den?" Zeela said.

"It's her," he whispered.

He took his beret and arranged it on his head, activating the ferronnière as he did so. The minds around him flared like so many miniature supernovas, throwing at him a radiation of competing emotions. Before he could filter it out, he caught a mental emanation from Zeela – something which he would rather not have read. He thrust this to one side, quelled the pulsing jealousy from the waitress to his left, and concentrated his probe on the advancing figure of the woman... what had the Endolon said she was called?... Sharl Janaker?

As he'd expected, and feared, Janaker was shielded.

"Can you read anything?" Zeela asked, leaning forward and touching his sleeve.

"No."

"Do you think...?"

"That she's a bounty hunter?" He nodded. "I'm sure she is." He felt sick.

As he watched, the woman stopped and turned to look behind her, and a second later Harper received another unpleasant shock.

A tall figure strode from the foyer of the hotel and joined her.

Harper swore to himself and sat back.

Zeela was watching him with alarm. "What is it?"

"Her sidekick," he said, "is a Vetch."

The alien was a good half metre taller than Janaker herself, clad in black leather and armed with a laser rifle strapped to its back. It walked like a military killing machine, which to all effects and purposes it was. It was also hideously ugly, with a proboscis that appeared to have been sliced into bloody strips, and huge, doleful eyes.

"I take it," Zeela said, "that that's not good?"

"You take it correctly, girl."

Harper had only ever seen a Vetch on one other occasion – a prisoner captured by Expansion marines after a border skirmish. The two races occupied bordering sectors of space, and rarely did the twain meet. He wondered what the hell the bounty hunter was doing with a Vetch accomplice.

He sent out a probe in the Vetch's direction, but the alien was shielded too.

Harper pulled off his beret, and with it the ferronnière. The minds around him became blissfully silent, and with them Zeela's.

"So... we get out of here?" she suggested.

He watched the pair cross the boulevard and pass from sight beneath the restaurant's striped awning. "Never a truer word spoken. Let's go."

He stood and strode from the balcony, entering the café and heading for the spiral staircase. He stopped at a sound from below: the Vetch speaking in guttural Anglais.

He turned on his heel, grabbed Zeela by the elbow and led her back to the balcony. He resumed their table with his back to the door, his heart tripping like a Geiger counter.

"Sit down opposite me," he said. "There's only one other table free, and it's out here. Lean forward and hold my hand like a lover whispering sweet nothings, okay?"

"That shouldn't be too hard," she said, and Harper flashed on the emotion he'd read in her head minutes earlier.

She said, "Please, you won't shoot them, will you?"

"It's okay, Zeela. I'm not armed. No bloodbath in the Boulevard Tea Room, I promise."

"But if you were armed...?"

"What do you think I am, a conscienceless killer?" he hissed. "I wouldn't take the risk when there are other options."

She took his hands and leaned towards him, looking into his eyes. Her glance took in the woman and the Vetch, who were seating themselves at the vacant table behind Harper.

He clutched Zeela's hand, surprised at how small it was. But then in comparison to him she was tiny, bird-boned. She could have passed for his daughter, and he wondered if their guise of star-crossed lovers might be a mistake which would only draw attention to themselves.

Janaker and the Vetch were conversing in Anglais. Harper listened, trying not to smile at what he heard.

Here they were, a trained killer and a bellicose Vetch, bickering over sandwich fillings.

"You know that egg makes you vomit," Janaker was telling the Vetch. "You're safer with meat."

"You humans don't know what meat is," the Vetch began.

"Just because your lot eat it raw – and still living."

Zeela whispered, "They sound just like man and wife."

"Shhh, Zeela. Listen..."

The mismatched pair were silent for a time, and then gave their order to the waitress. Seconds later Janaker sighed and said, "Well...?"

"Maybe he's up and left," the Vetch said. "He could be anywhere in the Reach."

"True. But you heard what the fat bastard said – he returns every few months."

"Which might mean we've got weeks to wait."

"Do you never cease complaining?" Janaker said.

"I am merely stating a fact," said the Vetch with a growl.

Harper whispered, "Have they looked our way yet?"

Zeela shook her head. "They're too busy bickering."

"Are they facing us?"

"The ugly alien is. The woman has her back to us."

Harper considered possible escape scenarios. The favourite, he decided, was to sit tight and wait until the pair had finished their meal and left. On the other hand, the longer he and Zeela remained here, the more chance there would be of Janaker recognising him.

Zeela pulled a disgusted face.

"What?" Harper asked, alarmed.

"Their orders have arrived," she said, "and the alien is eating... You should see it!"

"I'd rather not," he said.

"It's sucking a sandwich up its nose tubes!" Zeela hissed. "Oh, my..."

"Will you please be quiet and let me think?"

"I'm sorry." She looked suitably contrite.

A minute later he said, "Okay, this is what I want you to do. Pay our bill, then go back to the Endolon on Phreak Street."

"And then?"

"When you find the Endolon, tell him that the woman called Janaker is a bounty hunter out for my blood. He'll understand. Tell him – and this is important – tell him that if this pair returns asking after me, he's to tell them that the word on the street is that I left aboard my ship this morning bound for... for Beckett's World. That's vitally important. Beckett's World. It's in the opposite direction to where I'll be heading."

She nodded. "Beckett's World." She gripped his hand. "And then?"

"Then make your way to Cradle Seven on Macarthur Street. I'll meet you back there in thirty minutes or so. Got that?"

She nodded, again, determined. She stared into his eyes, then said, "You won't leave me, will you? You won't just take a cab back to your ship and leave without me?"

He returned her gaze, surprised that the idea hadn't crossed his mind. "No," he said. "No, I've come to a decision."

"Yes?"

"We're heading in the opposite direction to Beckett's World..."

"We?" she asked, wide eyed.

"Of course, *we*. In a few days, a week at the most, we should reach Kallasta if luck is on our side."

She almost leapt off her seat with delight. "Oh, Den!" she cried.

"Quiet!" he hissed. "We'll be going nowhere if the ugly twins laser my lights. Right, off you go."

"I think you should give me a kiss, for the sake of reality."

She leaned forward and puckered her lips. Harper kissed her chastely on the forehead. "Now go!"

With a smile she slipped from the table and entered the restaurant.

Oddly, Harper felt suddenly more vulnerable on his own. He played with the empty tea-cup, wondering if the pair behind him would be more likely to notice his presence now that he was alone.

He glanced down at the boulevard. He saw Zeela's slight figure emerge from beneath the red and white awning and merge with the surging crowd. She turned once, waved up at him, and then was lost to sight.

Harper swallowed his fear and listened in to the pair's conversation. They seemed to be discussing the relative merits of various firearms. "You get a cleaner kill with a Sholokov," the Vetch was saying, "even if its range isn't up to the Hoeneker."

"Give me the Hoeneker any day," Janaker said. "It's deadly *and* silent."

By the sound of it they had finished their sandwiches. With luck they would soon pay their bill and depart. But he should have known that that would just be too easy...

Janaker said, "I don't know about you, but I rather fancy another beer."

"You and your beer," the Vetch growled.

"Waitress!" Janaker called.

Harper braced himself to get up, turn around, and stroll casually from the balcony. He'd wait until the waitress arrived and the pair were distracted, then make his move.

Seconds later he heard the waitress approach their table. "And what can I get for you?"

He stood up and turned. The waitress was blocking access between the tables. He would be forced either to squeeze past the girl or politely ask her to make way... either of which would draw attention to himself.

He found himself striding across the balcony towards the waitress just as she nodded and moved back into the tea room. Luck, it seemed, was on his side. Breathing with relief, he slipped past the table occupied by the human and the Vetch. He sensed Janaker look up at him, and he could not stop himself from meeting her glance.

For the briefest moment their eyes locked.

He hurried from the balcony, his pulse racing. He strode across the tea room towards the spiral staircase, and for a second he thought his luck was holding and the bounty hunter had failed to recognise him.

Then a cry from the balcony indicated otherwise.

He dived for the staircase and, instead of using the steps, braced his elbows on the helical rail and launched himself, helter-skelter fashion to the ground floor.

He landed at speed and made a split-second decision. The option was left or right – out onto the boulevard, or through the kitchen...

Instinct told him *left*, onto the boulevard and the protective custody of the busy thoroughfare. He sprinted from the restaurant and slipped into the crowd, almost colliding with a rolling Ooom. He dodged around the sulphur-filled atmospheric ball, with its fish-like inhabitant staring out at him in pop-eyed alarm, then had the bright idea of using the sphere as cover. Beyond, Janaker and the Vetch burst from the tea room and looked right and left in desperation.

He ducked, grabbed the sphere and rolled it along the boulevard at speed, keeping himself between the bauble and his pursuers. The Ooom emitted a series of shrill squeaks, signalling its alarm, and Harper wondered if his actions would result in a diplomatic incident. Ahead and to his right, an alleyway gave access to the spaceport precincts. Harper released the sphere as he came alongside the alley, then launched himself through a throng of startled Glaydian blue-men. He sprinted down the alley, hoping he'd given Janaker and the Vetch the slip. A hoarse Vetchian cry, seconds later, informed him otherwise. He wanted to look over his shoulder and assess how close they might be, but elected to keep running. He expected a shot to skewer his spine at any second, and wondered whether that would be courtesy of a Hoeneker or a Sholokov...

The alley turned left and he rounded the bend with relief. He sprinted through a mass of pedestrians heading towards the spaceport. The problem with headlong flight, of course, was that it attracted unwanted attention. Citizens would turn and comment, creating a visible dynamic in the crowd... The difficulty was how to tell when he'd put sufficient distance between himself and his pursuers so that he could slow to a casual stroll. He judged that, at the moment, his pursuers were too close for him to do that with any confidence.

At least he was leading them towards the spaceport, which had a couple of advantages. One was that his pursuers might assume, naturally enough, that he was attempting to make for the 'port in order to flee aboard a departing starship. The other, more prosaically, was that from the precincts of the 'port a dozen exits issued to all parts of the city. Once he'd reached the crowded underground plaza he would be able to merge with the travellers and select his escape route at leisure.

That was the idea, at any rate.

He took a subway to the plaza. He glanced over his shoulder. There was no sign of Janaker or the Vetch. He allowed himself a relieved breath and slowed to a fast walk as he came to the plaza and merged with the crowd. This was not the first time in his life he regretted being so tall. He stood head and shoulders above the average citizen, and it would take an eagle-eyed bounty hunter only brief seconds to pick him out of the crowd. He stooped and headed for the nearest exit, a ramp leading to the old quarter of the city.

Just as he gained the exit, he chanced a look back. He saw the towering Vetch arrive at speed at the foot of the ramp, come to a halt and scan the crowd. Its monstrous head turned in his direction and, before he could move, the Vetch saw him and gave chase.

Harper turned and ran.

A minute later he emerged into the ancient street that ran parallel with Phreak Street. He turned right, heading towards Macarthur Street and the vehicle cradle. If he could lose his pursuers before reaching the cradle...

He dodged into an alley and seconds later came out on Phreak Street. He looked behind him. There was no sign of Janaker or the Vetch. He turned right and zigzagged through the crowds, keeping low. If he could make it to his car without being apprehended, then he was as good as free. A short drive up the coast and he would be off-planet within the hour, especially if he informed *Judi* he was on his way and ordered her to power up.

He took a circuitous route to Macarthur Street, confident now that he'd shaken off the bounty hunters. He hoped Zeela had managed to tell the Endolon of his ostensible plan to head for Beckett's World, and made it back to the vehicle cradle. If the bounty hunters approached the alien again, and then headed off to Beckett's World, then his way would be free to cross the Reach to Kallasta.

But, he reminded himself, Janaker and the Vetch had caught up with him years after he'd dealt with the last bounty hunter, when he'd assumed his trail would be cold. What were the chances that, first, they would believe the Endolon and, second, decide to hare off to Beckett's World solely on the alien's say so?

He decided it was fruitless to speculate, and that worrying over the minutiae of all eventualities would only increase his paranoia.

He came to Macarthur Street and hurried towards the towering, skeletal structure of the cradle.

Zeela was pacing back and forth in the tiny foyer before the elevator. The look of relief on her face when she saw him was almost comical. She ran to him and pressed herself to his chest, murmuring something he didn't catch. He clutched her hand and dragged her into the elevator.

"Did they see you?" she asked as they were whisked up to the fifth level.

He nodded. "As I left the balcony. I had to run."

"And they fired at you?"

"I kept to the crowds, so they didn't take the risk. How about you? You told the Endolon?"

She nodded. "And he said that if they did not return, then he would contact them at the Old Rose and tell them he'd heard you were heading for Beckett's World."

"Well done."

She sagged against the wall of the elevator. "Must admit, Den, that I'm not feeling too good."

"It's almost over. We'll soon be heading away from here."

She nodded and smiled weakly.

They came to level five and hurried along the catwalk to his ground-effect vehicle. Once inside he darkened the windows for privacy and felt a measure of relief as he drove down the ramp and along the crowded street towards the flyover. Five minutes later they were heading away from DeVries.

He activated his wrist-com and got through to *Judi*, ordering her to power up the maindrive for phase out within forty-five minutes.

Zeela lodged her head against the head-rest and smiled at him. "Just a week ago, if I'd looked ahead and seen myself running away from bounty hunters and heading for Kallasta..."

"You'd've thought you were dreaming?"

"It would have been beyond even my wildest dreams! I had no hope. None at all. And then you walked into the Rat and Corpse."

"Thank Krier Rasnic for that."

She frowned. "Odd how fate plays itself out, isn't it? He wanted to see you dead and steal your ship... and from that came my salvation."

"What did your parents say, Zeela? 'Life is mysterious'..."

He glanced at her hands. They were shaking in her lap. Aware of his glance, she clasped them together.

Thirty minutes later they rounded the headland above Port Morris and *Judi* came into sight, squat and silver on the emerald greensward. He drove up the ramp and assisted Zeela, weak on her feet now, towards the upchute.

"Are you sure you're going to be okay?"

She nodded. "I'll... I'll just go to my cabin, sleep a little..."

He led her along the corridor, told her to use the com beside her bunk if she needed anything, and hurried to the flight-deck.

He slipped into the sling and ordered *Judi* to phase out, and minutes later the idyllic scene of the bay and Port Morris vanished from sight. He stared into the shifting grey veils of void-space, and for the first time in an hour allowed himself to believe that they would get away from Tarrasay without being apprehended.

He called up a starscape of the Reach, and seconds later the grey void was replaced with a three-dimensional representation of this sector of space.

He ordered the point of view to pull out, so that fully half the Reach was in view, a gaseous drift of stars shaped like a stylised arrowhead. Some said that this was how the Reach had got its name, as the arrowhead resembled a devil's tail.

He plotted a route to Kallasta. He would be forced to stop at a few worlds on the way to refuel and take on provisions. He would call in at Clemency first, where he might be able to sell the steamboat engine and fund his onward journey to the far side of the Reach. The rain-forested planet was twenty light years from Tarrasay. And from Clemency...

His thoughts were interrupted by the com channel bleeping in the arm of his sling.

"Zeela?"

"I'm sick, Den... Will you please come?"

The communication ceased, and he pushed himself from his sling and hurried from the flight-deck.

He ran along the corridor and slapped the sensor beside the sliding door to her cabin. It opened to reveal Zeela sprawled across her bunk, blood dribbling from the side of her mouth.

He dashed across the cabin. Her skin was slick with sweat, the front of her shirt soaked with a thick bib of blood.

She tried to focus on him and smiled weakly. "Didn't think it would be this bad," she managed.

"Shhh," he ordered, scooping her up and hurrying into the corridor.

He carried her to the sick-bay and laid her on the slide-bed of the med-pod. He eased the slide into the machine, sat down and stared through the viewplate in the door as probes like miniature tarantulas inserted needles into her skin.

"Well?" he asked impatiently a couple of minutes later.

The med-pod was another minute before replying. "Chronic liver and kidney dysfunction, probable cause as yet unknown."

"Prognosis?"

Seconds elapsed and Harper wanted to scream at the machine to answer him. At last it said, "The patient requires treatment that is beyond present attainment. Suggest transfer to a Grade A medical facility."

He stood up and strode back and forth across the small room. "Okay, okay..." He stopped and stared through the viewplate at the tiny woman within. "How long before she needs the transfer?"

A silence, then: "Approximately twenty-four hours."

"Very well. Do all you can in the interim. Keep her stable. I'll get us to the nearest Grade A facility."

He sprinted from the sick-bay and along the corridor. He slipped into the sling and asked *Judi* about the medical facilities on Tarrasay.

"Negative. Grade C. I do not advise..."

"What do you suggest, then?"

Judi's soothing contralto said, "We are equidistant between two requisite facilities, at Cannon's World and Amethyst Station."

"Which is the closest? Amethyst, right?"

"Affirmative."

"Great. Head there, full speed. No holding back, okay?"

"Understood."

He braced himself, then asked, "And estimated time of arrival?"

The reply came. "Between twenty and twenty-four hours."

"Okay," he said, and tried to persuade himself that they would make it in time.

Amethyst Station... a vast star station eighteen light years from Tarrasay. He knew people there; in fact, an engineer who specialised in starship drives owed him a favour or two.

Of course, once there he would have to foot Zeela's medical bill, and Grade A medical facilities never came cheaply.

He was about to leave the flight-deck and return to the sick-bay when *Judi* said, "Den."

His heart lurched. "Go on."

"We are being followed," *Judi* said.

"But how the hell...?" There was just no way that Janaker and her hideous sidekick might have tracked him all the way to Port Morris and followed him into space at such short order.

Judi went on, "An Ajantan ship is trailing us at approximately two hundred thousand kilometres, Den."

He swore. "Very well. Take whatever evasive manoeuvres you can without compromising on speed. It's a priority that we reach Amethyst as soon as possible." He thought about it, then asked, "I wonder why the frogs didn't try to apprehend us on Tarrasay?"

"My guess is that they were wary of the authorities. There is a history of discord between the two planets."

"Well, thank the fates for small mercies," he said. "I wonder if they're more likely to try to take us on Amethyst Station?"

"That is improbable, given the fortress nature of the star station."

"Excellent."

He left the flight-deck and made his way to the sick-bay. Looking ahead, beyond Zeela's recovery... The Ajantans would be waiting for them once they left Amethyst Station. In which case, if he failed to shake the Ajantans in the void, then the only option would be to land somewhere and hope to ambush the frogs.

Unless...

There was another option, which he would be able to set in motion once he'd reached the star station.

He sat before the med-pod and stared through the hatch at Zeela, willing her to hold on.

CHAPTER FIVE

JANAKER SAT IN the bar of the DeVries spaceport, nursing her fourth beer and cursing her luck.

They had been *this* far from the bastard, sitting at the next table to their target, and had let him slip through their fingers. She'd looked up from her drink, seen the tall, dark human glance at her, and it had been a couple of seconds before recognition kicked in. Too many beers, she thought, and the fact that the last place she'd expect Den Harper to turn up would be on the balcony of the tea room. She'd forgotten the very first rule of being a bounty hunter: be prepared for every eventuality. She'd been lax, and Harper had taken advantage of that to get away.

She had been impressed with Helsh Kreller's reactions, however. He had bragged, back on Hennessy, that he processed reality faster than humans did – and on the evidence of the ensuing chase that was true. Only the intervening crowds that thronged the streets of this old world had slowed his progress.

The Vetch had insisted that they try the spaceport again, though Janaker saw little reason in wasting their time. On landing on Tarrasay they had checked the port for any ship corresponding to the one Harper had stolen, and came up with nothing. Nevertheless, Kreller said that he would check for recent departures.

While Kreller did the foot-work, Janaker drowned her sorrows at the bar and thought through the abortive encounter with the errant telepath.

She was on her fifth beer when Kreller's dark shadow loomed over her. She looked up at the alien's macerated visage. "Don't tell me," she said, "you drew a blank?"

Kreller sat down. "The only ship that phased out in the last couple of hours was a tanker bound for Cryos."

"I could have told you we wouldn't find he'd phased out from here, only you were too impatient and rushed off."

Bloodshot eyes regarded her, inscrutable. "How so?"

"Think about it. We're not in the Expansion now, nor are we in Vetch space."

The Vetch looked around the cramped room, at the humans garbed in what looked like ancient costume. Janaker had no idea what a Vetchian expression of disgust might look like, but she guessed that he was feeling disgust now. "That," he said, "is self-evident. Your point?"

"My point is that the rules that work in the Expansion and in your system don't necessarily apply here. Back home, you land your ship in a designated, government-run spaceport – and woe betide if you come down anywhere else, unless you have a damned good reason. Here..." She waved a hand. "Here, you can land anywhere and the authorities – such as they are – don't turn a hair. The only reason there are a few dozen ships at this port is that DeVries is a mercantile centre so it's convenient for them to land here."

"So you're saying that Harper might have come down anywhere on the planet?"

"And might very well be still here. Then again, if he has any sense he might have high-tailed it back to his ship and phased out."

He regarded her. "So... what now?"

She lifted her drink. "I've been thinking, helped by this stuff, while you've been running around like a headless chicken."

"A... what?" he snapped.

She said, "A term of approbation. I mean 'while you've been running around doing all the hard work'... Anyway, it struck me that it wasn't mere coincidence that Harper was at the tea room."

"It wasn't?"

"Of course not. What were the chances that in all DeVries he'd just happen to choose that café for refreshment? He was there for a reason – because he knew we'd be nearby, knew that the 'solicitor's representatives' had left word to contact them at the Old Rose hotel."

"Ah... so he'd spoken to the Endolon?"

"And decided, being a cautious individual, to stake out the Old Rose before committing himself to meeting us." She hoisted her glass. "So let's go back and have a little word with the overweight alien, shall we?"

They left the spaceport and took a rickshaw to the centre of DeVries, the Vetch muttering his dissatisfaction at this crude form of transport while Janaker looked around her in appalled wonder. The Reach... an anarchic melting pot where the ancient rubbed up against the modern, where all fashions prevailed at once and personal idiosyncrasies were seen as the norm. After the staid, regimented culture of the Expansion – where all exhibitions of individuality were looked upon as suspect, and the authorities clamped down on anything that hinted at radicalism – the melange that was DeVries struck her as chaotic and unsettling.

They arrived at Phreak Street – its very spelling destabilising her notion of the order of things – paid off the rickshaw driver and pushed through the crowds to the Endolon inn.

The Endolon was ensconced upon its throne, grey and adipose and revolting.

"Ah," said the creature as she and Kreller drew up stools and sat down, "the solicitor's representatives. I have just had word, through a third party, that Den Harper has had to leave the planet on urgent business. He is heading, as we speak, towards the rim and a planet known as Beckett's World."

Janaker smiled and glanced at the Vetch. He reached into his jacket, and at first she thought he was about to produce a weapon.

However, he merely leaned forward from the waist, his eyes closed as if concentrating, and said to the Endolon, "He was with a girl?"

"That's right, a tiny companion from..."

"From Kallasta," Kreller finished, his eyes still shut.

Janaker looked from the bloated folds of the Endolon's head to the meaty strips that hung from Kreller's face, wondering how the Vetch had come upon this information.

Kreller opened his eyes and stared at the Endolon. "This so called third party," he said, "did not exist."

The Endolon waved its four arms, giving the impression of being flustered. "I beg your pardon?"

"There was no third party," Kreller went on, surprising Janaker. "The girl returned here, less than one hour ago, and told you to inform us, should we return, that she and Harper were heading towards Beckett's World."

"But, my friend, I assure you..." the Endolon began.

The Vetch reached out a massive hand and clamped one of the Endolon's tiny arms. The alien's long mouth expanded in pain. "Unhand me! This behaviour is most uncivilised!"

"You are lying!" The Vetch leaned forward, speaking softly so as not to arouse comment from the other drinkers. "Now, tell me... where is Harper really heading?"

"I... I swear... I swear the girl did not say!"

Again the Vetch closed his eyes and leaned forward. He was silent for perhaps ten seconds, and Janaker thought she understood the reason for his actions.

So *that* was why the Vetch was accompanying her...

She slipped a hand into the pocket of her jacket and clutched her shield, more than a little pleased that Commander Gorley had insisted she keep it about her person at all times.

Kreller opened his eyes and flung back his head in a gesture she had come to recognise as the equivalent of a human nod. "You speak the truth, this time."

He released the Endolon's hand, and the creature gasped with relief and rubbed the outraged limb with its remaining three hands.

The Vetch turned to her. "Come, I've learned all I can here."

They rose and strode from the bar, and behind them Janaker heard the Endolon call out, "A flagon! A flagon, I say! And food, food!"

They emerged into bright sunlight and Kreller hailed a passing rickshaw. As the flimsy vehicle dodged through the teeming pedestrians, Janaker turned to the Vetch and said, "Commander Gorley forgot to mention that you are a telepath, Kreller."

The Vetch stared ahead. "Perhaps he considered it would be enough of a shock to your prejudices that he was teaming you up with a Vetch."

She bit back a rebuttal and said instead, "So what else did you learn from the mind of the Endolon?"

"Very little of consequence. Except, as of three months ago, Harper still had the same ship he stole from the Expansion five years ago. So, if he had the ship that long, then the chances are that he has it still."

Janaker nodded. "That's a fair assumption."

"I scoured the Endolon's mind, but it didn't know where Harper and the girl might be heading." He turned to her. "I do, however, have a suspicion."

"Go on."

"Harper told the Endolon that he'd saved the girl – Zeela, her name, by the way – from aliens on the world of Ajanta, from which they were fleeing, pursued by the Ajantans."

"Ah, so you think...?"

The Vetch flung back its head. "Yes. It would be logical, would it not, for Harper to take the girl back to the world from which she hailed – Kallasta?"

She nodded. "It's a... workable assumption, until we have more to go on. What now?"

"We phase out, attempt to lock on to Harper's ion trail, and follow."

She smiled to herself. "You're nothing if not an optimist, Kreller. And if we fail to trace his trail?"

"Then we scan the charts and plot a route to Kallasta."

She was silent for a time. "I take it that Harper and the girl are shielded?"

He glanced at her. "Harper certainly so. His standard issue ferronnière will have an integral shield. As for the girl..."

She stared at the alien. "But at the tea room...?" she began.

The Vetch looked away. "My amplification device was not activated."

She laughed derisively. "What?"

He turned his bloody gaze on her and said, "For the sake of my sanity I cannot have the device active at all times. The mind-noise would be intolerable. I had no reason to suspect that Harper or his companion might just happen to be dining at the next table..."

She shook her head, but forestalled her criticism. "Well, just be a little more circumspect in future, hm?"

The Vetch didn't deign to reply.

They came to the port, passed through rudimentary customs – laughably lax after the rigorous security checks of the Expansion – and boarded her ship minutes later. Fifteen minutes after that they gained clearance from the port controller and phased into the void.

Janaker instructed her smartcore to analyse all the ion trails from the ships that had departed Tarrasay from places *other* than the port in the past hour, then stared at the schematic that the 'core transferred to the screen. The image resembled a ball of wool with loose strands shooting off in all directions.

Kreller sat in the co-pilot's couch, watching her as she commanded the 'core to remove all the trails that issued from ships larger, and smaller, than Harper's. She looked up at the screen, and the ball of wool that was Tarrasay didn't look quite so chaotic now.

"Three trails moved from Tarrasay's orbit in the past sixty-seven minutes," she said. "Observe, one is heading into the core. The other two away from it, in the general direction of the rim and Kallasta."

To the smartcore she said, "Bring up a schematic of the sector and all the habitable worlds and star stations between Tarrasay and the rim world of Kallasta." She glanced at the Vetch. "My guess is that he'll make at least one stop between here and Kallasta, for refuelling if for nothing else."

Kreller flung its head back in an affirmative, then leaned forward and stared at the screen.

The schematic showed Tarrasay and Kallasta as shining points of light, with three smaller points in between. She brought up details of the first one, a star station known as Amethyst, eighteen light years from Tarrasay; the station was a vast chaotic hub swollen with modular accretions, a stop-over for ships in transit to the rim and a home to a million citizens. The second was a world known as Teplican, uninhabited according to the most recent records. The third world was Vassatta, a planet with a highly eccentric orbit around its primary.

Kreller said, "Amethyst Station is the closest, and therefore the most likely place Harper would stop."

She nodded, and brought up the schematic showing the ion trails leading from Tarrasay. She homed in on the two likely candidates, both indicating small ships in the category of Harper's, heading towards the star station.

Janaker smiled to herself. "We've got the bastard," she said. "Now we keep our distance and follow them to the station."

"And then?"

"Then we assess the situation and take it from there."

She told Kreller she was going to get a little shut eye and hurried from the bridge.

SHE WAS AWOKEN a while later by the insistent buzzing of her wrist-com. "Developments," Kreller said. "Get yourself to the bridge."

Her scout ship was small: the bridge, a lateral corridor giving onto two cabins, the engine-room aft and, on the deck below, a cargo hold and a storeroom. She stepped from her cabin and was on the bridge in seconds. She slipped into the couch beside Kreller and stared at the screen, which appeared to show a deep-sea fish, all warts and barbels. She glanced at the Vetch. "You didn't tell me you were into natural history."

He indicated the screen. "It's one of the ships we detected earlier, and it appears to be trailing Harper."

"You sure?"

"Well, it's an Ajantan ship, and Ajanta is where Harper rescued the girl."

"So you think...?"

"Clearly, they want her back – or intend to punish Harper for taking her. I've looked up information on their culture. They're a... a barbaric race, to put it mildly. In the Vetch system they would have been wiped out centuries ago."

She stared at him. "Don't you think that a little... excessive?"

"The Ajantans enslave the humans on their planet with a drug, to which the humans become addicted. Then the Ajantans take the humans and... and perform sexual congress upon these individuals. In the course of which, the aliens secrete chemicals which are poisonous to the human metabolism."

Janaker stared at the hideous Ajantan ship. "And the authorities allow this?"

The Vetch barked what might have been a laugh. "What authorities? The Reach is lawless... and apparently the humans on Ajanta are quite happy with the situation. They exist in a drugged bliss for years before they are... taken."

"Delightful," she said. She indicated the alien ship. "So how does this alter things?"

"I can discern both benefits and disadvantages."

"We can be pretty certain we're on the right trail," she said, "and so we just follow the Ajantans until they catch up with Harper. But... then the fun begins. We'll have to fight off the amphibians before we snatch the telepath."

"Just so. The situation is fluid, at the moment. My advice would be to hang back, assess the situation as it develops, and be ready to act at all times."

"I wouldn't disagree with that," she said. "Do you know the weapons capability of the Ajantans?"

He flicked his chin. "Negative. No information available. But as they are a star-faring civilisation, we would be safe to assume their ship possesses a fairly sophisticated armoury."

She slipped from her couch, fetched a beer for herself and a container of water for Kreller.

They sat in silence for a while, until Kreller said, surprising her, "You keep your bridge, if I might make the comment, in a state of disorder and filth."

"Now you're sounding like my mother," she said. "She was always telling me to clean my bedroom." She stared around the cramped bridge, at the discarded beer cartons, greasy food trays, the miscellaneous streaks of unknown fluid that marked the worn surfaces of the consoles and couches and made the deck a sticky mess.

She shrugged. "Home comfort," she said. "I've always worked alone in the past, haven't had to consider other people's refined sensibilities."

Kreller flicked out a hand. "And who are all these people?"

She stared around at the pix of all the women she'd known, going back years. Some images were old and faded, others new and shiny. "Lovers," she said.

Kreller leaned forward and stared at several images closely. He turned to Janaker. "They appear to be all women," he said.

"That's right."

At the last count there were two hundred – two hundred smiling faces staring out at her from all around the bridge, reminding her of all the pleasure and the pain, the good times and the bad.

"The term 'lover,'" Kreller said, "suggests that you mated with these people. But how is that possible?"

"Mated as in made love, yes. Though of course we can't mate to the point where we produce offspring." She looked at the Vetch. "Do you have a problem with that?"

He avoided her eyes. "We Vetch consider such practices immoral. The point of two beings coming together is to produce a litter."

She smiled. "And I always thought the point of two people – humans, at any rate – 'coming together' was to love each other and have fun."

"Such behaviour is against everything that is natural," Kreller said.

She sighed. "You sound like a few politicians from way back I've heard about, in unenlightened times." She shook her head. "Look, my kind of love happens, between two *natural* beings, so how can that be called *unnatural*?"

The Vetch looked at her. "You are a strange person, Sharl Janaker."

She smiled. "You're not the first one to say that," she murmured. "Right, I'm not going to be lectured at by an alien on how to live my life, so I'm out of here. Call me if anything happens. On second thoughts, don't bother. I need my sleep."

She pushed herself from the couch and hurried from the bridge.

CHAPTER SIX

MIRO TESNOLIDEK HAD been a human being, once.

Now no one was sure what he was – or even if he was still 'he' and not 'it.' Even Miro himself had no real idea what he had become.

Harper preferred to think of his old friend as still human, however, and to think of him as 'he', even though the label human might be stretching the definition. They had been through a lot together, before Miro's metamorphosis – and it had been Harper who had saved Miro's life back on Stanislav, three years ago. He often wondered whether it might have been kinder just to let him die.

Now Miro stumped around *Judi*, scoping its superstructure with his one good eye.

Harper followed, keeping his distance. Miro was unpredictable. There was no telling when he might lash out with one of his chitinous claws, not that it would be Miro doing the lashing.

In his lucid moments, Miro often joked that he was the only human-alien in the Reach with Tourette's syndrome.

"What do you think?" Harper asked, not for the first time.

Miro dragged himself around the ship. He growled something, or rather the thing he had become growled at Harper.

In his younger days, Miro had been tall and slim. Now he was grotesque, bloated. He had been tanned, muscular – but now very little of his skin was visible beneath the grating plaques of grey shell. He clanked as he walked. What had been his face – a very handsome face, as Harper recalled – was covered by a mask of warted tegument, through which one piercingly blue eye peered.

This eye shuttled back and forth, taking in the ship.

Not long after Harper had hauled Miro from the swamp on Stanislav, during the early stages of the metamorphosis, he had made the mistake of attempting to read his friend's mind... or what remained of it. He'd read the agony of the human being buried beneath... something else. That something else was alien, and seemingly as confused, as terrified, and in just as much pain as Miro himself.

Harper had vowed never to read his mind again.

"I think it can be done," Miro said now, surprising Harper with his cogency. He had moments of lucidity, but they came and went.

"But how quickly?"

The bright blue eye rolled to regard Harper. "A day, if I drop everything else."

Miro suddenly darted towards Harper. "*Yesh sankrat! Yesh! Yesh!*" An arm swung, terminating in a lethal claw. Harper ducked and the claw whistled millimetres above his head. "*Yesh!*"

Harper backed off, putting five metres between himself and the creature Miro had become. He stood and watched his friend warily. Miro slumped, the plates of his bloated chest rising and falling with his uneven breathing.

"*Yesh, sankratash!*" Miro cried, turning and stomping away across the ringing deck of the hangar.

Harper followed at a distance. They passed a couple of small starships in for repair, Miro's engineers and apprentices clambering over their superstructure.

Miro squeezed through a door into the room he used as his office. Harper paused outside and peered in through the window in the door. He waited until Miro had climbed into his cage and given a voice command for the bars to lock. Only then did Harper push through the door and sit down across the room from his friend.

Miro rested in a seat adapted from the sling of an old star-liner. An analgesic hypodermic on the end of a waldo dangled from the ceiling like a scorpion's tail. As Harper watched, the needle descended, inserted itself between the scales on Miro's pachydermous back, and released its sedative load.

"Ah... Christ, but that's better." Miro laughed. "I feel almost human again."

It never failed to amaze Harper how, despite his condition, Miro managed to maintain a sense of humour.

"It's good to see you, Miro," he said.

"And you too. It's been a year or more. What you been doing with yourself?"

Miro liked to hear the stories of Harper's travels across the face of the Reach; through them he lived vicariously, visiting worlds no longer open to him. "Crossed the Reach three times since we last met, Miro. Nearly won a fortune on Constance..." He told the story again, even though on meeting the mechanic less than an hour ago he'd told the same tale; Miro had seemed lucid then, but soon after had begun to phase. He often forgot what he'd heard just before the alien within him gained ascendancy.

"And you want work done on the old ship?"

He'd outlined his needs in detail earlier, too, but obviously Miro had forgotten. "I want weapons mounted, fore and aft. Void capable, with a range of up to a million kilometres. And not just pea-shooters. You said it could be done."

Miro shifted his bulk, heavy plaques scraping. "I did?" He nodded his domed head. "I don't see why not."

"You said it'd take a day, if you dropped everything else."

"I've got a quartet of decent Housmann Defenders that would fit nicely. That's not the problem, though."

"What is?"

"I could fit the mechanisms, no problem, and it wouldn't be expensive."

"What are we talking, including labour?"

"To you, a thousand."

Earlier, on arriving at Amethyst Station, he'd taken the ten thousand Ajantan units and changed them for a more stable currency, walking away from the deal with six thousand standard Reach units.

"I can afford that, but what's the problem?"

Miro leaned forward, his scales scraping the bars of his cage. "It's not the mechanisms, nor fitting them, that's the expensive part. It's the missiles themselves. They don't come cheap."

"How much?"

"A thousand each."

Harper whistled. "And I'd need at least four..." Which, along with the cost of fitting, would leave him with just a thousand standard units.

He had no idea how much Zeela's treatment might cost, but he guessed a lot more than one thousand. He had scant savings, few assets other than his ship itself... and the steamboat engine which he had been hoping to hang onto and sell later.

Miro said, "So... what do you say?"

"Let me think it over, Miro, okay?" He pushed himself from the padded chair and crossed the room to the viewscreen, and stared out into space.

He marvelled as always at the grotesque complexity of Amethyst Station. It was so called because, hundreds of years ago when it had been constructed by the engineers of Lansdowne in the Expansion, it was said to have resembled a purple, faceted gemstone. Over the centuries, however, since its sale to junk dealers in the Reach and its subsequent removal from Expansion territory, it had undergone a slow process of change, with a thousand accretions building up from its original core. It looked like some nightmarish coral reef now, shaped like a spinning top but hideously unbalanced, scaled and patched and extended with tentacles and pseudopods.

A bit like poor Miro himself, Harper thought.

He watched the tiny shapes of starships flitting from the void and heading for the letterbox openings of the reception berths.

Might one of them belong to the bounty hunters, he wondered, or the Ajantans?

He turned from the window and nodded. "Agreed. Go ahead and do the work. I have little choice, really."

Miro turned his bulk awkwardly to regard Harper. "You mind telling me what kind of trouble you're in?"

He'd done so already, an hour ago, but he didn't mind repeating his tale of woe. He told Miro about the Ajantans, and the bounty hunters, and how he had little hope of outrunning them both before he reached Kallasta. His only really hope was to stand up and fight.

"And this kid, this woman. You two...?"

Harper shook his head. "She's a passenger, that's all. I'm taking her to Kallasta, fleeing the aliens who think they own her."

"What she like?"

Harper described Zeela: slim, black, pretty...

"Oh, Christ, man... and you two aren't...?" He made a choking sound like an indrawn breath. "What's wrong with you, Den? Hell, if only I had the chance..."

He fell silent. Harper looked through the viewscreen to where starships came and went like scintillating insects.

As close as he had been to Miro Tesnolidek, he'd never told him why he'd gone on the run from the Expansion, what had happened to push him over the edge... what had made him the man he was today.

He'd told no one that, and doubted he ever would.

Miro said, "And this girl, you say she might not pull through?"

Harper shrugged. "I got her into a clinic as soon as we arrived. Grade A. The best money can buy. They said it was touch and go. The kid... she's in a bad way." He shrugged. "We'll see..."

"Tough," Miro said. "I hope she pulls through."

Harper smiled. "Thanks."

He was more than a little uncomfortable, talking medical matters and clinics with Miro. The fact was that his friend's condition could be cured, or at least ameliorated, if only he could lay his hands on sufficient funds. He needed a comprehensive somatic scouring, a stripping down to his skeleto-muscular frame and building back up again. Conservative estimates put the cost of his treatment at two million units. Some medics quoted five million. Harper had said that if ever he came into a fortune...

"I'll get the work done," Miro said. "I'll get my team working on it, pronto." His claw swung up to a camera lens in the corner of the room. "And don't worry, it's all in there. I might forget all hell and more, but my boys always check the cam."

"I appreciate that, Miro. I'll drop by tomorrow."

"See you then, Den. Hey, shake?"

Harper moved towards the cage and, in a game of trust that he'd never shied away from, he extended his hand through the bars and slapped his friend's chitinous claw.

He left the hangar and took a dropchute down to the radial slideway, then rode the slide to the station's core.

As HE MADE his way to the spindle where the hospital was located, his wrist-com buzzed.

"Den," *Judi* said, "just to update you..."

"Go ahead."

"I've been monitoring on all frequencies, and the Ajantan ship is in orbit around the station."

"What about Janaker's ship?"

"No sign of that one so far, but it might be hanging back. I'll keep scanning. Any further word on Zeela?"

"Not yet. I'll keep you posted."

He cut the connection. At least the bounty hunters hadn't followed him here, yet. The problem with the Ajantans was that he had no idea about their ship's capabilities – which was why he'd thought it wise to arm his own ship. When the Ajantans decided it was time to move in, he would be ready.

He arrived at the spindle and took a dropchute down to the hospital on level seventy-five. Six hours ago he'd called ahead and arranged for Zeela's admittance, squirting the med-pod's diagnosis along with his credit details. The fact that his bank balance was almost zero had worried him to begin with, until the clinic's admin department had assured him that they would consider his ownership of *Judi* as collateral.

The sliding door of the dropchute opened and he stepped through.

He passed through the identity check and made his way to ward twenty, his apprehension mounting. The physician and his medical emergency team on duty when Harper had arrived with Zeela had been non-committal and brusque. The medic had studied the med-pod's report, but admitted that he'd never come across dhoor withdrawal symptoms and couldn't possibly hazard a guess as to Zeela's chances. All he could say, all things considered, was that it was touch and go – and that if she had arrived at the hospital any later, then she would not have pulled through.

And if Zeela's treatment proved prolonged and exorbitant, what then? He'd considered this earlier, on leaving the hospital. The worst case scenario would be that he'd have to hire out his ship to cover the cost of her treatment, and remain with Zeela for an indefinite period on the station... which, with the Ajantans and the bounty hunters on his tail, was not an option he wanted to consider.

A nurse on reception took his details and indicated a seat. "Ms Antarivo is currently in the critical unit, Mr Harper. I'll have a specialist update you just as soon as possible."

"You've no idea how she's doing?"

"I'm sorry, Mr Harper. If you'd care to take a seat."

For the next hour he tried not to consider the possibility that Zeela might not pull through. He'd known her for less than a week, and yet they'd been through a lot together. He wondered if what he felt for her was similar to the bond that existed between a father and daughter.

He stood abruptly and began pacing the corridor. For Zeela to pass away now, after all the hardships she'd overcome... Harper believed in nothing other than fickle, arbitrary fate – and at times he wished fate would manifest itself as an incarnate form so that he could attack it, vent his rage and frustration in a physical act of cathartic violence.

"Mr Harper."

He jumped at the sound of his name. The nurse at reception indicated a door to his right. He hurried to it, knocked and entered.

He was surprised by the spaciousness of the room, and the fact that it looked out onto the star-flecked vastness of deep space. An elegant, dark-haired woman sat behind a triangular silver desk. She rose, rounded the desk and took his hand.

She introduced herself as Consultant Gina Di Mannetti, and indicated a seat.

On his way to the clinic, Harper had considered employing his ferronnière at this meeting, but decided against it. Physicians employed euphemisms, and if Zeela wasn't going to make it then he didn't want to read the raw fact in the head of some dispassionate consultant. He wanted euphemisms.

"How is she, Doctor?"

Di Mannetti smiled. "For a tiny, insubstantial wisp of a thing, addicted for years to an opiate-analogue, and suffering from multiple organ failure... I'd say that she's doing remarkably well."

"She'll survive?"

"We performed a liver and kidney flush this morning, Mr Harper, and a total blood transfusion. She'll be up and active in a day."

He took a deep breath and felt light-headed. He was aware that his smile must appear insane.

"Your quick thinking in getting her here undoubtedly saved her life," Di Mannetti said. "I must admit that I've never treated a case of dhoor withdrawal before, though I've heard of the drug. I specialise in the study of xeno-biological pathogens, and I consider myself fortunate that Ms Antarivo happened along when she did. I was due to leave the Station yesterday, but as fate would have it my ship was cancelled."

"Can I see Zeela?"

Di Mannetti consulted a screen on her desk. "Ms Antarivo is conscious, so I see no reason why not. If you would care to come this way."

Harper followed the physician from the room and along a wide corridor. They paused outside a door and Di Mannetti indicated an observation panel. He peered through.

Zeela lay on a bed, outfitted in a white shift. She appeared tiny, elfin – more like a child than a young woman.

He looked at Di Mannetti, who nodded. He pushed through the door and approached the bed.

Zeela looked up and her smile illuminated her features. "Den!"

They embraced, the girl stick-thin in his arms. "It's so good to see you!" she said.

"It's great to see you, too. You gave me one hell of a fright." He sat down beside the bed, clutching her hand.

Di Mannetti stood at the foot of the bed. "Ms Antarivo requires a few hours rest and recuperation, but I see no reason why she won't make a full recovery. Of course, there is the ongoing factor of her addiction to take into consideration."

"Zeela's still addicted?"

"Technically, yes. But I've been working on a relatively harmless synthesis of the addictive compound of the drug, which I'll prescribe when Ms Antarivo is discharged. If she takes this in decreasing doses for the next month, then I see no reason why her recovery should not be complete."

She looked from Zeela to Harper. "I'll leave you two alone for a while, Mr Harper. We have a few technicalities to discuss, so if you would return to my office in ten minutes..."

Di Mannetti left the room.

"I think by technicalities, Den, she means how we might pay for all the treatment."

He smiled. "Don't worry about that. I've got it all sorted out."

She brightened. "You have? But the ten thousand units from Ajanta wouldn't..."

"Shhh," he said. "I told you, it's all sorted out, okay? We'll have you out of here and on your way to Kallasta in no time."

"And what about the Ajantans?"

"No sign of them," he said, another white lie to add to the first.

"And the bounty hunters?"

"I think we safely gave them the slip on Tarrasay."

She smiled at him. "What have you been doing while I've been lazing around?"

"Looking up old friends, planning our route."

"We'll make it okay, won't we? I mean, what with the bounty hunters and the Ajantans after us."

"We'll make it okay," he assured her. "I'm taking steps to ensure that."

"Steps?"

"Later, when you're out of here. Right," he said, squeezing her hand. "I'd better go and see what Her Highness wants."

At the door, he waved and slipped from the room.

He found Di Mannetti's office, knocked and entered. He resumed his seat at the point of the arrowhead desk. "You mentioned technicalities?"

Di Mannetti looked from her screen to Harper. "Ms Antarivo's treatment has been intricate and expensive."

"How much?"

She smiled. "I'm delighted that you appreciate that healthcare is primarily a matter of business," she said.

"We live on the Reach, so what isn't?"

"To answer your initial question. The cost of Ms Antarivo's treatment, the operation, the drugs, the aftercare, and of course my own fees... would come to a little over seven thousand units."

He nodded, keeping his expression neutral in a bid to hide his shock. "I see..."

He would have a thousand left over after paying Miro's fee, and perhaps another thousand in scrip aboard the ship – but even if he could sell the steamboat engine here on Amethyst he would be unlikely to realise five thousand for it.

"That's... more than I was expecting."

"I take it that you do not possess the immediate funds with which to cover the cost?"

"You state the case with refreshing eloquence, Doctor."

She smiled and tapped her chin with an elegant forefinger. She said at last, "I understand that you work as a star trader?"

"That's correct."

She glanced at her screen. "And that you own your own starship?"

"Right. But I'm in no position to sell it in order to finance..."

Something in her expression halted his words. She said, "Selling your ship is not an option, Mr Harper. But there is another way."

"There is?"

"Ms Antarivo mentioned that you are heading to the world of Kallasta."

Intrigued, Harper nodded. "That's correct."

"In your travels have you ever been to the world of Teplican?"

"Teplican... The name's familiar. Wasn't there a colony there at one time, a hundred years ago? As I recall, the colonists left rather suddenly."

"There was a mass emigration from the planet perhaps ninety years ago. It wasn't particularly commented upon at the time. The various colony worlds are largely autonomous, and what they do rarely makes the news. But historians have since wondered exactly what happened."

"Which is very interesting, Dr Di Mannetti, but I don't see the relevance..."

"Evidence has come to light that there might have been a medical reason for the colonists' flight from their world. As I am a research xeno-biologist, this excites my professional curiosity."

"Ah..." Harper said.

"I was due to take a ship to Teplican yesterday, but the flight was cancelled and the next one will not be for another month, which doesn't fit in with my busy schedule."

"I see," he said.

Di Mannetti went on, "Now, the cost of a flight to Teplican is approximately that of Ms Antarivo's treatment, which I would be willing to underwrite, if..."

Harper stared beyond Di Mannetti, to the star-strewn blackness of space. As far as he knew, Teplican was thirty light years from Amethyst Station – the flight there would be a rather longer leg of the zigzag course he'd planned anyway, but would serve the same purpose as it was in the general direction of Kallasta.

He smiled, leaned forward, and held out a hand. "You've got yourself a deal," he said.

"TRY NOT TO show your alarm when you see Miro," Harper told Zeela as he assisted her across the ringing deck of the hangar. "Stay close to me and we'll be okay."

He could see Miro Tesnolidek hunched beside the blunt nose of the ship, looking more like an alien crustacean than a human being.

Zeela gripped his hand and stared. "But what happened to him?"

"I'll tell you all about it when we're under way," he said. "I've just got to look over a few things with Miro, then we'll be off."

Dr Di Mannetti said, "I've read about Tesnolidek. He's the only case of Stanislav parasitism to have survived."

"If you can call what he's become survival," Harper said.

"And I was beginning to feel sorry for myself..." Zeela murmured.

Harper smiled at her. Since picking her up from the hospital that morning, he'd experienced the strong desire to protect the tiny woman. Di Mannetti had assured him that she was making excellent progress, but even so Harper felt the need to cosset Zeela. He'd instruct *Judi* to keep her supplied with healthy meals and nutritious juices for the next week.

"What is Teplican like?" Zeela said as they approached the ship.

"It's a beautiful world, by all accounts," Di Mannetti said. "I've only seen 3Vs of it, but it looks idyllic."

"Just the place for a relaxing holiday, Den," Zeela said.

Harper nodded. "Ideal for a convalescent, I'd say."

Miro heard them, turned and shuffled forward. "Don't worry, folks, I've dosed myself up to the gills. I should be fine for the next thirty minutes."

As Harper made the introductions, Zeela smiled at the hunched, pustular shell that was Miro Tesnolidek. "Den has told me all about you," she said.

Miro growled a laugh. "You shouldn't go frightening a beautiful woman with horror stories, Den."

Harper indicated the ramp and said to DiMannetti, "*Judi* will see you to your berth."

"I'll go with you, Gina," Zeela said. "Nice to meet you, Mr Tesnolidek."

As the women strode up the ramp, Miro said, "Glad to see she's pulled through, Den."

Harper almost said something about the wonders of modern medicine, but stopped himself just in time. Instead he said, "How did the work go?"

Miro waved a claw at the ship. "Without a hitch, both the engineering and the programming. We slaved the operating system into the ship's core. All you have to do is give the command when you want to blast your enemies out of the sky. Come on, I'll show you the missiles."

Harper looked at his friend. Normally the only confined space where Miro allowed himself to entertain others was his office, where the restraining cage ensured he couldn't run amok.

Miro picked up on Harper's hesitation. "It'll be fine. I started a new course of drugs yesterday. They keep me relatively sane for stretches of thirty minutes. And I'd say I had another twenty to go before I lose it again." He indicated the ramp with a scabrous claw. "Anyway, there's something else I want to show you."

"'Something else'?"

He followed Miro into the ship and they took the chute to the engine-room. "We'll get to it," Miro said. "First, the hardware..." He crossed the engine-room and paused. "Well, what do you think?"

They stood in the shadow of a big silver breech cradle, a mechanism so ugly it possessed its own odd beauty. Nestled in the cradle was a stubby red missile. Miro tapped it with a claw.

"There's another housed on the port side, and two more at the prow. When you give the command, they externalise through the ship's carapace for all round targeting. But remember, you only have four of the beauties, so go easy."

"Range?"

"The manufacturer claims a million kilometres. If I were you, I would play safe and wouldn't fire until the target was under half that distance."

Harper nodded. "I'll remember that."

"I programmed *Judi* with the firing codes. She'll give you them once you're under way."

"I appreciate this, Miro."

"Anything for a friend," he said. "I hope you don't need to use them, but if you do, then I'm confident they'll do the job."

They made to leave the engine-room. "And the other thing?"

Miro lifted a claw and indicated the chute. They climbed aboard and dropped to the under deck. "Down here," his friend said, leading the way along the narrow corridor, his shell scraping the walls.

Harper knew where they were going, and what Miro had found. The Enigma of Hold Number Two, he called it.

As expected, Miro stopped before the arched hatch that gave access to the second hold – or, technically speaking, would have given access to the chamber had entry been permissible. He tapped the metal hatch with a claw and said, "The hold would have been the obvious place to house the first stern missile, Den. But, try as we might, we couldn't get into it."

Harper nodded. "As if I didn't know."

"So what gives?"

"I wish I knew. I've had the ship five years and the hold's been locked all that time. Ship's smartware core can't command it to open, and in the early days I tried opening it with a cutting tool."

"And?"

"I spent three back-breaking days at it and made a cut about a millimetre deep, then gave up."

"Might be treasure in there, Den. Who owned the ship before you?"

He was pretty certain he'd told Miro about the ship, back in the days before the accident, along with the enigma of the hold. "I stole it from an Expansion Commander," he said.

"I wonder what he hid in there...?" Miro mused.

They moved back through the ship and stopped at the top of the ramp. "Been a pleasure doing business with you, Den."

"As always," Harper replied. "And thanks."

"Shake?"

Harper smiled and slapped Miro's waving claw.

Miro lurched forward, brought the claw up above Harper's head – then laughed as Harper flinched.

"Got you that time!"

"You ugly bastard, Miro!" Harper cried. "Now get off my ship and clear the deck – before I give the command to phase out and fry you."

"Till next time, Den."

He watched Miro shuffle off down the ramp and cross the hangar to his office, then made his way to the flight-deck.

Zeela was waiting for him in the co-pilot's sling. "Hey, shouldn't you be getting some rest?" he said as he laid himself out beside her.

"I was bored, and anyway I haven't seen you for ages and I wanted to talk. Thank you for the clothes, Den." She smoothed her hands down the front of the one-piece he'd bought, along with a variety of dresses and suits, to celebrate her recovery.

"You like them? I wasn't sure..."

"They're great."

He smiled to himself. "Strap yourself in, then we'll phase out."

"And thank you for everything else, Den. I appreciate it."

He smiled at her. "Shut up while I get this thing up and running, will you?"

He gave ship the command to phase out and stared through the viewscreen at the empty hangar. Behind the far safety screens, he made out the faces of mechanics and engineers staring out at the ship as the clearance klaxon blared.

Judi said, "The Ajantan ship is on the far side of the station, Den."

Harper nodded. "Which suits me just fine."

"Hey!" Zeela said. "You told me there was no sign of the Ajantans!"

The scene flickered, and seconds later the scene of the hangar was replaced by the depthless grey of void-space.

Harper shrugged, affecting nonchalance. "There wasn't, when you asked. They turned up earlier today."

She ran a hand through her luxuriant hair. "And there I was, thinking it'd all be plain sailing from now on."

"Don't worry. I've made certain adjustments to the ship."

She was sarcastic. "Like another engine?"

"Like a weapons system that will blow the Ajantans to bits if they try to get too close."

Zeela sniffed. "Will serve them right for trying to kill us in their lair. Spoken like a true pacifist! My mother and father would disown me."

The phase out completed, he climbed from the sling. "I don't know about you," he said, "but I'm famished."

They ate on the flight-deck, enjoying an Amethyst Station speciality which Harper had stocked up with that morning: flatbreads stuffed with curried spinach, said to be the staple diet of the spacers who'd first worked on the Station after its removal to the Reach.

"So..." Zeela said, "you said you'd tell me about your friend, Miro. What happened to him?"

He thought back three years, to the time they'd ventured across the Reach to Stanislav on what he'd assumed was going to be just another routine trading trip.

"Back then Miro was a trader," he told her, "and we often worked together. There was a small scientific colony on Stanislav, studying the locals – the shilth, they called themselves, swamp-dwelling coelacanths. Anyway, we went in with provisions, cut a deal and were about to light out when Miro was attacked as he left the camp for his ship. I heard his screams as I was boarding ship, grabbed a weapon..." He shrugged, reliving those frantic, fear-filled few minutes. "I ran back to where I'd left him, just in time to see something dragging him off towards a swamp. I gave chase and followed Miro and whatever it was that'd grabbed him. The long and the short of it was, I fried the crab-thing and dragged Miro to safety, but..."

Zeela stared at him. "But...?"

He shrugged. "Sometimes I think it might have been better if Miro had died. I hauled him aboard ship and slammed him in the med-pod. The crab had cut him up pretty bad, and I had get him to a Grade A facility, fast."

"Where have I heard this story before?" she murmured. "Hope these things don't happen in threes..."

"To cut a long story short, there was little the medics could do for him, short of patching up the lacerations. He'd been infected, invaded by some xeno-parasite, and he'd already begun to metamorphosise. You've seen the result, three years on."

"And there's no cure?"

He told her that there was, at a cost of two million units or more.

"But it won't get any worse, will it? I mean, the alien won't take over entirely?"

"There's been no change in three years," Harper said. "So I suppose we should be thankful for small mercies. He takes drugs to ease the pain and keep the alien at bay. He has his good days, and his bad. Today happened to be a good one, I'd say."

She shook her head. "Wouldn't the Reach be a great place without aliens, Den?"

He looked at her, and shook his head. "No, Zeela, it wouldn't. It'd be impoverished. For every race like the Stanislav crabs, or the Ajantans, there are a hundred good, altruistic ee-tees. It's the diversity that makes the Reach what it is. In my experience, there are more bad humans than there are aliens. Believe me."

She smiled at him and stroked his hand. "You're probably right, Den," she said.

A little later she yawned and said she was going to turn in. "When are we due to arrive at Teplican?"

"In a little over thirty hours. Go and get some sleep."

He watched her move from the flight-deck and remained in his sling, staring out into the void. He felt relaxed, content for the first time in days. He was about to experience a new world – which was always a pleasure – and Zeela was on the mend.

An hour later *Judi* said, "Den, I'm picking up pursuers."

He sat up. "Pursuers? Plural?"

"Affirmative. One is the Ajantan ship."

"And the other?"

"I suspect that it's the vessel belonging to the bounty hunters, but that is to be confirmed."

Harper swore. "Great. How far away are they?"

"A million kilometres and half as far again, respectively."

"Very well. Warn me if they approach any closer – but not while Zeela is on the flight-deck, understood? I don't want her getting alarmed."

"Understood, Den."

Harper settled back into the sling and stared into the void.

CHAPTER SEVEN

JANAKER HAD SEEN many star stations before – all of them in the Expansion, of course – but none like Amethyst.

"Would you look at that," she said.

"It's the ugliest example of human spatial architecture I've ever seen," the Vetch said. "And that's saying something."

"I can just detect an Expansion station somewhere in there," Janaker said, "but it's been built on and added to over the years. It looks lopsided, as if it shouldn't work."

"Asymmetry doesn't matter in space," Kreller reminded her. "Function is all."

"I know that," she snapped.

She thought the station looked like a spinning top to which a child had glued an assortment of mismatched oddments, blocks and cylinders, without the slightest aesthetic consideration. She wondered how safe it might be. According to the information cached in her ship's core, Amethyst was home to more than a million citizens. It looked like an accident waiting to happen.

She watched a variety of ships, big and small and every size in between, come and go from the station's docks, a façade of dull metal marked with a dozen entrance bays.

"So... you know where Harper is?" she asked.

"I traced his ion signature to the station, then lost it among thirty others. They approached the docks, then their trail became tangled."

"How long ago did they arrive?

"Going by the degradation of the signature," the Vetch said, "around forty-eight hours ago."

"And they haven't been and gone in that time?"

"I have scanned no ion signatures leaving the station in the direction of the Rim."

She stared at the ugly agglomeration of the station. "So they could be anywhere in there now?"

"They might have docked in one of the dozen hangars you see before you."

"Well, that narrows it down a little," she said, doubting that the alien would pick up on her sarcasm. "We sit here until they emerge, right?"

He turned and stared at her. "I want to go in there and find them, now."

She nodded, giving the impression that she was considering his proposal. "And why is that, when we can just sit out here and wait for them to emerge? We know where they're going, after all."

"Time is important. We are facing a remorseless foe in the Weird, and we need every weapon in our armoury, sooner rather than later."

"One single telepath," she pointed out, "will hardly make that much difference."

"You forget that our remit was to return with the telepath *and* the ship."

She looked at him. "The ship?" She tried to recall if Gorley had said anything about the telepath's ship. "Why's the ship so important?"

The Vetch hesitated, and in that second Janaker knew that the alien was holding something back. "Every ship, every armament, in the fight against the Weird is important."

That was screwy. "Not *that* important, surely? One ship? It isn't as if it's that big or powerful."

He stared at the screen. "I am merely obeying orders, Janaker."

She stared out at the racked letter-box openings to the hangars, docks and repair shops in the face of the station. "Okay, so we go in there blind and just hope to stumble across Harper and the girl or their ship?"

Kreller tapped his head. "You forget my ability, Janaker. We dock at the lowest level and work our way up. It shouldn't take me long to read something about Harper and the girl in the minds of the workers and engineers. With luck we might even find their ship, if Harper hasn't taken the precaution of berthing it in a secure, enclosed area." He snorted. "If they have such on *this* kind of set up."

It would take a lot of unnecessary time and effort, as far as she was concerned – but she had to admit that a part of her was curious to see if the station's interior was as chaotic and *ad hoc* as its exterior. She had always lived on rural worlds, by choice, and she wondered how people could live in such an ugly, enclosed environment, without sky and sea and countryside.

She recalled the pursuing Ajantans and asked Kreller, "Any sign of the aliens?"

"They're keeping their distance; more than a million kilometres away."

She nodded. "Playing a waiting game," she said.

Kreller contacted the station's docking authorities and gained permission to berth. Janaker slotted her ship into the approach run, behind a tanker that had seen better days, and stretched out on her couch.

Kreller said, "Amazing. No accreditation required, no security checks..."

"And if it's anything like Tarrasay, no identity scans when we pass through customs," she added. "This is the Reach, after all."

The Vetch made a disgusted, venting snort through its many facial tentacles. "And I thought security in the Expansion inordinately lax, compared to that in Vetch territory."

"Remind me never to take a holiday in Vetch space," she said. From the little that Kreller had said about the authorities that ruled the Vetch, they seemed even more fascistic than the Expansion authorities.

They docked in a vast hangar and walked down a ringing umbilical to passport control – which consisted of a bored official who waved them through without bothering to insert their proffered data-pins into her terminal.

Kreller indicated an upchute access which gave onto the next level. "Now we make our way up, one deck at a time, and I scan the personnel. I will need to concentrate, so no unnecessary questions, please."

She nodded, suddenly tense, and touched the pistol on her hip. "One thing before you start," she said, "when we find Harper, we stun him immediately and I'll deal with the authorities, okay?"

He considered this. "I would rather we follow him to his ship and deal with him there. Then I will take his ship and return to the Expansion while you return with him aboard your ship."

She looked at him. What was it about Harper's vessel that was so important, all of a sudden? She nodded without replying as they rode the upchute to the second level.

Beside her the Vetch had tensed, leaning forward slightly, his head moving from side to side. The upchute bobbed to a halt and they stepped out. They were in a cavernous hangar swarming with grease-stained mechanics and engineers with soft-screens. A dozen big ships occupied gargantuan cradles and racks. Janaker scanned the ships for any sign of Harper's vessel, but his wasn't among them. As they watched, a liner slipped through the rectangular entrance at the far end of the chamber, blasting through the vacuum-impermeable membrane with a roar of auxiliary drives, and came to rest in the exact centre of the deck.

They made their way around a gallery catwalk that looked down on the busy deck. Kreller was silent, turning his head this way and that, his eyes half closed in concentration.

They made a complete circuit of the hangar and came to the upchute access. She said, "Nothing?"

He flung back his head in an affirmative. "We ascend."

They stepped into the upchute and rose to the next level. She stepped onto the catwalk of another hangar, this one given over to the refuelling of vessels: umbilical hoses hung from the ceiling, each one pulsing as fuel was pumped from reservoirs into the ships' tanks. Only a dozen personnel worked here, and the Vetch didn't bother making a circuit of the hangar. "Nothing," he said, and indicated the upchute.

"Two down and ten to go," Janaker said to herself.

The next level was a storage hangar filled with ships that appeared to be mothballed, attended by a lone curator who Kreller quickly scanned and dismissed. The fourth level was another busy repair shop replete with vessels big and small in various stages of reconstruction. They made the requisite circuit and returned to the upchute.

One hour later they hit paydirt.

They stepped onto the catwalk enclosing a hangar on the seventh level, and the Vetch gripped the rail and leaned forward. He half-closed his eyes and turned his head from side to side.

"What?" Janaker asked a minute later as he opened his eyes and straightened up.

"Harper had his ship fitted with a weapons system," he said. If he possessed a mouth, she thought, he would be smiling now. Only his wide eyes indicated his pleasure. "It is my guess that Harper armed himself against the Ajantans."

Janaker snorted. "He killed the last bounty hunter sent after him," she pointed out. "I guess he'd have no qualms about killing another." She looked around the deck. "When did they leave here, and do you know if they were heading directly to Kallasta?"

The Vetch flung back his head. "All I read in the mind of a mechanic was that Harper phased out some hours ago." He indicated an office at the far end of the hangar. "The... human who dealt with Harper is in there. I need to get closer to read him. I would like to know exactly what weapons system Harper had fitted."

She glanced at the Vetch. "The way you said 'human'... you sound almost doubtful."

He hesitated, then said, "The creature is human... or was human, once. Now I'm not so sure. It seems to have been taken over by something – something alien. From time to time this *thing* asserts cognitive dominance. It makes it hard for me to read its... his... mind."

Janaker stared through the rectangular window in the wall of the office, but made out no one inside.

Kreller led the way to a flight of stairs and they descended. As they were crossing the deck towards the office, the door swung open and something limped out.

Janaker stopped in her tracks and stared.

Her first feeling was one of revulsion, quickly followed by pity. The thing before her had obviously been human once, but something terrible had happened to him. It was as if half of his body had been grafted onto something vaguely crustacean, but bloated and alien. Even the right side of his body, which still resembled a human being – in form if nothing else – was scabbed with overlapping plaques of shell. Only his right eye had survived whatever had happened to him; the rest of his face was lost under a pebbled, chitinous tegument.

"What happened to...?" Janaker murmured.

"His name is Miro Tesnolidek," Kreller murmured. "He is... hard to read. I see an alien swamp, read the trauma of an accident..."

The creature limped towards her, the plaques scraping against each other with a painful, grating sound. He paused a few metres from where she and Kreller stood.

"How can I help you?" Tesnolidek said. What had been his right hand, but was now a giant claw, gave a galvanic twitch as if barely under his control.

And the touching thing was that his voice – muffled though it was beneath a scab of shell – was deep, rich, and beautiful.

Kreller leaned forward and scanned the man. Janaker said, "We are friends of a star trader called Den Harper."

The man screamed, took a quick step forward, his outsized claw flying in threatening arc. "*Veshank! Kretch! Nassa...*"

He stopped his advance as if with great effort, and said, once again in his beautifully modulated baritone, "I'm sorry. Sometimes I have little control over..." The claw waved. "You were saying?"

She and Kreller had backed away, and now the Vetch murmured to her, "I'm getting nothing. Keep him talking while I..."

She smiled at Tesnolidek and said, "I quite understand. We are friends of Den Harper. We understand that he was here, that you did some work for him. We were wondering where..."

"Friends of Den's?" Tesnolidek said. "Den has few friends. He would have mentioned it if..." His one good eye flicked towards the Vetch.

"We met him just recently, and we'd like to meet up again. Did he mention where he was heading after leaving here? We understand his destination was Kallasta, but..."

"I'm sorry. I do not discuss the travelling plans of friends with... strangers."

"I assure you..." Janaker began, frustrated.

"My friend is a very private person. He has few friends. I am fortunate to count myself one of them." He stopped there and the claw flew to his head, clashing with the chitin that covered his skull.

"*Yesh!*" he screamed.

He swayed, regained his balance and stared at Janaker. "My head... I can feel – one of you? What are you doing?"

They backed off. Kreller said, "I assure you..."

"I can feel you in my head! You bastards! *Yesh – yeshank! Kresh!*"

When Tesnolidek struck it was lightning fast and Kreller – for all his vaunted rapid response times – was unable to defend himself. The creature leapt forward, struck out once, twice, his great claw a blur. Kreller staggered back, jets of blood as dark as port wine sluicing across the deck. Tesnolidek, or whatever he had become, pounced and struck again, slicing through Kreller's leather tunic and scoring a long gash in the meat beneath.

The Vetch screamed and fell to his knees, then toppled onto his side, and only then did Janaker act. She drew her pistol and fired a blinding laser beam. It struck the chitin that covered the creature's chest, stunning him – even though the weapon was set to kill – and knocking him backwards a couple of metres.

It was enough to bring Tesnolidek to his senses. He stopped, as immobile as a statue, his one eye taking in what he had done. He cried out, turned and dragged himself back towards the office door.

Already the attack had brought mechanics and engineers running. While Janaker stood, frozen with shock, two mechanics attended to the fallen Vetch, applying first aid and spraying synthi-flesh over the alien's lacerated torso. Another took her to one side, murmuring that a med-team had been called. She stared through the window of the office and saw Tesnolidek crawl into a silver cage, incarcerating himself. A mechanic followed him into the office and turned a dial on the cage, locking the mechanism.

She said to a mechanic, "What... what is he?"

"Human, most of the time." The man was clearly as shocked as she was, his voice shaking as he spoke. "The alien in him is prone to... to violence. For the most part he can keep it under control, but..." He gestured to the slick of blood on the deck, and the Vetch lying on his back.

Minutes later a med-team rushed into the hangar and surrounded the Vetch, soon followed by a security patrol. She and the mechanic gave statements, and she watched as the cage containing Tesnolidek was wheeled from the office and loaded onto a buggy. Tesnolidek regarded her with his one good eye, a hand and a claw gripping the bars.

Perhaps she should have felt anger towards the creature that had attacked her colleague, but all she felt was sympathy.

The medics carried Kreller to the upchute and she followed. They rose two levels and when they emerged the medics slid the stretcher onto a waiting buggy. Dazed, she accepted a lift and the next few minutes passed in a blur as they raced along wide corridors, citizens of the station alerted by the buggy's penetrating siren.

She turned to one of the medics and asked, "Will he...?"

"Impossible to say. He's strong, so with luck... and we do have the finest surgeons in the Reach working here."

Kreller was wheeled into surgery and an official took Janaker's credit details.

Later she sat on a hard chair in the corridor and waited. She slumped in the seat and considered what had happened, and was vaguely troubled to realise that her shock, her numbness, was occasioned less by any sympathy she felt towards the Vetch than by a simple revulsion at the attack and the resulting bloody mess. All things considered, she realised, she didn't care one way or the other if Kreller lived or died.

And she was shocked that she could feel this heartless towards a fellow sentient being.

She found a bar next to the clinic, sat in the gloomy half-light and stared out into space. She drank one beer after another, then slumped in her seat and slept. She jerked awake some time later to find that four hours had elapsed.

She returned to the hospital, found a nurse and asked after Kreller. She was told that he'd come through the operation and was recuperating. He was sleeping at the moment and would be up to receiving visitors when he awoke.

She took a seat and stared down the utilitarian corridor. The plastic seats, featureless walls and antiseptic stench brought back painful memories. She thought back ten years, to the time when she'd sat in a similar corridor on a far away planet, this time waiting for word of someone she cared about passionately. Kara had been the love of her life – they'd been together three years; a record for Janaker. That night they'd arranged to meet at a restaurant to celebrate their anniversary, and when Kara was late Janaker had not worried in the slightest: she was always late.

Thirty minutes later Kara had walked in... only it was not Kara but her sister – with the news that Kara had suffered extensive head injuries in an air-taxi accident.

They'd gone straight to the hospital and waited for hours and hours in the dead, featureless trauma ward, only to be told by a sympathetic nurse that Kara had passed away on the operating table.

For the next year she'd gone through a dozen lovers, fixating on petite blondes as if trying to find what she'd lost, and of course failing.

Her wrist-com chimed. "Janaker." It was Kreller's graceless growl.

"Kreller. You're...?"

"I am fine. There have been developments."

She shook her head, confused. She repeated the word, and the Vetch said shortly, "Get yourself in here, now."

She found the reception desk and asked if she could see Helsh Kreller, only to be told that they were experiencing some difficulty with the patient.

She hurried past the desk, attended by a harassed nurse, to a private room where Kreller was pulling on his lacerated jacket and struggling to get out of bed.

"Sign all the waivers they're demanding, Janaker, and pay these people! We're getting out of here, now."

"We really think Mr Kreller needs at least another two days..." the nurse began.

"I'll be fine! Now sign the waiver, Janaker!"

She nodded to the nurse, who provided a softscreen. Janaker scribbled her signature, then paid three thousand units with her data-pin. She helped Kreller into his jacket, easing the material over the hardened cast that encased his torso, and assisted him from the room.

They limped from the hospital, Kreller pushing her hand away.

"What the hell, Kreller...?" she began.

"I read a nurse back there. Harper's given a ride to the doctor who was treating the girl, Zeela, in lieu of payment. They're heading for Kallasta, but by way of a planet called Teplican. It's uninhabited, but for a small scientific team. We can apprehend Harper and the ship there."

She looked at him. "And you're sure you're up to this?"

"A few cuts might stop a human," he spat, "but not a Vetch."

You nauseating macho prick, she thought as they stepped into a downchute and dropped to the hangar and her ship.

CHAPTER EIGHT

THE *JUDI HEARNE* fell through a thin layer of cloud and sailed over a mountainous continent, following co-ordinates supplied by Dr Di Mannetti. High, sharp ridges like scimitars passed by in silence. Ahead, a vast green plain extended towards an ocean.

"It's beautiful," Zeela said. She leaned forward in the co-pilot's sling, staring through the viewscreen.

Harper agreed. "I never tire of visiting new words."

Di Mannetti stood between the slings, smiling to herself. "It's every bit as picturesque as the 3Vs suggested."

"I wonder why Teplican has never been resettled?" Harper said.

"Other than gorgeous landscapes and vast oceans, there's not a lot more here. The planet is low on metals and ores, and while it's clement and the soil fertile, it's too far off the star lanes to make it a profitable agricultural location."

"What were the original colonists doing here?" Zeela asked.

"They were a religious sect," Di Mannetti said, "persecuted by the Expansion. They came to the Reach in search of sanctuary, and claim to have found it here."

Harper glanced at the doctor. "And you said they left the planet around ninety years ago? How long had they been here?"

"No more than fifty years, I gather. And they left over a period of two years. I want to investigate a theory that there was some health scare which prompted the evacuation. They left aboard the same two colony ships on which they came to the planet. The odd thing was that, instead of heading further into the Reach – which you would have expected from a persecuted minority – they returned to the Expansion."

"Yes. Very odd."

"Even odder," Di Mannetti went on, "is that they passed *through* Expansion space and entered Vetch territory."

"Any idea why?"

Di Mannetti shook her head. "The historian who pieced together the events from all those years ago, from radio transcripts, second-hand reports and hearsay, has no idea – not even a theory. The human-Vetch conflict had yet to kick off in earnest, but there was still an uneasy truce between the races. The Vetch didn't like human vessels straying into their territory, and they made their feelings plain by blowing these strays out of the sky."

"And you think that's what might have happened to the colony ships?"

"Since no more was ever heard from them," Di Mannetti said, "that's the working hypothesis."

They left the mountains in their wake and drifted over the rolling green plain, dotted with darker expanses of forest and threaded with the silver filaments of rivers. A great lake came into view, backed by low hills. The remains of a small city or township nestled around its far shore, surrounded on three sides by forest.

"That was the capital of Teplican, such as it was. Around ten thousand citizens made it their home before the exodus."

"And now no one lives there?" Zeela asked.

"Not a soul. The only people there at the moment are part of a small scientific team, numbering around twenty individuals."

Harper said, "What about sentient natives?"

Di Mannetti shook her head. "Teplican was never home to sentient life-forms."

"Curiouser and curiouser," Harper said. "Had there been native aliens, then inter-species conflict might suggest why the colonists left."

Di Mannetti smiled. "I'm afraid it's not going to be that simple."

The ship flew in low over the water, heading for the deserted township. According to Dr Di Mannetti the scientific team had set up camp in the town's main square, and Harper instructed the ship to make landfall there.

"You'll remain here for a few days, I take it?"

Harper considered the question. It all depended on whether either the Ajantans or the bounty hunters decided to follow them to the planet's surface. He said, "We'll keep our options open. Our priority is getting to Kallasta, after all."

"But we could stay here for a day or two, Den," Zeela said.

"We'll see. Right, will you leave the deck while I bring the ship down?"

Zeela climbed from her sling and said to Di Mannetti, "Den can be *so* dictatorial at times."

Di Mannetti smiled at Harper and followed Zeela from the flight-deck.

Harper eased himself back in the sling, glanced over his shoulder to ensure the women were out of earshot, then said, "*Judi*, what's the situation with the pursuing ships?"

"There is no sign of either the Ajantan ship or that of the bounty hunters."

Harper thought the news too good to be true. It was as if his pursuers were playing with him, hanging back beyond range before a tactical strike.

"Very well... Inform me if either of the ships show up, okay?"

"Affirmative."

He considered the situation. "And if the Ajantan ship does appear in the vicinity... and elects to fire at us, intercept with a missile and then follow it up with a retaliatory strike."

"Understood. And the bounty hunters?"

"They're very unlikely to launch a strike," Harper said. "If they do locate us, they're more likely either to arrest me and hand me over to Expansion custody, or try to account for me one-on-one." That way, he thought, the bounty hunters could claim his ship as their own.

The ship slowed, hovered over the main square, and came down gently. Harper felt the cushioned impact of its ramrod stanchions and heard the jets' diminuendo.

He stared through the viewscreen at the deserted square. A line of timber store-fronts, ramshackle and rotted over the decades, contrasted with the dozen silver domes belonging to the scientific team. The scene was notable for its air of desertion. He had expected the square to be busy with scientists, or at least one or two of their number to be in evidence.

He considered the evacuation of the planet almost a century ago, and the current quietude which hung over the place, but dismissed his thoughts as fanciful.

He left the flight-deck and found Zeela and Di Mannetti at the top of the ramp, staring out at the quiet square. Bright afternoon sunlight and a warm breeze were a refreshing change after breathing the canned air of the ship for the past few days.

They made their way down the ramp and stood in the square, staring around them at the tumbledown timber buildings and the globular domes. The square had the aspect of a vacated film-set.

Zeela said, "Where is everyone?"

"I wasn't exactly expecting a welcoming committee," Di Mannetti said, "but nor was I expecting there to be no one here."

"What's that?" Harper said.

Seconds later the growl of an engine grew louder and a small run-about came into view around the bend of an overgrown road.

"Ah," Di Mannetti said with a note of relief, "no doubt the scientists returning from a field trip."

The open-topped buggy crossed the square and drew up before them, bearing a silver-haired man in his sixties and a young Oriental woman. The latter stood up and braced her arms on the windshield, smiling a greeting.

"Dr Mannetti! But we thought your flight had been cancelled."

"It had, but then I hitched a lift from this kind starship captain."

"I'm Director Xian Ti," the woman went on. "My deputy, Dr Lionev."

Di Mannetti made the introductions. "We were beginning to wonder where you all were."

"You've arrived at an opportune moment. My team has made what we hope will be a breakthrough. We've set up a secondary camp ten kilometres north, around the lake. If you'd care to accompany us...?"

They made arrangements: Di Mannetti was to travel with Xian Ti and Lionev in the buggy, while Harper and Zeela would follow in his ground-effect vehicle. They would remain at the new camp overnight. Xian Ti assured them that there were provisions enough for three extra mouths and room aplenty in an accommodation dome.

Harper gave the ship instructions to secure itself, then packed a bag with supplies for himself and Zeela and steered the vehicle down the ramp. He could not stop himself from glancing up into the clear blue sky as Zeela climbed in beside him.

There was no sign of the pursuing bounty hunters or aliens.

"What's wrong, Den? You've been quiet ever since touchdown."

They followed the buggy along the long, curving track – which might have been a metalled road, once, but was now overgrown with short grass laced with multi-coloured flowers. A herd of small animals, like sheep-sized rodents, cropped the vegetation. To their right, sunlight sparkled on the placid surface of the lake.

Harper smiled at Zeela with what he hoped was reassurance. "I'm fine. A little tired."

"Worried about the bounty hunters, and the Ajantans?"

He laughed. "No, not at all. I heard from the ship earlier, and there's no sign of them, Ajantans or bounty hunters alike."

"We've lost them?"

Why was he uneasy to acknowledge the possibility, as if to do so would be to tempt fate? "For the time being," he said.

They drove on in silence.

At last Zeela said, "What if they find us again, Den? What would be the best case scenario then?"

He glanced at her. "Meaning?"

"I mean, can we really lose them both in void-space, or will it come to using the missiles?"

"If they found us again... then I'd seriously think about using the missiles."

"And if they come after us down here?"

He gripped the wheel. "I'll think about what to do if and when it happens. But we'll be fine."

She nodded. "You're still worried, though?"

He turned and smiled at her. "No, Zeela, I'm confident that the ship has managed to outrun them."

She laid a hand on his thigh and rubbed it up and down. He remained clutching the wheel, wishing she'd desist.

Five minutes later a collection of blister domes, smaller than those back in the township, came into view around the curve of the lake. They were strung out alongside what looked like an artificial mound, a long bank of bare earth rising to a height of ten metres.

Xian Ti's buggy pulled up beside the domes and Harper came to a halt alongside.

"I'll show you to the accommodation dome, and then perhaps you'd like a guided tour before we eat?"

The accommodation dome was larger than the others and was filled with bedrolls and a central, enclosed shower unit. They stowed their bags next to vacant bedrolls and emerged to join Xian Ti in the sunlight.

She led the way up the gently sloping mound behind the domes.

Harper followed, curious as to what the 'breakthrough' might be. The mound appeared man-made, certainly not a feature formed by nature: the plains around the township were rolling, and had thrown up no other similar hillock.

But why might the colonists have constructed such a mound or barrow – and what relevance, if any, might it have on the mystery of their sudden exodus?

"A cursory satellite survey of the planet discovered this feature," Xian Ti was saying as they climbed. "But it wasn't until a few days ago that we got around to examining the data."

"What is it?" Di Mannetti asked. "It's certainly not natural, is it? So the colonists must have made it." She hesitated. "It has the look of a burial mound."

Xian Ti nodded. "It certainly does, but it isn't."

"I take it that you *do* know what it is?" Zeela asked.

Xian Ti smiled. "We certainly do," she said, approaching the crest of the rise.

She stopped at the summit and pointed.

Harper joined her, pulling Zeela up beside him, and stared at the sight Xian Ti was indicating with an outstretched arm.

"So," she said, "what do you think?"

They were looking down along the length of what might have been a narrow metal building perhaps a couple of hundred metres long by twenty wide, a construction without a roof and divided internally by a dozen bulkheads. Only then did Harper realise what it was.

Di Mannetti got in before him, "A starship..."

Beside him, Zeela laughed. "Of course!"

"It had me guessing at first," Xian Ti admitted. "We suspect that its upper panels were wrecked when the ship came down, so at first sight it doesn't resemble a ship at all."

Harper turned to Di Mannetti. "But didn't you say that the colonists left the planet aboard the ships they came in?"

Di Mannetti looked at Xian Ti. "That's right, isn't it? So this ship can't have belonged to the colonists."

"It isn't of human design," Xian Ti said. "Nor does it belong to any of the alien races known to the Reach, the Expansion, or to explored space beyond."

"It's not Vetch?" Harper asked.

Xian Ti shook her head. "Most certainly not. They don't go in for such florid designs. Look."

She was pointing to a fin that had collapsed into the structure of the ship halfway along its length. "You can't really see from up here, but if we go down to get a closer look..."

They descended the far side of the mound, coming down inside the tangled metal of the ship's nose-cone which had ploughed the mound of earth.

They picked their way through the remains of the ship, moving carefully down twisted corridors and across buckled decks. It was hard to credit that, more than a hundred years ago, some alien race unknown to humanity had navigated the vessel across space and fetched up here.

They arrived at the foot of the vast fin, canted at an angle and towering above them. "Observe the engraved patterning."

Harper reached out and traced a series of whorls and curlicues decorating the fin.

"Eerily beautiful," Di Mannetti said.

"Do you know when it came here?" Zeela asked. "How long ago?"

Xian Ti said, "My team has worked it out, approximately – we reckon it arrived about a hundred years ago."

"A little before the colonists left," Di Mannetti said.

"Did it crash," Harper wanted to know, "or did it land?"

Xian Ti shrugged. "We don't know. We think it came down with some impact, hence the damage to its superstructure."

"Do you know if it was a void-ship?"

"Again, no, we don't."

"But... its crew, passengers," Di Mannetti said. "They must have survived. Or, if not, then be buried somewhere."

"There are not the slightest signs of any alien remains," Xian Ti said. "Nor of any stores or possessions aboard the ship. And we haven't located where any aliens might be buried. We've found a cemetery the colonists used, but all the graves are human."

"So," Zeela said, "what happened to the crew?"

"Another mystery to add to all the others," Xian Ti said. "Where did the ship originate? Who did it belong to? Why did it come here, if this *was* its intended destination?"

"And did its arrival," Di Mannetti said, "have any bearing on the colonists' exodus?"

"Exactly, doctor – that's the important question."

Harper moved off by himself towards the stern of the ship, picking his way cautiously through eroded girders and fallen panels. Judging by the size of the door-frames, and the width of the corridors, the ship had belonged to beings slightly taller, and broader, than the average human – which wasn't much help in working out which race that might be.

He came to the end of the ship and stood beneath the flaring cone of one of four great engines; even these had an ineluctably alien design, a baroque line that made the cones resemble ancient church bells. He turned and looked back along the length of the ruined ship: the human figures appeared tiny amidst the skeletal superstructure. Zeela saw him and waved. She picked her way towards him with a comical high-stepping gait.

"What do you think?"

"I think the universe is full of mysteries, Zeela, some of which we will work out in time, and others we won't. This is why I couldn't live a safe life on one planet, and never travel among the stars. And to think," he went on, "the mystery of this ship will be multiplied a thousand times across the face of the galaxy."

She looked around her in wonder, and smiled at him.

He took in the ship and the humans swarming over it; their small party had been joined now by the rest of the scientific team, scouting among the wreckage with monitoring instruments and cameras. The supergiant sun was going down over the far horizon, illuminating cloud layers of gold and silver. The light around the alien ship was golden, magical.

Something struck him as odd, then, but for the life of him he couldn't work out what. There was something not *right* about the scene – which struck him as strange because he'd never seen anything like this with which to compare it. His inability to nail what was bothering him was irritating, as if it were an optical illusion which refused to resolve itself.

"What's wrong, Den?"

"I don't know... I have the strange feeling that there's something not right about this."

She laughed. "Not right? What do you mean?"

"That's just it. I don't know." He laughed with her.

She looked around, then out across the rolling plain, and back again. "I know..." she said slowly. "It's the grass. Or rather the lack of it. Look, nothing's growing within the ship, or for metres around it."

As soon as she said this, he knew she was right. "You genius! Why couldn't I see that?"

She cocked her head and looked at him. "You did *see* it, Den, but you just didn't make the comparison."

"Well done. Come on, let's see if Xian Ti knows what's happening here."

They rejoined the main group as they were making their way back up the slope towards the encampment.

At the top Xian Ti and Di Mannetti paused, allowing Harper and Zeela to catch up.

"We've just noticed," he panted, "that there's nothing growing in or around the ship. Radiation?"

Xian Ti shook her head. "We've ruled that out. The area is clean. I have a couple of people working on the problem as we speak. We suspect some xeno-microbial infection, but won't be sure for a while yet."

"Perhaps the infection that might have driven the colonists away from here?" Zeela said.

"We can't rule anything out at this early stage," Xian Ti said. She indicated the line of blister domes far below. "Shall we eat?"

As the twilight deepened and a bright swathe of stars came out overhead, they sat around a light-wand and ate a surprisingly good vegetable stew from pre-heated trays. Xian Ti broke out a canister of passable red wine. Conversation, predictably, centred on the wreck and its link, if any, to the leave-taking of the colonists. A couple of outspoken anthropologists mooted the possibility that the aliens and the humans had fought or, if not, that at any rate there had been some conflict between the two camps which had necessitated the colonists leaving the planet. Xian Ti countered this with the observation that there was no sign, in the township or elsewhere, of conflict. She favoured the theory that the aliens had brought some form of virus inimical to the human population. "Conflict, if you like, but not intentional," was how she phrased it.

"That's what I hope to investigate over the course of the next month," Di Mannetti said.

Harper asked, "I take it that there's nothing back at the township, no records, memoirs or whatever, that refer to the colonists' plans to leave?"

A woman shook her head. "I've been through the com-archives and found nothing relating to their decision. The odd thing is, though, that I have found a lot of discs, pins, and cores wiped or just empty. It's as if... and I'm sticking my neck out here... the colonists went through the records and cleared them before leaving."

"As if they didn't want anyone to know why they were going," Di Mannetti said.

"We don't know that for certain," the woman said. "But it's a working hypothesis."

"When we discovered the alien vessel," Xian Ti said, "I sent someone back to Amethyst to check the records."

"Hoping to find...?" Harper asked.

Xian Ti sipped her wine and said, "I'm not from the Reach, Mr Harper. I was born on a world in the Expansion. I didn't come here until I was twenty..." She made a waving gesture with her free hand. "It's a long story, which has no place here. Anyway, I recall reading reports, stories, about mysterious crash-landed starships – of unknown alien origin – fetching up on half a dozen or so worlds of the Expansion many years ago. So when we made the discovery, I recalled these stories and sent someone to see if they could work out if there might be a link."

"It would be intriguing if the other ships were of the same origin," Di Mannetti mused, "and what their effect was on the worlds where they landed."

"That's what I hope to find out." Xian Ti looked across at Harper. "If you don't mind my saying, I take it you're not from the Reach?"

Harper felt immediately defensive. "Is it that obvious?"

"You speak Anglais with a familiar accent. Are you from the world of Denby, by any chance?"

He smiled. "Your ear is excellent. Yes, I am."

"I visited the planet a few times in my teens," she said. "I can't say I was impressed."

"Oh, I don't know... For a grim, sunless, impoverished industrial world, it wasn't that bad. All things considered, though, I'd rather move from world to world across the Reach."

"You're a star trader," Xian Ti said, leaning forward. "How romantic! Why did you leave the Expansion, Mr Harper?"

He shifted, uncomfortable now that the conversation had veered to his past. "For the reasons most sane people leave the Expansion," he said. "Probably for the same reason you left."

She nodded. "I found I couldn't practise my science without some government officer continually questioning not only my findings, but my theories and working methods. I had to toe the party line... so, when the opportunity to work on a planet in the Reach presented itself, I took it. Then I sought political asylum, and as I was a high-ranking scientist I was granted citizenship on Henderson, and never looked back. I have absolutely no desire to return, have you?"

Harper shook his head. "Only to spit in the eye of the bastards who..." He stopped himself from completing the sentence, and for a few seconds an uneasy silence reigned.

Talk returned to the work being conducted here, and Harper sat back and drank his wine. He considered the bounty hunter out there who, if she didn't want to shoot him dead, would attempt to return him to the Expansion authorities so that they could do the dirty work.

He sensed Zeela watching him, but didn't acknowledge her.

They turned in a little later, as two moons rose over the starship earthworks. Harper lay on his bedroll under the moon-silvered dome, considering whether to take his leave of Teplican tomorrow or the following day. They could always explore the township, which might prove interesting in itself, and have the benefit of taking them away from the scientists. Xian Ti's probings had unsettled him; he was sure they were innocent enough, but he was unused to speaking of his past to anyone.

In the darkness, Zeela moved closer to him and reached out. She found his chest and pulled herself closer, so that her lips touched his shoulder. Harper lay still, unwilling to reciprocate. He stared at the smeared highlights of the moons on the curve of the dome, and was relieved fifteen minutes later when he heard the soft sound of Zeela's breathing in sleep.

Perhaps an hour later, unable to sleep, he eased himself from the bedroll, found his boots, and crossed the dome to the hatch. It slid open silently at his approach and he walked out into the warm, moonlit night.

He stood beneath the massed stars, taking deep breaths. The earthworks rose before him, the soil dark in the light of the moons and the stars. He paced towards the slope and climbed, and at the top turned and stared down at the line of domes and the calm surface of the bay glittering to his left.

He sat down, staring out over the scaled water – and minutes later the call he'd been fearing ever since leaving the ship came through. His wrist-com buzzed and he gave a start, cursing.

"*Judi*?" He took a breath. "They've found us, haven't they?"

"Affirmative, Den," *Judi* said. "The Ajantan ship appeared in orbit one minute ago."

"And the bounty hunters?"

"No sign of them, yet. But the Ajantans must have phased in hours ago on the blindside of the planet—"

His stomach tightened. "How do you know?"

"Because they sent down a shuttle, and I estimate that it will arrive within fifteen minutes. I was unsure whether you'd want me to expend a missile on a shuttle."

"Good question. Let me think." He was standing up now, staring into the heavens above the far township, as if he might be able to see the descent of the Ajantan shuttle.

If he blasted the shuttle out of the sky, then who knew how the Ajantans aboard the mothership in orbit might react. If they had missile capabilities, then they might retaliate by firing on *Judi*.

Fifteen minutes... Even if he ordered *Judi* to power up immediately, fetched Zeela and raced to the township, he wouldn't make it inside fifteen minutes.

"Do you have any idea where the shuttle might come down?"

"Plotting from its entry trajectory, I surmise it will make landfall in the forest behind the township."

"Right." He hurried down the mound towards his ground-effect vehicle. "Don't fire on the shuttle, okay? It'd be a waste, and there's no telling how the remaining Ajantans up there might react. I have a laser with me, so I'm coming back to the township.

One thing – how long does night last on Teplican?"

Judi replied, "Eight hours."

He reached his car and slipped into the driving seat. "So it'll be light in another..."

"Sunrise in four hours."

He started the engine and steered away from the domes. He found the overgrown track and accelerated around the bay towards the township.

He would have the benefit – or the hindrance – of darkness. It all depended on the Ajantans' night vision. For his part, he would activate his ferronnière and hopefully pick up the aliens' cerebral signatures at a range of two hundred metres or more.

"Alert me when the Ajantans land," he said, cut the connection and concentrated on the moonlit track.

He had considered instructing *Judi* to phase out and make herself scarce, but decided against the order. The ship, in situ in the square, would act as a draw for the Ajantans – and he would be ready for them.

Five minutes later the township came into view. In the moonlight, it might have been a sleeping settlement on any backwater colony world. He pulled off the road before he came to the square and slipped his car in between two timber buildings. When he cut the engine, the silence was absolute.

He was about to climb from the vehicle when he heard a distant, muted roar. "*Judi*?" he whispered into his wrist-com.

"The shuttle has landed approximately one point five kilometres inland."

"Right... If you detect any Ajantan individuals, keep me informed. Text only from now on."

"Understood."

He unclipped his laser from the rack in the rear of the car, then hurried through the silent, moonlit town towards the square. Seconds later he passed between two leaning buildings and made out the welcome sight of his ship, squatting in the moonlight. He looked around, searching for a suitable vantage point. He felt energised, alert. He thought back four years to when the bounty hunter had been on his trail, and how that had ended. He recalled feeling hyper-aware back then, adrenalised by the chase. He'd wasted no time considering the morality of what he was planning to do. As he'd told Zeela – it had been a case of kill or be killed. The same was true now: what the Ajantans had planned to do to him and Zeela on Ajanta disqualified them from any consideration of compassion or mercy. It was kill or be killed, and this time he had the added incentive that he was fighting for Zeela's life, too.

He found a likely building and climbed the steps onto a wraparound veranda. He tested the front door, which swung open at his touch. He stepped quickly inside. Windows looked out over the square and to the left and right: he would have a perfect view of the approach of the tree frogs.

He slipped his ferronnière from his jacket and looped it around his head. He slid the activation stud, took a deep breath and scanned. Nothing. Absolute mind silence.

He checked the charge of his laser and powered it up. He leaned against the wall, peering through the front window. All was silent again, *Judi* and the scientists' domes an incongruously modern intrusion into a scene that might have pre-dated the age of star flight: a moonlit square, ancient weatherboard buildings, a placid lake...

His wrist-com throbbed, and a line of text scrolled across the screen: *Two Ajantans have emerged from the cover of trees at eleven o'clock relative to my position and at a distance of three hundred metres and closing. Now approaching the square...*

Seconds later the cerebral signature of their alien minds flared in his consciousness. He winced, almost fell to his knees with the pain; he detected nothing at all like human emotions, but a screeching mind-noise like migraine. He stepped across the room and leaned against the frame of the side window, peering out.

His wrist-com throbbed again: *Ajantans one hundred metres away and closing...*

As they approached, so their mind-noise increased. It was like a nightmare he'd suffered once or twice, no doubt occasioned by accidental contact with alien minds: a feeling that his human consciousness was being overwhelmed by a chaotic alien sensibility which threatened to drive out his rational, human-centred view of reality. He wondered if this was what Miro Tesnolidek lived with every day of his life.

He fought to quell the feeling now, and concentrate on the view through the window. His pulse pounded deafeningly in his ears. He was sweating, the laser slick in his grip.

And here came the first Ajantan...

The alien bobbed into view fifty metres away, sliding with silky, reptilian fluidity along the side of a building. It wore a silver covering on its chest and carried some kind of rifle. His tele-ability told him that the second alien was out of sight on the far side of the building.

The mind-pain increased, distracting him. Once he had them both in view, he could dispense with the ferronnière.

He considered taking out the first Ajantan right away, but decided that would only alert the second alien, spook the creature and send it scuttling back into the cover of the forest. The last thing he wanted was to chase the alien through a darkened wood.

The first Ajantan came to the corner of the building and peered around, looking across the square to the ship. It spoke into some kind of hand-held com device then moved off at a brisk trot towards the ship. The second Ajantan remained hidden behind the building - judging by its cerebral signature - no doubt covering the first. He was dealing with experienced combatants.

He stepped silently across the dusty floorboards towards the front window and peered out.

Judi communicated. He read: *An alien approaching, twenty metres, fifteen...*

He whispered, "I see it."

The Ajantan reached *Judi* and moved around her, stopping from time to time to peer up at the viewscreens. It moved with an easy bobbing gait which gave it the appearance of being constantly cautious, ready to take flight at any second.

It made a circuit of the ship and stopped, turning to look around the square. At one point its sweeping gaze took in the building where Harper was concealed... and moved on. He realised he'd been holding his breath, and released it with relief.

He swore to himself, urging the second alien to show itself.

The alien beside the ship raised a hand again, speaking into its com. He felt the agonising locus that was the second alien's mind move away from where it was hiding and approach the square. At last...

Seconds later a smaller Ajantan scurried across the square and joined the first.

Harper raised his laser, took aim. His left hand shook. He was unable to concentrate with the white-noise of the alien minds in his head, so he lowered the rifle and switched off his ferronnière. The immediate cessation of the screeching migraine was blissful.

He took a breath. He felt calm, poised, without the alien mind-noise in his head. He raised the laser again and aimed at the Ajantans. The bigger one first. He flashed on the scene in the alien lair, at the rotting remains of the human corpses strewn around the perimeter. These were two Ajantans who would never again have the pleasure...

He sighted the larger alien, aimed at the centre of its skull, and fired.

The blue vector lanced across the square. He saw the alien's head dissolve in an atomised spray of fluid, and a split second later fired at the second Ajantan. He hit its chest. His beam lanced off its silver garment – obviously body armour – and ricocheted into the air. The alien rolled and came up firing. A bolus of fire screamed across the square and hit the window frame to Harper's right. He fired again, this time aiming for the creature's head, and missed.

The Ajantan surprised Harper by racing towards him, firing as it came. He had expected the alien to retreat, seek cover. He had to hand it to the bastard...

Three quick gouts of fire set the façade of the building ablaze, and Harper retreated to the back of the room. A doorway gave access to a moonlit rear room. He stepped into it and crossed to a door, kicked it open and ran outside. He rounded the house to the square and stopped at the corner. He peered round. The alien was climbing the steps to the veranda with extreme caution. Harper raised his laser, sighted the creature's head, and fired.

The alien turned at the same time, just as laser vector blew its skull apart.

Harper sank to his haunches and took deep breaths. He felt his pulse pound through his body, and wanted to laugh out loud in the heady relief of having survived. He stood up and approached the Ajantan's corpse. It had fallen across the blazing veranda and within minutes would be consumed by the pyre of its own making.

He walked across the square to the ship and inspected the remains of the second alien. It lay spread-eagled amidst the debris of its cranium, and despite its humanoid shape he could see it as nothing other than animal.

He raised his wrist-com and got through to Zeela.

It was a minute before she answered, fuddled by sleep. "Mmm...? Den? But where are you?"

"Listen. Get Di Mannetti to drive you back to the township. We're leaving."

"But... where are you, Den?"

"At the ship. There's been developments. The Ajantans came down."

"Den!" She sounded frantic. "What happened? Are you...?"

"I'm fine, but I can't say the same about the Ajantans. Just get yourself down here and we'll be on our way."

He cut the connection before she had time to reply.

He was about to command *Judi* to lower the ramp when he heard a sound behind him. He turned – but too late. Something hit him across the back of the head. He cried out and fell. While he was down and struggling to get up, he felt someone wrest the laser from his grip and pull his wrist-com from his arm.

His initial confused thought was that one of the scientific team had followed him down here and for some bizarre reason attacked him...

He turned sluggishly and sat up.

"Stop!"

The sound of the voice told him that his assailant was not human.

He looked up and saw an Ajantan five metres away. It held both his laser and its own bell-muzzled incendiary weapon, levelled at him.

Very clever... or had he been stupid to deactivate his ferronnière when he had? The Ajantan shuttle had contained three aliens, with one hanging back to cover its fellows.

And Zeela and Di Mannetti would get here in ten minutes or so, and drive straight into the mess he'd allowed to develop.

His only hope was that *Judi* had been monitoring events and would get through to Zeela to apprise her of the situation.

Failing that... How could he hope to disarm the alien when it possessed two weapons and his wrist-com?

He would begin by talking to the alien, establishing a dialogue, and hope that its command of his language extended beyond the single word it had used so far.

He was unable to tell, by staring at its face, just what emotions might be passing through its alien brain. Its big, dark eyes stared at him and its long mouth hung open to reveal two rows of needle-sharp teeth.

He had summarily killed two of its fellow... He wondered if it might seek revenge.

"What do you want? You followed me..."

The alien twitched, raising its weapons. It hissed, "The girl!"

Harper shook his head, feigning ignorance. "What girl?"

"You took her! The girl. Our..." It spat a word he had no hope of catching, something sibilant in its own language. "The girl..." it went on, "belongs to us!"

"She belongs to no one. You do not own her."

"We own her! By Ajantan law she is our..." That word again, which sounded like *shisk*...

Harper smiled. "But we are no longer on Ajanta," he pointed out, "so your barbaric laws no longer hold."

The alien fired. The bolus of fire roared past Harper's head, missing him by a metre. He flinched away from its heat, feeling the skin of his face burn and his hair singe.

"Where is girl!"

He could always claim that Zeela was no longer with him... but he thought twice about this. If the Ajantan believed him, then it just might consider him surplus to requirements and, to avenge its dead fellows, execute him on the spot.

He might be better able to overcome the alien if he could lure it aboard his ship.

"The girl is in there," he said, indicating *Judi* over his shoulder.

"Get her out!"

Harper smiled to himself. "Very well... Either let me enter the ship and find her, or give me my wrist-com." He pointed to the device which the alien had strapped around its own arm.

The Ajantan hesitated, watching him with its vast eyes. It blinked, its eyelids nictitating sideways.

Of course, Harper thought, it could always order me to lower the ramp, then kill me and enter the ship in search of Zeela...

"No!" it said at last.

"No to what?" he asked. "To me entering the ship, or you giving me my wrist-com."

It blinked again and spat, "Both!"

Harper smiled. No fool, this one...

"Okay," he said, "then how about this: we both go into the ship to find her?"

Surely, in the confines of the ship, he'd sooner or later have the opportunity to overwhelm the Ajantan?

The alien regarded him inscrutably, assessing the idea.

At last it bobbed its head. "Yes," it said.

Harper let out a relieved breath. "Good. So... I'll need my wrist-com to order my ship to lower the ramp."

The alien was considering the request when, seconds later, the sound of an engine intruded upon the dawn hush. Harper cursed his luck.

The engine's roar increased as the vehicle approached the square.

The Ajantan crouched lower and backed off. It covered Harper with his own laser and swung the incendiary device in the direction of the approach road.

This changed things. Harper worked on the assumption that when Zeela and Di Mannetti drove into the square, unsuspecting, the alien would have no second thoughts about killing him and the doctor and taking Zeela.

He felt impotent, seated on the ground with his head throbbing painfully. But what would the alien's reaction be if he climbed to his feet? He elected not to find out.

The alien spat, "Who is... this?"

Harper shook his head. "I don't know."

To claim ignorance was the safest option. He could always have tried to spook the alien and said that whoever it was was well armed... But then the Ajantan might have thrown caution to the wind and fired on the car as soon as it appeared.

Seconds later the vehicle came into view between two buildings at the far end of the square.

With a kick of hope, Harper saw that there was only one person in the car – Di Mannetti, seated behind the wheel. That could only be *Judi's* doing; she had assessed the trouble he was in and communicated the fact to Zeela.

But where was she?

The car slowed and came to a halt twenty metres from the alien. The creature's domed head rotated from Harper to the car.

He calculated what he would do now if he were the alien, and he didn't like what he came up with. He, Harper, was a dangerous liability who could be dispensed with. But how long would it take the alien to realise this?

Should he act now, surge to his feet and charge in a zigzag sprint towards the Ajantan and trust that its aim was aberrant?

In the car, Di Mannetti sat very still behind the wheel, then raised her hands above her head.

It was probably a sensible thing for her to do, in the circumstances – but, Harper realised sickeningly, it freed the alien to act.

The Ajantan turned to face him, lifted the laser and fired. Harper rolled sideways, but the blue light slammed into his flank with indescribable pain. He cried out and hit the ground. He heard a piercing cry, followed by a second blast of laser fire. He thought that the Ajantan had turned the weapon on Di Mannetti, but when he forced his eyes open and looked at the alien he saw that it was no longer upright. It lay on the ground, in several pieces, and a slight, slim figure was running across the square towards him, a laser rifle clutched to her chest.

He tried to sit up and reassure Zeela that he was fine, but the pain in his side stopped him. He looked down, shocked at what he saw. There was a gaping hole in the material of his jacket, and a corresponding laceration in the flesh beneath – and a mass of puce innards, highlighted in the light of the rising sun, was bulging from the wound.

Zeela paused before him and he was shocked by the horror on her face. She reached out and cupped his cheek. He saw her lips move as she said his name, but there was something wrong with his hearing. Everything was silent. And his vision was failing too... Zeela's grief-stricken face was fading. Again he tried to struggle upright. He wanted to tell her that he was fine, but another wave of pain shot through his body and oblivion claimed him.

HE CAME TO his senses briefly.

He tried to sit up, but his forehead touched

something. He was in darkness, but the pain had ceased. Then he understood. He had died and they had buried him on Teplican... Only he hadn't died because he was still alive. He was in a coffin. They had buried him alive!

He felt something crawl over his naked chest, then a sharp pain. He lost consciousness.

He came awake again, and light flooded the narrow confines where he lay, and with the light came awareness of his situation. He was not in a coffin. He touched his flank, where earlier he'd seen his guts tumbling out. He felt a slight scar. He pressed, amazed. There was no pain. He raised his head awkwardly and looked down the length of his body. Between his feet he could see the hatch of the med-pod.

And through the hatch he saw Zeela smiling in at him.

He lay back and closed his eyes. He recalled her grief-stricken face on Teplican, which had convinced him that he was dying... Now her smile celebrated his resurrection.

Later she opened the hatch and pulled out the slide-bed.

She stood back, staring at him. "The med-pod said you'd pull through, Den. But I didn't believe it. All the blood, the..."

He sat up, swivelled off the slide-bed and stood, conscious of his nakedness. His clothes were piled neatly next to the med-pod and he dressed while Zeela watched him.

He felt weak and dizzy. He reached out and said, "Come here."

She came, and he held her head to his chest.

"*Judi* contacted me," she said. "We were on our way to the township, so we had to double-back for a laser. On the way down we planned what to do. *Judi* told us that the alien had you in the square, so Gina dropped me off and I crept between the buildings... I saw the Ajantan shoot you, Den. I thought you were dead. I never thought I could kill anything, but seeing it do that to you..."

"You're a crack shot, girl."

She shook her head. "You should have seen the laser. It practically fired itself. All I had to do was point it in the right direction. And then, when I saw you, the wound... Gina took over. She fixed you up, stopped the bleeding. We carried you onto the ship and put you in the med-pod."

He sat on the slide-bed, taking deep breaths. "How long have I been in there?"

"Almost three days."

He cocked his head, heard the thrumming of the maindrive. "We left Teplican?"

She nodded. "I consulted with *Judi*, and we thought it best. We didn't want another Ajantan shuttle coming down."

"Good work."

"We're heading for Vassatta, Den. The last port of call before Kallasta. *Judi* said you might be able to sell the steamboat engine there, and anyway we need to refuel."

"You've thought of everything, between you."

"And the good news is that there's no sign of the Ajantan ship, or the bounty hunters."

"It's almost too good to be true," he laughed. "Next you'll tell me you've fixed a four course meal to celebrate my recovery."

"Well, *Judi's* done that, Den. You hungry?"

"Famished."

They made their way to the flight-deck, Harper testing his body as he went. To say he'd been lasered in the guts three days ago, he felt remarkably well. He still felt a little shaky, but he suspected that that was because he hadn't eaten for ages.

They sat in their slings and ate from pre-heated trays.

"I owe Di Mannetti my thanks," he said. "One day I'll call in on her at Amethyst station."

"I told her all about the Ajantans, how you saved me from them. She said to say hi when you came round, and wished us a safe journey to Kallasta."

"What have you been doing for three days?"

She shrugged, a forkful of pasta poised before her lips. "Keeping a vigil by the med-pod, taking the stuff Gina gave me for the withdrawal."

He glanced at her. "How are you feeling?"

She laid her fork on the tray and held out a small hand. Her fingers trembled. "I get hot and cold sweats all day, I'm finding it hard to sleep, and I'm all shaky." She shrugged. "But I'm fine. Gina said that in a few weeks the effects will wear off and I'll be back to normal."

He watched her as she ate. She took small mouthfuls, chewed deliberately, from time to time sipped her juice. They'd been through a lot together over the course of the past week, and he wondered if he would miss her company when he dropped her off at Kallasta. Well, he *would* miss her, of course – the question was, how long would it be before he slipped back into the old routine and *no longer* missed her?

"*Judi*," he said. "When are we due to reach Vassatta?"

"In twenty hours and thirteen minutes."

Zeela said, "*Judi* told me all about Vassatta while you were recovering. Have you been there before?"

"Once, many years ago. It was summertime, then, but it'll be very different now."

"*Judi* said it's winter there." She thought about it. "It must be strange, living on a planet where the winter lasts for a hundred years, and the summer only ten."

"I expect it seems normal to the inhabitants. They must think it very strange to live on a world where the summers and winters last only months."

"But a winter that lasts for a *hundred* years!" she said. "*Judi* said it's a beautiful place."

"Well, it was in summer. I took a party of tourists to see the Blooming. After such a long winter, the summer comes fast and the plants, dormant for so long, flower all across the world. It's a spectacular show that covers vast plains and mountains..." He smiled at the recollection. "The tourists seemed very happy that they'd witnessed it."

"I wonder what it'll be like now, in winter?"

"Just as beautiful, or so I'm told, in its own way. Stromgard, the capital city, is built on a system of ice-canals. I'm looking forward to seeing the place. I just hope we can off-load the engine."

"*Judi* thinks we will. She said you have contacts there."

"I have contacts on most planets on the Reach," he said, "but whether they'll buy from me, or can put me in touch with people who can... that's the question."

The life of a star trader, he thought. It would be nice, once he'd returned Zeela to her homeworld, to get back into the routine again.

"Den," *Judi* said a minute later. "We have company."

Beside him, Zeela stiffened. He said, "Details, please."

"The Ajantan ship. I suspect it's been trailing us since we left Teplican, but out of detectable range."

"How close is it now?"

"One and a half million, and gaining."

Zeela sat up. "What do we do, Den?"

He thought about it. "*Judi*, why do you think they're showing themselves? If they've been following us all along since Teplican... why play catch up now?"

"They wish to apprehend us before we make landfall at Vassatta?"

Harper grunted. "I don't like the word 'apprehend.'"

Judi was silent for five seconds, and then said, "All is explained, Den. The Ajantans are attempting to contact us."

"They are?" he said, surprised. He raised his eyebrows at Zeela, who pulled a worried face.

"Very well," he said. "Put them through."

Seconds later the grey void dissolved, giving way to the darkened interior of the Ajantan ship. Three tiny frog-figures, strapped into high couches, stared through the viewscreen.

Zeela said something under her breath.

"*Judi*," Den said, "don't reciprocate with visuals. Sound only."

"Understood."

The central Ajantan figure leaned forward and spoke in a series of hisses.

"*Judi*, respectfully ask it to speak in Anglais, if it wishes to communicate with us."

"Affirmative," *Judi* said.

The central alien cocked its head, evidently listening. It pointed to the viewscreen with a long, thin forefinger and spoke again, still in its own language.

Judi said, "It says that you killed their only interpreter, Den. One moment, while I install a translation program."

Seconds later the alien spoke again and a line of text scrolled across the foot of the viewscreen.

"We charge you with the murder of three... [untranslatable] Ajantans. You are criminals under Ajantan spatial law. We request the immediate handing over of the girl."

"*Judi*, transmit this: Under human spatial law, the Ajantan treatment of humans on the world of Ajanta is deemed a criminal offence. Under no circumstances will I submit to the demand to hand over Zeela Antarivo."

Judi transmitted his reply, and a minute later the Ajantan replied.

"We request the girl... ensure her release... we will stop at nothing..."

"Tell them that threats will not succeed in altering my decision."

The three Ajantans spoke to each other, then the central alien turned to the screen and spoke. The text read: "If you do not give us the girl... the girl who is *shisk*... we will take offensive action. You have been warned."

"Please ask them to define the term 'offensive action.'"

"Affirmative."

A minute later the alien spoke. "If you fail to comply to our demands, we will destroy your ship."

Den said, "How far away are the Ajantans now?"

"A million kilometres," ship said.

Worriedly, Zeela asked, "Is that close enough for them to...?"

Harper interrupted. "I don't know if it's close enough for them to successfully fire at us, but... *Judi*, is the Ajantan ship within range of us to ensure its destruction if we fire within the next thirty seconds?"

"A computation of the current distance, and the destructive capabilities of a single missile, suggests that there is a sixty-five per cent chance of the Ajantan ship suffering complete destruction."

Harper stroked his chin. "I don't like those percentages."

The Ajantan spoke again. "We will give you one minute, standard, for you to make your decision. Hand over the girl or suffer the consequences."

Harper looked at Zeela. She was staring, wide-eyed, at the aliens on the viewscreen. She clutched the frame of her sling.

He said, "I'm going to say that I agree to their demand, but don't worry..."

She stared at him. "Okay, Den."

"*Judi*," Harper said, "tell the Ajantans that I agree. Say that we are slowing down, and we will beam the docking protocols to them within minutes."

"Affirmative."

Harper watched the reaction of the trio on the viewscreen. They bent forward as one as *Judi* relayed his capitulation, then sat back and spoke amongst themselves. From their alien body language it was impossible to determine any sign of triumph.

"*Judi*, proceed to decelerate, and inform me when the Ajantan ship is close enough so that, when we fire, one hundred per cent destruction is assured."

"Understood."

"And close the visual link, please. I've seen enough of the Ajantans for the time being."

The seconds ticked by. The silence lengthened. He turned and looked at Zeela. She was staring at the viewscreen as it flickered and, a second later, showed only the marmoreal void.

"I don't like the idea of wiping out an entire ship and its crew," he said. "But I must admit that, in the circumstances, as the ship in question does belong to the Ajantans... I won't lose that much sleep over my decision."

Zeela nodded. "I'm with you there, Den."

"Den," *Judi* said. "The Ajantan ship is within..." It stopped suddenly, then said, "Alert! Alert! The Ajantan ship has launched a missile." So that had been their motive all along, to get within range and avenge the deaths of their colleagues.

Harper sat forward, pulse racing. "Evasive action?"

"Negative. We're travelling too slowly to avoid impact."

"Then... can you intercept with a missile of our own?"

"Affirmative."

"Then do it!"

Harper gripped the frame of his sling. "And patch through a visual of the Ajantan ship."

Almost instantly the image of the alien ship, bloated and wattled like a particularly ugly example of a deep sea fish, appeared on the viewscreen.

Zeela gasped. Something was heading directly towards them, a sleek black torpedo that had already covered half the distance between the ships. A simulation, Harper thought, as the missile itself would be too small to see in the void.

A second later *Judi* launched their own missile, and almost instantly the viewscreen bloomed with the resultant detonation as the missiles collided. The ship rocked as if caught in a storm and Harper held onto his sling as he was tossed from side to side. When the flash subsided, Harper stared at the Ajantan ship and made a snap decision. "*Judi*, fire two missiles, one after the other."

"Affirmative."

"Den?" Zeela asked.

"In case they try to intercept the first," he said.

He stared at the screen. A stylised missile sped into view, heading straight for the alien ship – closely followed by a second.

"Look!" Zeela cried.

The Ajantans had responded with their own intercept missile. A black streak left their ship, crossed the gulf and impacted with the first outgoing missile. The screen flared a sudden orange. The ship yawed, and Harper and Zeela tipped in their slings. He stared at the screen, searching for the second missile. Then he saw it, streaking through the detritus of the detonated missiles and closing in on the alien ship.

He leaned forward, fists clenched, willing the missile to strike its target.

A second later it impacted, and the resultant explosion created a blinding white light on the viewscreen, which *Judi* thoughtfully muted... though it could do nothing to prevent the subsequent blast-front that reached the ship and tossed her bow over stern. The slings tightened, cocooning their occupants, and Zeela screamed while Harper closed his eyes. They hung upside-down for long seconds, like spiders in a vibrating web, until *Judi* righted herself and rode out the storm.

Minutes later, though it felt much longer to Harper, the ship settled.

"Damage?" Harper enquired.

"Minimal. No shield breaches. Slight antennae damage."

"And the Ajantan ship?"

The viewscreen showed what remained of the alien ship, an oddly stylised confetti of metal in the shape of a sphere, radiating slowly as the expanding blast-front carried debris through the grey of void-space.

"Very good," Harper said. "Okay, full speed ahead to Vassatta."

Beside him, Zeela was very quiet. She reached out and took his hand.

CHAPTER NINE

JANAKER WOKE SUDDENLY, dragged her wrist-com from the bedside unit and stared at the dial. She'd been asleep for ten hours.

She sat up, and only then realised what had awoken her. The ship was going through a patch of turbulence. Flight through the void was normally smooth, so this could only mean that they were dropping through the atmosphere of their next port of call, Teplican.

She strapped on her wrist-com, pulled on her jacket and staggered from the cabin. The ship yawed and she careered from wall to wall as she made her way along the corridor to the bridge. The ship was on auto, and should have negotiated entry with more finesse than this. Teplican must be one hell of a stormy world, she thought.

Helsh Kreller sat in the pilot's seat, staring through the viewscreen. As Janaker slumped into the co-pilot's couch – irritated that the Vetch had appropriated *her* seat – she saw that they had yet to phase from the void.

She glanced across at Kreller. "I thought we were making landfall?"

The Vetch gestured at the swirling greyness and snapped, "Does it look as if we are?"

She squinted at the viewscreen and made out what appeared to be scraps of debris. "So are you going to tell me what's going on?"

The Vetch stared ahead. "Harper used a missile on the leading Ajantan ship," he said, "and destroyed it."

She stared at him. "The *leading* Ajantan ship? Just how many of them are out there?"

"There were two," he said. "I detected the second just three hours ago, hanging well back, before Harper destroyed the first one."

"Destroyed..." she echoed. "You're not joking, are you?"

"Of course I am. And what you see out there, those scraps of bulkhead and superstructure, and no doubt pieces of pulverised Ajantans, are figments of my imagination. As is the turbulence of the aftershock we're riding."

She stared across at him. "What the fuck," she said, "has got into you since we left Amethyst?"

He was silent for a time, then said, "You could have reacted a lot faster than you did."

She blinked, wondering what the hell he was talking about. Then she had it – Tesnolidek's attack back at the station. "I reacted as fast as I was able to, Kreller. The monster moved before I knew what was happening."

"You stood frozen, like a statue."

She laughed. "Listen to you! He was attacking you, Kreller – and I didn't see you get out of the way very fast, for all your claims of superior reactions."

The Vetch turned to stare at her. "I am sure that, before you fired, you hesitated."

"I was in shock, you bastard. I didn't expect the attack. The very fact that I fired when I did probably saved your life. And why the hell," she said, "would I deliberately hesitate? What are you trying to say?"

"You never wanted me along on this mission."

She nodded. "True. I could have done this alone, without all this running around. Simply followed Harper to Kallasta and apprehended him there. But just because I didn't want to be accompanied by an ugly, bad-tempered bastard like you doesn't mean to say I want you dead. Get a fucking grip, Kreller!"

They sat in silence for a long time as the aftershock of the alien ship's destruction abated. She asked at last, "How long before we land on Teplican?"

Kreller stared into the void. "We don't."

"I beg your pardon?"

"I said, we don't land on Teplican. We orbited the world some six hours ago and I decided that the wisest course of action was to avoid the planet."

"Just when have you been making the decisions, Kreller? I seem to recall, back on Hennessy, you said that we were to work as equals."

"You were sleeping. I made an orbit of Teplican, and what I saw down there decided me."

"What you saw down there?"

He tapped the console set into the arm of his couch, and the scene on the viewscreen changed. She saw a blue world striated with thin cloud. He touched the controls again and the image magnified: a continent loomed, an inland lake.

"I traced Harper's ion trail to where he landed not far from the base of a human scientific team. They are studying an alien ship... Look."

The image jumped and Janaker made out the skeleton of a ship beside the lake; it had evidently been there for a long time, interior spars and girders corroded, panels fallen in or removed.

Kreller adjusted the magnification and homed in on a fin which had slipped sideways, allowing them to see the pattern etched on the metal of its surface.

She looked at the Vetch. "So this is what decided you not to land?"

"That is correct. It would be... dangerous for us to do so."

"Would you mind explaining exactly why that is, Kreller?"

"I recognise the ship," he said, "or rather the scroll-work on its superstructure. Several ships identical to this one landed in Vetch territory many years ago. They were very mysterious – as they were without a crew. They and the areas around them were quarantined, declared no-go areas, and it is only in the last few years that we have come to understand what the ships... harboured."

She nodded, recalling something Commander Gorley had told her back on Hennessy. "Weird mind-parasites," she murmured.

"Exactly. Which is why I decided against landfall."

"They might still be... active, after so long?"

"According to scientific reports," he said, "the parasites can lie quiescent for more than a century."

"So Harper and the girl, and the scientific team down there..." She didn't finish the sentence. "Did you say Teplican was uninhabited?"

"I accessed your ship's smartcore. Records indicate that it was inhabited until shortly after the Weird ship arrived, approximately one hundred years ago."

"So the colonists..."

The Vetch twitched his head in an affirmative. "The colonists, if they were infected, carried that infection to the Reach, and maybe beyond."

"But that was a hundred years ago, right?" She shook her head. "The colonists would be dead by now..."

Kreller said, "My people's scientists are working on the theory that the Weird parasites can pass themselves through generations, lying dormant in their hosts until they give birth, and then infecting the newborns."

"Lying dormant..." she echoed, "until when?"

The Vetch spread his massive hands. "Until they deem the time is right? Until they have spread through the Reach, through the Expansion, through Vetch space, infiltrating our respective command structures?"

She shivered mentally. "That doesn't bear thinking about, Kreller."

"It is nevertheless a scenario that we must take into consideration in our fight against the Weird. And it increases the value of telepaths like myself... and Harper," he finished.

"If he hasn't gone and got himself infected," she said.

"Quite."

She glanced at him. "You've read infected minds, right?"

"Correct, back in my home system."

"And... what did you do then, when you found...?"

He looked at her, his big bloodshot eyes unreadable.

"It was incumbent upon me to... liquidate the infected," he said.

She nodded. "Right."

"When we apprehend Harper, I will scan him, and if he *is* infected..."

He let the sentence hang, then cleared the image of the alien ship from the screen and gestured at the void. "When Harper destroyed the first Ajantan ship, the second hung back beyond Harper's range. We are following the remaining Ajantan ship. I have no idea of whether the aliens are aware of our presence. As for Harper, he's no longer heading straight for Kallasta, but for the world of Vassatta."

"So what do we do? Wait until he leaves Vassatta and head for Kallasta?"

The Vetch was silent for a time, before replying, "I am reluctant to do that. The remaining Ajantan ship is much larger than the first. I fear that they will have revenge in mind for the destruction of their fellows' ship. If they are armed with missiles..." He gestured. "At present they are being cautious and hanging back, but that might change."

She nodded. "So we make landfall on Vassatta and try to apprehend Harper there?"

"Harper *and* his ship," he said. "I think that is the wisest course of action."

She almost asked him, then, about Harper's ship and his inordinate interest in it, but decided not to press the issue. He was still prickly about her so-called hesitation on Amethyst Station. The matter would no doubt arise when they eventually apprehended Harper.

She pushed herself from the couch. "I'm hungry," she said. "You eaten?"

The Vetch made a grunting sound. "I should have brought my own food along," he said. "It is an oversight I am beginning to regret. I will have meat, if you have any. And water."

She fetched two self-heating trays of food from stores, along with water and a couple of beers for herself.

"YOU ARE A strange woman, Sharl Janaker," said the Vetch.

She opened her eyes and sat up. A greasy tray slid from her chest and joined all the others on the deck.

"I was almost asleep," she said, yawning.

The Vetch was staring at her.

"What?" she said.

"I would like to know how you square your radicalism with the fact that you work for the Expansion authorities, which in your own words is a 'repressive, totalitarian organisation'?"

She found a half-full carton of warm beer wedged between her hip and the couch and took a long swallow. She waved the empty container at him. "In my early days, I admit, that did bother me."

"But not now?"

She pursed her lips, thought about it for a nano-second, and said, "Nope."

"And why is that?"

She shrugged. "I worked it out this way: whatever I did, in whatever field I worked, I'd always be working in some way for the regime I despise – or even if I wasn't directly working for the Expansion, then the very fact that I was a tax-paying consumer would be contributing to the success of the regime.

The only thing I could really have done would have been to flee the Expansion."

"For the Reach, like our friend Harper."

She nodded. "But the opportunity never arose."

Kreller regarded her and said, "But there are degrees of... complicity, shall we say? You could be a tax-paying consumer running a artist's commune on Hennessy, and your conscience would at least be a little cleaner than it is now, no?"

She sat up, riled by this virtuous prig who, on his own admission, was a fully paid up member of the fascist elite in his own system. "Way I see it, Kreller, is this: I work as a bounty hunter because I have... morals."

"I don't see..." he interrupted.

"Other bounty hunters, Kreller, go after their man, or woman, and if the subject dies during the chase then so be it. Part of the job. Way they see it, the subject was scum anyway so he or she's just dead scum now. But me... I've never killed a subject, Kreller. I don't work that way, and my controller knows that. And because I'm good at my job, I always get my man, or woman."

"And take them back to the authorities so that they can carry out what you were too squeamish to do."

"They shouldn't have broken the law in the first place..." she muttered.

The Vetch made an odd gesture. He held two fists in the air and brought them together so that they were joined but misaligned. He said, "I hear what you say, Janaker, but it doesn't quite fit. You might not kill the criminals yourself, but you return them to the authorities who do." He stared at her and, before she could respond, went on, "I have a theory about you."

She snorted. "Oh, yeah?"

"Yes." He indicated the pix of her lovers that covered every available vertical surface of the bridge. "Look, all these woman, the people you have engaged in sex with over the years."

"You make it sound so romantic, Kreller. I loved some of those girls, you know?"

"Have you noticed something about them?"

She shrugged, staring around at the smiling faces. "They're all cute?"

"They are all," he said, "of a certain type. Small, blonde, and younger than you are, or rather were – going by the images in which you appear alongside them."

"So what are you getting at, Kreller? What's this great theory of yours?"

"My theory is that in engaging with these women, these physically small women, you are sublimating your guilt at working for a masculine fascist organisation."

She stared at him, open-mouthed. "And what the fuck do you, a fascist alien prick yourself, know about human psychology, or come to that women's psychology?"

"I know enough to believe that on some deep strata of your psyche you seek out lovers who are smaller than yourself, physically weaker than yourself, and maybe even mentally vulnerable, because this is a way of re-establishing some form of... control in your life, of compensating for the fact that, every working day, you are subjugated by the Man, in the form of the Expansion authorities." He waved a hand with insufferable arrogance, and finished, "This might even account for the reason that you chose to be homosexual in the first place."

She contained her anger, turned in her seat and stared at the bastard. "Listen up, you ugly fucker... For your information I didn't choose to be lesbian – it's who I am. I was attracted to girls from an early age, okay, before I knew the first thing about the political make up of the Expansion. So that fucks your theory, doesn't it?"

He gestured, turning a placid hand. "It in no way disproves my theory that you are sublimating your guilt by seeking out small, physically weak, partners."

She stood up and paced the bridge. "I have no guilt, Kreller, and I've *always* been attracted to small women – from the age of around twelve, okay? So you can stick your moralising psychology lessons up your arse, which can't be any uglier than your fucking face, okay?"

"I seem in some way to have offended you," Kreller said. "If so, then I apologise."

Janaker stared at the Vetch. "And you call me strange?" she said. "I've had enough of this. Call me when we get to Vassatta."

She hurried from the bridge and made for her cabin.

CHAPTER TEN

THEY CAME DOWN slowly and made landfall at the ice-bound spaceport of Stromgard. As the docking ring clamped around the ship, making it clang like a struck bell, Harper and Zeela stood on the flight-deck and stared through the viewscreen.

"I've never seen anything like it," Zeela said. "What's that stuff falling through the air?"

"It's called snow," he said. "Frozen rain." He smiled at her wondrous expression. "But then you've always lived on warm planets, haven't you?"

She nodded absently. "I've never been cold in my life. I've read about it, of course."

"Then you're in for an interesting experience. Fortunately I have enough suitable clothing for both of us."

The city of Stromgard and its adjacent spaceport sat in the middle of a vast plain that extended for thousands of kilometres in every direction. To north, south, east and west the icy wilderness was broken only by the occasional town and village. Harper wondered what kind of hardy soul would voluntarily sequester themselves so far from civilisation, and in conditions so inimical to human life. Existence in the capital itself was extreme enough, but to live out on the ice plains many hundreds of kilometres from Stromgard... Only a certain type of person would do that, he decided; people desperate for work, sociopaths, or those unlucky enough to be born out there and know no other way of life.

Stromgard itself was situated to the west of the spaceport, the city a series of monolithic, multi-storeyed granite buildings forming canyons at the bottom of which were the famed ice-canals. Orange lights glowed in a million windows, but even so the overall effect was one of bleakness. A greater contrast to their last port of call, the sunlit world of Teplican, Harper could not imagine.

He ordered *Judi* to arrange refuelling, and learned from the port authorities that they were tenth in line for that service and could expect a wait of at least eight hours.

"Which will give us plenty of time to do what we have to do here before phasing out," he told Zeela.

"*Judi*," he said. "Any sign of the bounty hunters?"

"They have recently phased from the void and are currently in orbit."

"Okay... inform me if they make landfall."

"The chances are, Den, that they would come down on the blindside of the planet."

"I know, and that's what worries me."

He took Zeela to the storeroom, where he kept a wardrobe for every planetary temperature, and dug out a couple of snug body suits. Zeela, being so small, was engulfed in hers, and he had to roll up the legs and arms in order for her to wear suitable snow boots and big mittens. The effect was little short of comical.

"Are you sure," she said as she trudged after him to the exit, "that this is really necessary?"

He turned to her. "Have you ever experienced temperatures of fifty below zero?"

"*Fifty* below?" She shook her head.

"It's so cold that if you spat, it'd freeze on the way down and shatter when it hit the ground. Your eyeballs would freeze in their sockets."

She stared at him, then asked, "And you say there's no daylight on Vassatta?"

"Not during the hundred years of winter, no."

"Darkness for a hundred years..." she murmured to herself.

He passed her a face mask and said, "Under no circumstances take it off outside, okay? Your face would freeze within seconds."

She nodded and pressed the mask to her face, then pulled up her hood and fastened it around the mask. Only her big caramel eyes showed through the visor, watching him.

He donned his own mask and slapped the sensor on the bulkhead. The hatch slid open and a blast of icy air whistled into the ship. The port authorities had connected a catwalk from the top of the ship's ramp to the terminal building, five metres above the grey sheet of ice that covered the tarmac.

They passed through customs in minutes and emerged into the city of Stromgard.

Zeela looked up. She pointed with a thick mitten, and Harper craned his neck. The buildings on both sides of the ice-canal seemed to go on for ever. High up, between the granite eaves, a strip of space showed a million scintillating stars.

There were few people abroad; Harper counted a dozen brave citizens, lagged like boilers, shuffling along raised walkways on either side of the ice-canal. Hard to believe that it was noon in Stromgard. At intervals along the ice-canal, flames flared at the top of high columns, providing light. Harper explained that beneath the northern plains was a vast reservoir of oil. "They've been drilling it for centuries and it hasn't dried up yet."

A silver, arrow-shaped sled drew up before them, its engine growling. They climbed into the rear and Harper relayed an address to the driver.

The motor powered up and they were off, the metal runners sending up a spray of silver ice shards on either side. They sat back and watched the inimical facades of the towerblocks strobe by, lit garishly by the open flames.

Harper couldn't help contrast the city now, locked in deep winter, with the Stromgard he'd visited almost ten years ago. Then it had been late summer; the canals had been filled with water, busy with boats, and the mansions' facades embroidered with thick rafts of an ivy-analogue shot through with bright crimson blooms.

"Bjorn runs a haulage business on the outskirts of Stromgard," he told her. "He ferries goods and passengers to the outlying townships. He's sometimes away for days. With luck we'll catch him at home."

"And do you think he'll be interested in the engine?"

Harper shrugged, the gesture almost lost in the padded suit. "I'm sure he'll take it off our hands.

Whatever we make on it will be clear profit, after all. I'll be happy with whatever I get."

Zeela was silent for a time, then said, "I can't wait to get to Kallasta."

"It'll certainly be warmer than this."

She looked at him. "When do you think we'll arrive?"

He thought about it. "It's a couple of days away from Vassatta, and if we leave here later today..."

She nodded. "And then... what do you plan to do after Kallasta?"

He stared through the side-panel at the spray of macerated ice and, beyond, the sheer, dark walls of the buildings. "I have no set plans," he said. "I'll return to the core, tour the marts..."

She nodded again and fell silent.

Harper stared out at the passing buildings. Seen from above on their approach, the city resembled a discus, circular and raised in the centre. The mansions which occupied the inner city were taller than those on the outskirts, though the gradation was very gradual. The city was shot through with the radial spokes of the ice-canals, and like most cities across civilised space the outlying districts were given over to industry. Now they were passing dozens of low, dark warehouses, silvered by the abundant starlight.

They came to an intersection where six ice-canals met, and the junction was busy with traffic. Harper made out vast ice-liners piled with cargo, which spanned the breadth of the canals and moved with surprising speed. Barriers came down before the ice-taxi in order to allow a caravan of liners past, then lifted. The taxi started up again, crossed the intersection, then pulled into a slipway beside the main canal.

Harper paid the driver in local currency and helped Zeela out.

The Bjorn Halstead Haulage Company occupied a busy terminal building beside the intersection. Harper led the way into a garage lit by a central oil stove as big and hot as an open furnace. Mechanics serviced vehicles of all sizes, from two-berth sleds to triple-decker liners.

They crossed to a glass-fronted office and Harper asked after Bjorn.

A thick-set bearded man asked gruffly, "Your business?"

"If you could tell Bjorn that Den Harper would like to see him."

"And your business?"

"Oh, tell him I'm here to sell him iced lemon sorbets," he said.

Beside him, Zeela raised a mittened hand to her face mask and laughed.

The official glared at Harper, lifted an old fashioned phone and spoke briefly into the mouthpiece. Seconds later he pointed across the garage to a flight of wooden steps. "You're in luck. He hasn't set off yet."

Harper thanked the man with exaggerated politeness and crossed the garage to the stairs. At the top was a tall timber door, and Harper was just about to lift the ornate knocker – in the shape of a Norse god's headpiece – when the door was snatched open and a giant filled the threshold. The man looked like a figure from Norse mythology himself – perhaps Thor or Odin – a towering bear of a beast with long silver hair and a flowing beard.

He roared, "Harper! Lemon sorbet indeed! Come here!"

He towered head and shoulders above Harper and took him in a crushing embrace. He moved on to Zeela, who barely reached his ribcage, and thankfully adapted his greeting. He bent down and shook her hand, then stood back and welcomed them into his home.

They stepped over the threshold and peeled off their padded clothing. A great open fire burned in the hearth of the long room, and heavy timber furnishings – settees and throne-like armchairs – were piled with what looked like genuine furs.

Bjorn Halstead poured three mugs of rich, spiced coffee while Harper made the introductions. "Zeela is a friend, in transit to Kallasta," he said.

"Ah, in transit," Bjorn said; even his voice was larger than life, guttural and stentorian, each word like an axe biting into hardwood. "Which is how I met Harper when I left Vassatta five years ago. You see, every Vassattan must leave his homeplanet once in his life – on a pilgrimage called the harrassa – in order to see what lies beyond and so appreciate how wonderful Vassatta is. I was on the world of Kempsey, if I recall, and the local beer and bookmakers had conspired to rob me of my funds. Harper here, he kindly ferried me to Amethyst Station where I worked for a month to pay him back. And here you are again, five years later, to sell me lemon sorbet!"

Harper and Zeela sat on a cushioned settee before the blazing fire, but Bjorn strode back and forth as he spoke, taking great strides from the fire to the long window overlooking the ice-canal, and back again. It was a restless pacing Harper recalled from the haulier's time aboard ship, when he had spun tall stories of life on Vassatta and his exploits on the out-flung ice-canals.

"But what is it you're really here to sell?"

Harper produced a data-pin and tossed it to the giant, who slipped it into a wall console and read the result on a small screen. He strode to the window and stared out, his back to them.

Harper drank his excellent coffee and smiled at Zeela, who held her mug in both hands and took small sips.

Bjorn turned from the window. "I'm always needing engines. But the price?"

Harper suggested five thousand standard units – half the price he had asked of the merchant on Ajanta.

Bjorn roared, "But you're almost giving it away, man!"

Harper smiled and recounted how he'd been duped by the Ajantan merchant but how, thanks to Zeela, he had recovered his funds and escaped from the planet.

"So for all your diminutive stature, girl, you have spirit, no?" He stood, grasping his beard and regarding them.

"But I think you're telling me half a tale, yes? I think you're on the run – certain parties are in pursuit. Am I right?"

Harper stared at the Nordic giant; he had often wondered, during their time together five years ago, whether it had been Bjorn Halstead who was the telepath.

"How the...?" Harper began.

Bjorn moved from the window and thumbed over his shoulder. "Seconds after your cab pulled up, it was followed by another. Now two individuals are freezing their balls off across the canal, keeping a keen eye on this place. Or rather," he went on, "one set of balls are being frozen... if such aliens posses balls. The second individual is a woman."

The coffee seemed to turn to ice in his stomach. Zeela made a small sound of pained surprise at his side.

"They are on your trail, no?" Bjorn asked.

Harper stood up. "The woman is tall, broad, with dark hair? And the alien even taller?"

"The woman is wrapped from head to foot, but there is no denying she is Amazonian. Only her..." Bjorn made a cupping gesture before his chest, "tells me she is female. As for the alien... Yes, it's taller, and tougher – the ugly beast is accustomed to cold and goes without headgear, which I would suggest it should wear if only to spare unwary citizens from the hideousness of its face."

"It's a Vetch," Harper said with a sinking feeling. "The pair are bounty hunters."

He crossed to the window, pressed himself against the thick drapes, and peered out. Sure enough, Janaker and the Vetch stood on a raised walkway on the far side of the ice-canal, staring across at the garage. Seconds later Janaker ducked into a small ice-sled, its flank emblazoned with a lightning fork. The Vetch remained standing in the bitter cold.

Zeela said, "Den? Is it..."

"Janaker and the Vetch," he said, moving from the window.

Bjorn stared at him. "Bounty hunters, hm?"

Harper looked up at the giant. "I told you, five years ago, that I was a telepath. What I omitted to mention was that I was on the run from the Expansion authorities."

Bjorn nodded. "That story can wait. The pressing matter now seems to be, how to spirit you away from here without them giving chase?"

He thought about it, then moved to an adjoining room. He returned with a bundle of clothing.

"Now, get out of those flimsy, off-world garments and climb into these. Don't worry, they'll fit. The belonged to my son and daughter."

"But why...?" Harper began, already peeling off his padded jacket.

"When you've got rid of your old stuff, give them to me. I'll have a couple of my men wear them and leave the building. With luck it will draw off the bounty hunters, no?"

Harper smiled. "Ingenious."

Zeela was struggling from her garments. She divested the rolled-up trousers and began climbing into a silver one-piece which fitted her much better. Harper took up his own new garment and pulled on the leggings.

"You've timed it just right," Bjorn said, glancing at a tall clock standing against the wall. "I'm due to pilot a liner out to Ostergaart and beyond. You're coming with me."

"How long will the journey take?"

"All round? Just over a day – Reach standard. We pass the spaceport on the way back. I'll drop you off there."

A minute later they were both wearing the silver one-piece suits, and already Harper could feel their superior quality. He was in danger of asphyxiating so close to the open fire. He backed away and donned his face-mask, drawing the one-piece's hood over his head.

"Follow me," Bjorn said, and led the way from the room.

They hurried down the wooden stairs after the giant. He gestured them towards a door at the back of the garage, then crossed the oil-stained concrete, addressed a knot of mechanics, and handed over the padded garments.

Harper pushed through the door, followed by Zeela, and found himself standing on the edge of an open loading bay before the lighted cab of a huge ice-liner.

A keen wind whistled along the bay, but in the Vassattan protective garments he didn't feel the slightest bit cold. The door swung open behind them and Bjorn strode out in his own stained one-piece.

"Magnus and Knut are suiting up and will leave the garage in minutes," he said. "With luck the woman and her animal will leave us be."

The giant climbed a metal ladder on the flank of the liner and opened a hatch at the top. Zeela followed him up, and Harper brought up the rear. He squeezed himself in through the hatch after Zeela and found himself in a corridor which ran the length of the liner. They followed Bjorn until they came to a hatch at the end of the corridor, which he pushed open and ducked through.

They were in the lighted cab which resembled less the working end of a juggernaut than the sybaritic flight-deck of a starship. The furnishings matched those in Bjorn's lounge, settees, armchairs and fur rugs. The only indication that this was the cab of an ice-liner was a bank of controls ranged before a delta windscreen. Bjorn had even personalised this working area with an armchair as huge as a throne.

Harper removed his mask, lowered his hood, and unzipped his one-piece. He sat with Zeela on a settee by the windscreen and watched as Bjorn slipped into his pilot's chair.

"I'll get this thing started, then we can relax a little, no? Have you eaten? Then later we'll eat and you can tell me all about your adventures so far."

He pulled at control levers and seconds later the liner's engines thundered into life. The vehicle throbbed and shook as Bjorn backed it from the bay with a wailing of warning sirens, then eased it into a slipway that joined the main radial canal.

He flicked a switch and pointed with a big hand at an overhead screen. The image showed an ice-canal and its traffic. "That's the scene to the rear," Bjorn explained, "and it would seem that the bounty hunters have gone, no?"

Harper examined the street scene for Janaker and the Vetch. There was no sign of their ice-sled.

He stared ahead through the main windscreen. They were high up here, staring down at the silver ice-canal as it stretched as straight as a ruler to a distant vanishing point. They were leaving the area of low warehouses behind and streaking through a silver-blue ice-field lighted by nothing more than the stars and three small moons.

Bjorn left the driving seat and pulled up a chair. He caught Zeela's concerned expression and laughed. "Don't worry. This thing drives itself, once we're locked into a canal. It's a hundred kilometres per hour from here until the first stop, two hundred kays north of here. After that we swing east and deliver machine parts to the oil works at Tromso on the New Oslo plain. From then on its south again on to Stromgard, with just a couple of stops before home."

He moved to the back of the cab and returned with containers of food, which he handed to Harper and Zeela: crisp-bread and hard cheese, and what tasted like strips of dried fish, washed down with bottles of what Bjorn declared as the finest lager in the Reach – or at any rate the finest he'd ever tasted.

Harper told Bjorn about his escape from the Expansion, his life on the run, the many worlds he'd visited and the close shaves he'd had with the bounty hunter the Expansion authorities had sent after him. He elected not to describe how that particular chase had finished.

Bjorn heard him out, then gestured with his half-full bottle. "But that was years ago, Harper. And now they're after you again... Why? You don't think they've been after you all along, and just happened to find you again after all these years?"

"That's the worrying thing. I don't. For the past couple of years I haven't exactly been trying that hard to cover my tracks. Perhaps it was stupid of me, but I felt that they'd given up the ghost when I evaded the original bounty hunter. So, as you say, why now?"

"And two of them. One of them a Vetch... But I thought the Vetch and the Expansion were deadly enemies?"

"They were, once upon a time. In recent years there's been a cooling off of hostilities, an uneasy truce. But yes, it's strange that they should send a human-Vetch team." He smiled. "And if that was not bad enough, Zeela is on the run from a nasty bunch of aliens."

"Well I was," Zeela said, "until you blasted their ship to smithereens."

The big man was wide eyed. "I never had you down as a bellicose sort, Den."

"When needs must. Do you know what the humans of Ajanta suffer at the hands of the Ajantans?"

"My knowledge of the ways of the Reach," Bjorn admitted, "is deplorably scant. Tell me."

For the next hour, before the liner stopped at the town of Ostergaart, Harper regaled the haulier with the story of Ajanta, with Zeela contributing graphic details from time to time.

While she detailed her day to day life, in thrall to the aliens and the dhoor alike, Harper considered his order – just a day ago – to fire upon the Ajantan ship.

The situation, he realised, had been comparable to what had happened with the bounty hunter. He'd fought for his life on that occasion, and killed the mercenary as a result. Scale up the situation, replace one human with an unknown quantity of aliens, add the same imperative to save one's skin... and the result was that it was an 'us or them' scenario with only one logical option. No... he told himself... he did not feel the slightest guilt, or regret, for the loss of life he had caused.

Zeela was interrupted, a little later, by a computerised voice issuing from the control console. "Ostergaart in ten minutes. Repeat, Ostergaart in ten minutes..."

"Come, and I'll show you how we drop. Suit up, as this will be a little cold."

Intrigued, Harper followed the giant from the cab and along the lateral corridor. At the far end they descended a spiral staircase to a cavernous cargo hold.

Three workers drove fork-lifts back and forth, ferrying packing crates to a raised platform on the left of the hold. Bjorn led the way across the chamber and paused before the platform as the last of the crates was slotted into position.

Bjorn moved to a control box set against the metal wall and depressed a red stud. The platform began to rise slowly with its cargo of crates, and at the same time a corresponding hatch in the side of the liner hinged open with a sigh of ramrod hydraulics, revealing what appeared to be the interior of a shipping container. As they watched, the platform lifted the crates and slotted them into the container.

Bjorn gestured to a viewscreen in the flank that looked out over the icy wastes. Harper peered back and saw the bulky rectangle of the container obtruding from the flank.

Bjorn pointed ahead, to a collection of lights and oil-flames a kilometre further along the ice-canal. "Ostergaart," he said. "Now, we don't actually have to halt in order to drop the provisions."

"I see..." Harper said, and understood why they'd had to suit up for the operation.

Ahead, a cat's-cradle device of metal spars appeared beside the ice-canal, and seconds later he and Zeela flinched in unison as something smashed into the flank of the liner.

He turned quickly, and where the container full of crates had been was now an empty rectangle open to the long Vassattan night and the blasting icy wind.

Bjorn laughed and slapped the controls, and the hatch lowered itself and sealed the hold. "It's a method of delivery that goes back thousands of years," he said. "To the railways of Old Earth, if the legends are to be believed."

He gestured to the spiral staircase. "Come, after that we deserve a drink. Have you ever tasted Vassattan vodka?"

They retraced their steps to the warmth of the cab and resumed their seats. Bjorn poured three ice cold glasses of vodka and proposed a toast. "Skol! To old friends – and new friends – and to the thwarting of ugly bounty hunters!"

Harper drank to that, and Zeela took a tiny, experimental sip of the clear liquid. She coughed and spluttered and pulled a disgusted face, and Harper slapped her back and tried not to laugh.

"But that's awful!" she cried. "Like poison!"

"Perhaps something a little milder," Bjorn said, and fetched a beer from the cooler.

They sat and drank as the ice-liner raced through the Vassattan night. Bjorn grew quiet and mellow under the influence of the alcohol, and spoke of his life on the ice planet.

"I was lucky to be born at a time which meant I would live to see summertime," he said. "Citizens of Vassatta born after summertime never see its like. They experience only one long lifetime of winter."

"It must have been amazing," Zeela said.

Bjorn shook his head as if in retrospective wonderment. "The years leading up to the Time of Thaw were filled with excitement and anticipation. Everything we knew, the way of life that had lasted for a hundred years, was about to come to an end. The ice, which was the entirety of our world, would vanish... It was too great a concept to comprehend. And then..." He laughed. "The thaw began. The sun appeared as a small red coal in the distance, growing ever brighter as the days and weeks progressed. The temperature slowly rose. And the ice melted. It was a little frightening, I must admit, to see everything we had relied on to make our world what it was slowly... vanish. And then daylight came to Vassatta, and the ice melted completely, and the Time of Blooming came to our world – and with it a million tourists from all around the Reach.

"The colours!" he went on. "I am not a man much given to beauty and aesthetics, but even I was reduced to tears as I gazed out across the former ice plains and beheld a million multi-coloured blooms."

"It sounds... magnificent," Zeela said.

"And following the Time of Blooming," Bjorn said, "the Time of Burning."

"Burning?" Zeela asked.

"On its wild elliptical orbit," Bjorn said, "Vassatta passes so close to Vass, our red dwarf sun, that the daytime temperatures reach seventy-five Celsius. We take refuge underground, in the system of vast caverns that riddle the crust of the planet. Here we wait out the Time of Burning – but not before the brave, or the foolhardy, amongst us have remained on the surface to witness the depredations of the sun's heat. I," he went on, "was one such. There was no way that I was going to miss out on a once in a lifetime experience like the Time of Burning."

Zeela leaned forward. "What was it like?"

Bjorn sipped his vodka reflectively. "It was... appalling, and terrifying, and humbling, Zeela. A small group of us cowered in the shadow of a cave, well away from the burning rays of the sun, and we watched as the light intensified, and the heat climbed steadily – and the beauty of the flower-covered plains shrivelled and blackened and gave off poisonous clouds of rank black smoke, which eventually drove us underground. When we emerged, some seven years later, it was to witness a miracle. Vassatta was moving steadily away from the sun, and it was the Time of Second Blooming, when the desiccated seeds of the first Blooming germinated again in an even richer, brighter display of abundant colour."

He laughed. "Listen to me! I'm sounding like one of our poets... But the Second Blooming is soon over, as Vassatta pulls away from Vass and begins its long voyage into space, and the ice returns, little by little, and the skies darken and the long night comes once again to our world."

"This is when I came to Vassatta with the tourists," Harper said, "to witness the Second Blooming – and astounding it was too." He recalled the fecund display of riotous, polychromatic vegetation in complete contrast to the icy mantle that now covered the face of the planet.

Bjorn looked up from his drink and smiled at them. "I for one was secretly pleased that winter – the winter I knew so well – was upon the world again. I am an ice person, my friends. I was born to ice and I shall die to ice; it is my world, and I know it well."

Zeela mock-shivered and gazed through the viewscreen. "I would never be able to live here," she whispered.

"But you come from a warm world," Bjorn said. "I would never be able to tolerate the heat, the constant summers... And daylight *every* day!"

He finished his vodka and stood up. "It is late. First thing in the morning we arrive at the refinery of Tromso, where we do stop to unload goods and take on passengers. And the refinery is a sight to behold. I will awake you at four, and we will breakfast and watch Tromso hove into view. Come, and I'll show you to your sleeping quarters."

They moved along the lateral corridor until they arrived at a door to their left, which gave onto a small room with a window looking out over the starlit ice-fields. There were no beds in evidence, but

Bjorn answered this riddle by sliding open a door to the right, and another on the left, to reveal a cupboard-bed in each.

"You'll sleep well. I find the thrumming of the skis on the ice a soporific. Good night."

The cupboards were little rooms in themselves, with a margin before each bed which contained a sink, a table and a container for clothes.

Zeela yawned. "It seems like an age since we last slept, Den."

He looked at his watch. "You're right. Eighteen hours. Goodnight, Zeela."

She smiled. "Goodnight, Den."

He pulled the sliding door shut behind him, and a low light came on to illuminate the chamber. He undressed and washed, and slipped in between heated sheets. He switched off the light and considered leaving Vassatta tomorrow. Before that he would see if Bjorn was interested in the engine, and if so have *Judi* attend to its removal and storage at the port.

He heard the sound of a door, sliding, and a few seconds later a small voice. "Den?"

"Mmm?"

"I can't sleep."

He sighed. "I was almost dropping off."

"I'm sorry."

He listened. A silence, followed by soft tapping at his door. "Den?"

"Mmm?"

"I wonder... can I come in and talk?"

"We should sleep. We have a long day ahead of us tomorrow."

"I know, but just for a few minutes..."

He considered what he'd read, inadvertently, in

her head on Tarrasay... "No," he said. "Zeela, I'm dog tired and I need to sleep."

Another silence, followed by, "Why are you being like this?"

He sighed. "Like what?"

"Like this. Cold. Reserved. As if we haven't shared anything over the past week and more."

"That's not true. But I'm tired now. And I have a lot to think about."

"Den," she said after a short silence, "what's wrong with you?"

"There's nothing wrong with me."

"I know what it is," she said. "That time on Tarrasay, at the café. You put on your ferroni-thingy, and... and you didn't like what you read in my head, did you? You didn't like the kind of person I was."

He sighed in exasperation and rubbed his eyes. She was wrong, very wrong. The fact was that he *had* liked the kind of person she was. That was the problem.

"Well?" she said.

"Zeela..."

"Yes?"

He tried not to laugh. "Come here."

She slid the door open. The light came on, showing Zeela in a short undergarment that came to just above her knees. She stood regarding him with big eyes. He patted the bed. "Sit down."

She sat down, regarding her dark hands pressed together on her lap as if in prayer. She looked up.

"Zeela. I'm sorry. I'm not being cold, or reserved. At least, I hope I'm not. And when I read your mind – briefly and accidentally – it wasn't that I didn't like what I read in there."

She looked up, hopefully. "Well, then..."

He tried to formulate the words that would tell her about himself, his life, in a way that would not hurt her. He said, "For the past few years I've lived alone, aboard the ship. Moving from star to star, planet to planet. Trading. And, for the first couple of years, running. And in all that time I've... I've been content with my own company. I don't want... complications. And I wouldn't want to burden anyone with the dangers that being with me would bring."

She stared at him, wide-eyed. "As if we haven't gone through dangers together already, and survived them!"

"I know. I'm not expressing myself very well." He gathered his thoughts. "I'm thirty, Zeela, and you're not yet eighteen. I'm too old to... It wouldn't work. It would end... unhappily, for one of us, both of us. The best thing, the only thing would be if we were to remain as friends."

"Friends?" She spat the word, staring at him incredulously. "As if everything we've shared didn't matter?"

"Of course it matters! It's just..."

She reached out and grabbed his hand. "I want you to do something, Den. I can't really express with words what I feel, not very well. So... so use your device and read my mind, read what I'm *really* feeling."

Her small hand felt very hot in his. He stared at her, feeling waves of hopelessness sweep over him. How could he begin to tell her what he had experienced, all those years ago?

He shook his head. "I'm sorry, Zeela. I can't do that. You don't realise how painful it is, to read another's mind. Why do you think I ran away, back then?"

"You ran from the Expansion," she said, "from what they made you do. Not from a woman–!"

Before he could stop himself, he cried, "For chrissake, that's exactly what I was running from, you little..."

She stared at him, wide eyes, as if he'd slapped her. "I'm sorry," she murmured. She pulled her hand away.

"No, *I'm* sorry. I... Look, one day I'll explain. When we've outrun the bounty hunters and we have plenty of time on Kallasta, then I'll explain."

She nodded, eyes downcast, not meeting his gaze. "Okay, Den," she said quietly.

Seconds later she slipped from the bed-chamber and slid the door shut.

He lay in the darkness, cursing himself, and it was a long time before he slept.

"Tromso! Tromso!" Bjorn yelled.

Harper came awake instantly, sitting up and wondering where the hell he was. It was the second time he'd awoken recently to find himself in a confined space. He felt the thrumming of the skis conducted through the superstructure of the ice-liner. He was hundreds of kilometres north of Stromgard, coming into the oil refinery at Tromso on the New Oslo plains.

He dressed quickly, rinsed his face at the sink, and emerged to find Zeela stepping from her own bed-cupboard. She smiled at him brightly, as if their conversation last night had never taken place.

By the time they reached the cab, Bjorn was back in his seat at the controls. He indicated a small table bearing spiced coffee, crisp-bread and hard cheese. "Breakfast. I trust you both slept well?"

"You were right about the effect of the skis," Zeela said. "I was fast asleep as soon as my head touched the pillow. What about you, Den?"

He glanced at her. "I was a little longer getting to sleep," he said, then whispered to her, "I was visited by a demon in the night."

They ate standing up and staring through the windscreen.

"Tromso," Bjorn said proudly. "What do you think?"

The darkness was banished by a thousand burning fires which illuminated a complex web of silver pipes like a giant's metal puzzle. Between the pipes Harper made out granite buildings, seemingly entangled in the pipe-work. The city-refinery extended for kilometres across the plain – in fact for as far as the eye could see – washed with the orange light of the burn-off chimneys.

"Ten thousand citizens work here," Bjorn was saying. "And the refinery produces the oil which keeps the planet going."

Zeela asked, "And how long will the reserves last for?"

"Experts estimate they're good for another thousand years."

"And after that?" Harper asked.

Bjorn nodded, his face grave. "Vassatta is viable only through the continued supply of oil," he said. "Without it, the planet would freeze – or rather we, the inhabitants, would freeze. So when the oil runs out, life on our world will be impossible, and my descendents will have no option but to leave. Vassatta will become a ghost world," he went on, "an epitaph to our brief time here."

He smiled. "But that will not be for another thousand years, maybe more, and before that there will be many Bloomings that my grandchildren, and their grandchildren, will witness and enjoy."

Just twenty Bloomings, Harper thought soberly.

Bjorn eased the ice-liner into a slipway, and the vehicle rang to the sound of fuel being pumped into the liner's empty tanks. Through the viewscreen they watched as a file of muffled workers, coming off shift, shuffled towards the liner. Presently they heard footsteps below and the sound of the passengers' voices.

"They're heading for Stromgard at the end of a six week shift," Bjorn said, "where they'll party for a fortnight until work begins again."

"It must be a hard life," Harper said.

Bjorn smiled. "This is Vassatta. To off-worlders, all life here seems hard." He laughed. "Now we swing homeward. Two more drop-offs before here and Stromgard, and a stop at the spaceport where we'll say goodbye."

They were on their way again thirty minutes later. An hour after that Zeela was leafing through a pictorial atlas of the planet and Harper was reading the Sagas, the epic prose-poems penned by the first human inhabitants of Vassatta. Bjorn turned in his seat and said, "I don't want to alarm you, but..."

He indicated a screen which showed the view of the ice-canal behind them. "This is magnified," he said. "The sled is perhaps three kilometres away. The thing is, it shouldn't be there." He pointed a calloused finger at another screen. "There's the schedule, and the next vehicle is a liner, two hours behind us."

Zeela jumped up from the settee and joined them at the controls. "Do you think...?"

Bjorn nodded. He increased the magnification, and the pursuing sled expanded. "I do. It's the same make of sled as your two friends had outside my place yesterday. Too much of a coincidence for it *not* to be the bounty hunters."

Harper tried to keep the fear from his voice. "And I thought we'd given them the slip. But how...?"

"They're tenacious, and skilled," Bjorn said, with not a little admiration. "They would do well hunting skarl across the southern plains. It's a pity they can't be persuaded to remain here."

"That would be one solution," Harper said. "The other, that we somehow evade them."

Bjorn nodded. "I'm taxing my brains to that very end, my friend."

"How far are we in front of them, in terms of time?"

Bjorn shook his head. "A matter of minutes only." The Vassattan looked from Zeela to Harper. "But I have an idea..."

Harper said, "Go on."

"It would work, and leave the bounty hunters chasing shadows." He paused. "I've done it myself, in my younger days. Granted, it's not exactly comfortable, and you must hold on for dear life for fear of earning a body-full of bruises... but the alternative is not worth considering."

Zeela stared at him. "Would you mind explaining?" she pleaded.

Harper said, "I think Bjorn's trying to tell us that we're about to be delivered, like a container of goods, at the next drop point. Am I right?"

Zeela gasped.

The big man grinned. "It's the only way, and cannot fail. From there – a small pumping station town called Eklund – you can catch the next liner that's scheduled to halt, which should be no more than a six hour wait. That will take you directly to the spaceport."

"I have a better idea," Harper said. "I don't like the idea of arriving at the port to find the bounty hunters waiting for us."

"But how can you leave Vassatta if you don't go to the port?" Bjorn asked.

"We don't go to my ship," Harper said. "The ship comes to us."

He asked Bjorn for the exact geographical location of Eklund, and the big man consulted his screen and relayed the co-ordinates. Harper tapped them into his wrist-com. "And when will we be arriving at Eklund?"

"In a little over twenty minutes," Bjorn said.

"In that case I'll get my ship to arrive on the ice plain outside Eklund in thirty minutes. The bounty hunters will have passed the town by then."

Bjorn laughed.

"What?" Harper asked.

"And the only reason you sought me out was to see if I wished to purchase a steamboat engine! Which, at five thousand units, I would very much like to... If your ship has time to off-load it, that is."

Harper smiled. "I'll contact *Judi* with instructions," he said, "and I'll not accept a single unit for the engine. It's a gift, and I'll hear no protests."

Bjorn regarded him, then stretched out a hand. "In which case I will accept, with thanks."

They shook, and Harper activated his wrist-com. He got through to *Judi*, relayed the co-ordinates, and told her to meet them on the ice-plain a kilometre north of Eklund in thirty minutes. He explained the situation, adding, "And come in on a circuitous route, avoiding the ice-canal so that the bounty hunters don't catch sight of you."

"Understood."

"And before you set off, have the port authorities unload the engine and store it for one Bjorn Halstead."

"Affirmative."

They left the cab and made their way down to the cargo hold. Bjorn strode to the bulkhead and slapped the controls. They stood back as the platform folded itself from the wall.

Through the viewscreen Harper watched the ice-bound land race by... and soon they would be placing themselves in a container which would be whisked by mechanical grabs from the liner as it sped by without stopping.

Zeela, as if guessing his thoughts, smiled bravely.

They watched as workers fork-lifted half a dozen containers onto the platform. Bjorn crossed the hold and came back with an empty container and a roll of plastic bubble-padding which he wadded inside. "To make for a more comfortable ride," he said. "When we did this, way back, we went without a container and just held on. I know, the stupidity of youth!"

Zeela looked at the container dubiously. "But what if it tips and cracks open?"

"It won't," he assured her. "I'll wedge it between two sturdier crates. Don't worry, you'll be fine."

Harper glanced at his wrist-com. They were due to pass Eklund in ten minutes.

Bjorn asked, "Are you armed?"

"No, and I hope we have no need to be."

Bjorn nodded. "Excuse me a moment." Harper watched the giant as he strode across the hold and slipped through the exit.

He returned minutes later with a laser pistol in one hand and a bottle of Vassattan vodka in the other. He passed Harper the pistol. "Simple stud operation, three settings: disable, stun, and kill. It's set on stun now." He gave Zeela the bottle of vodka and explained, "The receiving station should be empty, but in case there's someone about, give them this from Bjorn Halstead. I'll call ahead to see if it's manned, and if so warn them to look out for a surprise package."

"For a second," Zeela said, "I thought it was a parting gift."

"Well, if there's no one at the station it's all yours. To keep you warm on your voyage between the stars."

She laughed. "Thank you, but I think I'll stick to juice all the same."

Bjorn glanced at his watch. "Five minutes. We'd better be crating you up."

He lifted the empty crate onto the platform and wedged it between two others. Zeela jumped in first, nestling herself down in the bubble padding. Harper turned to Bjorn and they shook hands again. "Thank you for everything."

The Vassattan smiled. "Good luck, and call at Vassatta again if you get the chance. You'll always be welcome."

"I'll be in contact from my ship when we're safe," he promised.

He climbed into the crate beside Zeela, hunkering down and pulling the bubble-padding around him.

Bjorn handed him more padding, then saluted farewell. Harper arranged the padding around his head as Bjorn closed the lid and darkness descended. In the warm, silent confines of the crate, Zeela worked a hand through the padding and found his leg. He reached out and took her hand, gripping the pistol in his right hand.

"Promise not to drink all the vodka by yourself," he said.

"Promise, Den."

The crate jerked as the platform rose and inserted itself into the container. Harper lifted his hand and peered at his wrist-com. The illuminated screen told him that Eklund was a minute away.

"Den."

"Mmm?"

"Why are we crated up like animals in an ice-liner on a world a million miles from nowhere?"

He had to laugh. "Put like that, our situation does seem rather bizarre. *Hell!*"

It felt as if a runaway bulldozer had smashed into the crate. He expected it to disintegrate and smash them to a bloody pulp. He gripped Zeela's hand as she yelled. They rattled like peas in a drum, despite the padding. Seconds later all was still.

"You okay?"

"Think so, Den. Just shocked, that's all. I wasn't expecting such an impact. You?"

"No broken bones. I'm fine."

"And I managed to keep hold of your precious vodka."

"Well done. I just hope there's no one out there to share it with."

"Shall we take a look?"

He pulled the padding away from above his head and reached up. He pushed, and the lid popped. Weak grey light filtered through the remaining padding, which he batted away and struggled to his feet. He looked around, expecting to see amused workers staring at his sudden jack-in-the-box appearance.

The crate and half dozen others stood in a building that looked like a grey metal box, a hundred metres by fifty. Slit windows on all four walls looked out over the plains and the ice-canal. Through the windows at the far end, Harper made out the lights of a small town.

There were no workers in evidence within the station.

"Looks like we have the place to ourselves," he told Zeela as he helped her out.

She looked around and brrr'd her lips, her breath pluming in the icy air. "Wonder if there's a heater in this place?"

He pulled up his hood and donned the face-mask.

"How long before *Judi* gets here, Den?"

He consulted his wrist-com. "If everything goes to plan, in around ten minutes."

"What do we do? Stay put or make for where we're meeting her?"

"No need going out there before we need to. We'll give it five minutes, and set off then."

He jumped down and walked around the ugly cradle mechanism that had caught the platform. He approached the closest slit window overlooking the ice-canal and peered out on a desolate, deserted scene: the cold stone canyon of the canal with a grey strip of frozen water in between.

He wondered why he was feeling jumpy, nervous.

The bounty hunters would have raced by and would be kilometres south of here by now, and soon *Judi* would swoop down to carry them away. Nevertheless, the bounty hunters' tenacity to date engendered apprehension. The sooner *Judi* arrived, the better.

"Den," Zeela called from the far end of the chamber. "Slight problem."

He hurried across to her. "What?"

She indicated a corrugated metal door. "It's locked."

"Good job Bjorn gave us this. Stand back."

He set the gauge on the pistol to kill, backed off five metres, aimed at the locking mechanism and fired. The metal flared, popped, and dripped. He approached the door and kicked at it without ceremony. The corrugated rectangle swung open, admitting a freezing wind.

He peered out. Fifty metres away was a line of low granite buildings, and beyond them a gargantuan series of silver pipes. Half a kilometre beyond was where *Judi* would land in a matter of minutes.

He was about to suggest that they set off when he heard something – the sound of an engine above the soughing of the wind.

Zeela tensed. "What was that?"

Without replying he sprinted back to the slit window overlooking the ice-canal. He felt a surge of panic. "I don't believe it..."

Zeela was beside him, standing on tiptoe to peer through the window. "What?" She sounded desperate.

A two person ice-sled had come to a halt on the canal twenty metres from the receiving station. "The sled," he said.

"But is it theirs?" she cried.

He recognised the gold lightning blaze on the flank of the vehicle. "It's theirs," he said.

The sled was pointing back along the ice-canal, so evidently they had sped past the station in pursuit of the ice-liner, realised their mistake and doubled back.

But how the hell had they worked out that he and Zeela were here...?

A wing-hatch swung open and the woman eased herself out. The Vetch followed, towering over her. They were armed, and staring directly up at the station.

The ice-canal was perhaps five metres deep – so the bastards would have to climb out before they could approach the station. Metal ladders, stapled into the stone, dropped to the ice at intervals of two hundred metres. It would take them a minute to reach the nearest one.

He grabbed Zeela's hand. "Let's get out of here."

They ran across the ringing concrete and slipped through the door.

"Which way?" she said.

He was already hauling her down a concrete ramp that fell towards the town. The problem with sprinting on Vassatta, he discovered to his regret seconds later, was that every outdoor surface was coated with treacherous ice.

Their feet shot out from under them and they tumbled painfully. Zeela cried out. Harper rolled, cursing the pain that shot up his spine. The same ice that had thwarted their sprint now aided their unceremonious slide on their backsides all the way down the ramp. At the bottom Harper dragged Zeela to her feet. "You okay?"

She nodded. "Never better."

"This way. And this time we don't run, okay?"

Hand in hand they moved cautiously along a darkened alley between the receiving station and a granite building. He looked quickly over his shoulder. There was no sign yet of Janaker and the Vetch.

If they could lose themselves in the township... or, better still, head out to the ice plain where there was no illumination to betray their presence...

"This way," he panted, pulling her after him.

They darted down an alley between two squat, one-storey buildings, keeping their footing only with difficulty.

"Den."

"Yes."

"You... you're going to be," she gasped, "proud of me... if we survive."

"How's that?"

"Tell... tell you later."

"I can't wait."

He raised his wrist-com and snapped the activation command. "*Judi*, where the hell are you?"

"Approaching Eklund," *Judi* said. "Half a kilometre from rendezvous point and closing."

At that second, all around them, the night lit up.

"Duck!" Harper yelled, dragging Zeela to the ground.

They hit the ice and a lapis lazuli laser beam bisected the air above their heads. He rolled and in the same motion returned the fire. A hundred metres away he saw the Vetch dodge into a doorway. Janaker was behind the alien, caught in the open. He aimed and fired, intent on nailing the bastard. The beam missed by centimetres but had the fortuitous effect of bringing her up short. She slipped and fell. Harper fired again. The woman rolled, and a hand shot from the doorway and dragged her to safety.

Harper grabbed Zeela, hauled her upright and sprinted towards the end of the building. The relief when they reached the corner and turned was such that he felt like whooping with elation. He restrained himself and kept on running.

Zeela gasped, "Where... where now?"

"Where the bastards don't expect us to go – around the block so we end up where we started."

"Is that wise?"

"Any better ideas?"

They came to the corner of the gable end and turned, running as fast as they were able along the ice-covered ground. The danger was that the bounty hunters might reach the end of the row and turn the corner before he and Zeela could reach the end of the street... in which case they'd be in plain sight again.

He looked over his shoulder. The street was deserted, eerie in the light of the stars.

"And... and what then?"

"We go round the back of the receiving station and call *Judi*."

They came to the end of the building and flung themselves around the corner, pressing themselves against the ice-cold granite and hauling in lungfuls of freezing air. The station was a hundred metres away across open ground. To cross it would be dangerous... but Harper judged that it was the best possible option.

"Okay," he said, "Let's go!"

Expecting to feel a laser beam cauterize his backbone at any second, he gripped Zeela and ran across the ice towards the station, its dim interior light beckoning like a beacon. At one point the ice was so slick they began to skate and Harper went with it, releasing his grip on Zeela's hand and holding out his arms to keep his balance.

Seconds later they came to the station. He was tempted to seek the immediate refuge of its interior – but doing that would succeed only in trapping them like rats in a barrel. They would be in view for longer as they scuttled along its façade, but the bounty hunters had yet to show themselves. Perhaps the fact that he was armed had given them second thoughts about pursuing?

They made their way along the front of the station and, seconds later, reached the corner. He slipped around it, pulling Zeela after him, and laughed aloud with relief.

He sank onto his haunches and got through to *Judi*. "Change of plan. Lock onto our position and land in the ice-canal. Got that?

"Affirmative."

"And come down with the ramp extended and the hatch open. We might have to jump aboard. And as soon as we have, phase out. Understood?"

"Understood. Estimated rendezvous time, fifty-seven seconds."

Less than a minute. He looked up. The canal was ten metres away. The bounty hunters would hear the ship's arrival, of course, but if he and Zeela made a run for it before their pursuers got within laser range...

"As soon as the ship comes down," he said, "we sprint for it and dive aboard. You can do that?"

She nodded.

It was the longest fifty-seven seconds of his life.

What seemed more like five minutes later he heard the deafening grumble of *Judi*'s maindrive as the ship streaked over the roof of the station and sank towards the canal. Her running lights sequencing like a calliope, *Judi* lowered herself towards the strip of ice, ramp lolling like a tongue beneath the dark arch of the hatch.

"Let's go!" Harper yelled.

They pushed themselves from the wall and sprinted across the open area towards the canal.

The first laser beam missed him by a metre. The second was so close he felt its heat searing the air beside his head. He cried out and slipped, and only this saved the third beam from splitting his skull. He dropped his laser. It skittled away across the ice. He slid on his belly towards the pistol, gripped it, rolled onto his back and returned fire. He saw Janaker duck behind the station – but the Vetch was made of bolder stuff. It came out into the open, raised its rifle...

Harper fired, and more by luck than good marksmanship hit the bastard in the dead centre of its chest. The alien screamed, punched backwards by the impact.

Zeela grabbed his hand, pulled him to his feet and cried, "Look!"

Harper looked, and wished he hadn't. *Judi* was settling on the canal, canted nose forward as her engines melted the ice beneath her stanchions – but two hundred metres away, and heading straight towards *Judi*, was a speeding ice-liner.

Zeela yelled again and pulled him towards the canal. When she reached the edge she took off, seemed to hang in the air, spread-eagled for an age, then landed with a sickening thump at the top of the ramp. She slid, almost lost her grip, then reached out and grabbed the hatch's metal flange and pulled herself aboard.

A laser beam melted ice centimetres from Harper's head. He rolled onto his back and fired three successive shots. All of them missed Janaker, but succeeded in sending her scuttling into the cover of the station.

Harper pushed himself to his feet and sprinted.

Zeela was standing now, exhorting him at the top of her lungs to jump.

He looked to his left. The ice-liner was screaming ever closer as it applied its brakes in a futile attempt to slow before it impacted with the starship. He reached the edge of the canal. The open hatch was four metres away. A laser beam lanced past him, pinged off *Judi*'s metalwork. Zeela bent herself double and screamed, "Jump!"

He dived, yelling, and impacted with the ramp. He slid. Something grabbed him, pulled him up the ramp. Zeela, crying in desperation. Another laser beam struck the ship as it lifted with a sudden, deafening whine of motors. He rolled aboard and peered down. The ice-liner screamed by underneath, its microwave antennae and a couple of fins excoriating *Judi*'s underbelly.

More laser beams criss-crossed through the night air. He peered down. The Vetch, impossibly, was on its feet and firing alongside Janaker. Harper glanced at his laser pistol. It had been set to kill, but now read *stun*. Of course... when he'd dropped it on the ice, the impact must have altered the setting.

You're one lucky, ugly bastard, he thought.

He pulled his head in and rolled. "Close the hatch and phase out!" he screamed, and a second later the hatch slammed shut.

He felt the familiar lurching sensation in his gut as they phased into the void.

Across the chamber, Zeela was sitting against the wall, her face tear-streaked – and she was laughing like a maniac.

"Den!" she cried. "Den?"

Smiling, weary now but elated, he said, "Zeela?"

"I... I told you you'd be proud of me, didn't I?"

He laughed. "You did. But...?"

She pulled something from the pocket of her one-piece and held it aloft.

"I didn't break the vodka, Den!"

Laughing, he crawled across the floor and hugged her to him.

LATER, AS THEY sped through the void towards Kallasta, they sat side by side in their slings and Harper sent a recorded message to Bjorn Halstead on Vassatta. They raised their glasses and Harper proposed a toast. "To Bjorn Halstead – hero of heroes!"

"To Bjorn!" Zeela said.

She took a mouthful of vodka and spat it halfway across the flight-deck.

CHAPTER ELEVEN

"Stop firing!" the Vetch yelled.

His command was redundant, anyway, because seconds later Harper's ship stuttered visually and phased into the void.

She stood on the ice, staring up at where the ship had been. Down in the canal the ice-liner raced north, the roar of its engines diminishing. Janaker holstered her laser and hugged herself against the biting wind. Despite her thermal suit, gloves, hood and goggles, she was freezing. Kreller stood beside her, dressed as he had been from the start in his leather jacket – lacerated thanks to the attention of Tesnolidek back on Amethyst Station – without gloves or protective headgear.

She raised her wrist-com and instructed her ship to pick them up. It gave an arrival time of thirty minutes and she wondered if she'd survive that long. She gestured to the building behind them and hurried into its shadow. At least here they were out of the wind.

She sat against the wall on her haunches, hugging herself. The Vetch squatted beside her.

She glanced at his chest, where days ago Tesnolidek had sliced him to the bone, and a few minutes back Harper had lasered him in the sternum. The Vetch seemed to be unbothered by the wound, despite the mess of singed hair and scorched flesh.

She pointed at the wound. "You okay?"

Kreller grunted. "I'll live."

She stared at him. "There's something I don't get."

"What's that?"

"Harper destroys an Ajantan ship, kills God knows how many aliens aboard it... and yet when it comes to firing at us, he sets his laser to stun."

The Vetch turned his bloodhound gaze on her. "Have you thought that maybe his laser was set to kill – kill humans, that is? But I am a Vetch. I am... stronger."

She snorted. "You're made of the same stuff as I am, Kreller. You're flesh and blood. Had his laser been set to kill, you'd be dead meat now."

"In your dreams," Kreller muttered.

Fuck you, she thought. She shook her head. "It's not the actions of a man who killed the last bounty hunter sent after him," she said. "But that was four years ago. Perhaps he's changed in that time?"

She looked around at the wind-swept desolation of the station. The wind keened like a soulful musical instrument. "Who the hell, in their right minds, would chose to live on a world like this?"

"Those born here, those who know nothing else." He stared at her. "I am from a world like this one."

"Well, that'd explain thing or two."

"Meaning?"

She smiled, gesturing at his uncovered head. "Your tolerance to cold."

"I am from the world of Zankra, born of a noble clan. I was destined to follow my mother into the military, but I showed an aptitude for the sciences. And then, while I was studying, I was singled out for the surgery that would bring forth my telepathic ability. That was before you were even born."

She grunted. "And how long have you been tracking down Vetch infected with the Weird parasite?"

"We have known of the Weird for two of your years, so for just a little under that."

"And how many of the infected have you..." she recalled the word he had used "... liquidated?"

"To date, three."

"High-ups in the Vetchian hierarchy?"

"Two were scientists working in the arms industry, the other a Marshall in our space fleet."

She nodded, thinking about the humans in the Expansion infected unbeknownst to themselves and their loved ones... For all her dislike of the Expansion authorities, the thought of anyone harbouring a Weird mind-parasite filled her with horror and pity.

She glanced at her wrist-com. Her ship should be here within minutes. "So, Kreller... You've dissected my psychology, derided my sexuality. What about you? Are you married, or doesn't the term apply to the Vetch?"

He stared into the icy darkness. "We do not marry. We mate. We have a partner for months only, long enough for the female to conceive."

"Ah, and after that the woman is left to rear the brood?"

He looked at her. "Child-rearing, in my culture, is the responsibility of the male of the species."

Somehow, try as she might, she just could not imagine Kreller changing nappies.

She grunted, "And I'm sure you'd make a fine father, Kreller." She squinted at him. "Are you? A father, that is?"

"My rank within my cadre prohibits patriarchy, at least for another ten of your years. After that, maybe I will settle down and raise a family for a couple of years."

"A couple of years? And then your offspring will be old enough to fend for themselves?"

He nodded. "Unlike your feeble, puling pups which take many years to mature."

"We're all products of our biology and environment," she said, "and there's nothing we can do to change that."

The Vetch grunted. "It is just that some races, Janaker, are superior compared to others."

"I was about to ask you if you had any comparisons in mind, but look," she pointed, "the ship."

She stood up and walked from the lee of the building, the sudden wind slicing the exposed flesh of her cheeks and taking her breath away. She watched her ship come down, then hurried across the ice and up the ramp.

SHE LAY BACK in her couch and drained her fifth carton of beer.

She was at that pleasant stage of drunkenness that came just before maudlin introspection set in. The many mistakes of her past were forgotten in a pleasant haze of anaesthesia, along with the uncertainty of her future. All that remained was the present... and she was seated in her command couch surrounded by her ship, so the present was okay.

She even managed to push the irritation of Helsh Kreller to the back of her mind. He was alien, anyway, so what did he amount to? He wasn't even a real man, so she couldn't truly bring herself to hate him, for all that he was an insufferable, macho bastard. She would complete this mission, bring Harper kicking and screaming back to the Expansion, then find a resort somewhere and relax with a few weeks of beer and girls.

"The Ajantan ship?" Kreller's shadow loomed over her – and just when she was enjoying a quiet drink.

She ripped open another carton and greeted him. "Why not try a beer? Go on. Never know, you might like it."

He looked at her. "That is unlikely. I asked about the Ajantan ship."

She waved at the screen. "Somewhere out there. But don't worry, I told my ship to keep its distance."

Kreller eased his bulk into the co-pilot's couch. It creaked under his weight. "How far are we from Kallasta?"

"Just under a day." She took a long swallow of beer, closed her eyes and lay back.

Seconds later her wrist-com buzzed and the ship informed her of an incoming communiqué.

She sat up. "From?"

Surely Harper wasn't trying to contact her?

Her ship said the call was coming from the Ajantan vessel.

Kreller looked at her. "Open communications," he snapped.

"I was just about to, for chrissake," she muttered, and then said to her ship, "Okay, patch them through."

The viewscreen flickered and the bridge of the Ajantan ship appeared, a gloomy aqueous chamber like something at the bottom of a frog pond. Which was appropriate, she thought, when she saw the three Ajantans facing her. The central alien spoke, a series of almost inaudible fluting sounds, and she instructed the ship to translate.

Seconds later a computerised female voice rendered the words intelligible.

"We respectfully enquire as to the reason you are following us?"

Janaker leaned forward. "We are *en route* to the world of Kallasta," she said.

"You have been following us for the past three days."

"Our route to Kallasta happened to follow your own route."

"The coincidence is remarkable," said the Ajantan. "We suspect that you too are following the ship carrying the human male and female."

"Negative." She paused, choosing her words with care. "But why are *you* following their ship?"

The three Ajantans conferred, and at last the central alien turned to face the screen. "The human male is in possession of our property."

"In possession of *what*?"

"The human girl, who is our property."

She opened her mouth to say something, stopped herself and sat back in the couch. "I understand," she said at last, diplomatically. "And you intend to get back your... property."

"Affirmative."

"And the human male?"

"The human male is responsible for the destruction of an Ajantan ship. For this crime, he must pay the penalty."

"Which is?"

The aliens stared at her. Together they said one word, "Death."

"I understand."

"And we hope," said the central Ajantan, "that as a fellow human, you will have no argument with this."

She glanced at Kreller and said, "We have no desire to interfere in the affairs of another... judicial system," she finished.

"For that we are grateful, and farewell."

The screen flickered and Janaker was once again staring out at the void.

She remembered the beer clutched in her hand, took a long drink, then said, "They consider the girl their *property*?"

"Who are we to question the cultural arrangements of an alien race?" Kreller said.

She stared at him. "What kind of lily-livered morality is that, you bastard? Even the Expansion has outlawed slavery... and who knows what the Ajantans want with the girl."

"My main concern," Kreller said, "is Harper and his ship. We cannot let the Ajantans capture him."

"Well, at least we agree on that."

He said, "We are armed, correct?"

"With enough firepower to take out the Ajantan ship and more to spare," she said. "I feel like doing it now..." But that, she knew, was the beer talking.

Kreller gestured. "We will monitor the situation and assess our options," he said. "We know that they want the girl, so they will not fire on the ship for fear of killing her."

"Will you please tell me, Kreller, why you're so obsessed with Harper's damned ship?"

He stared at her. "Not now. When we have the ship, I will demonstrate."

Before she could begin to ask him what he was talking about, he pushed himself from the couch and strode from the bridge.

Janaker stared into the void and chugged her beer. *Full speed ahead to Kallasta*, she thought.

SHE CAME TO her senses some time later and sat up, her head pounding. Kreller was in the co-pilot's seat, intent on the console before him. She ran a hand through her hair and rubbed her face. A dozen beer cartons littered the floor at her feet. No wonder she felt as if something had exploded inside her head.

She looked at the viewscreen. Void-space swirled, but something was not quite right out there. Presumably they were approaching Kallasta, in which case the void should have showed as an orderly series of whorls designating the gravity well of a planetary body. But the grey swirls before her were knotted in a tight vortex normally seen spinning around the event horizon of a black hole.

"Kreller?" she said.

"There is an anomaly," he reported.

"I can see that," she snapped. "Kallasta, right?"

"Right, but there is something down there that is distorting the normal flow of the space-time continuum."

He gave the command to phase from the void, and a minute later they were staring down on a placid green-blue world. Kreller tapped at the console. The scene jumped. She leaned forward and stared at an aerial mountain view of snow-capped peaks and verdant valleys. Nestled in the lap of a central vale was what she took at first to be a lake – but the water in the lake was not blue but an opaque, milky white.

"What the hell," she said, "is that?"

The thing was perfectly circular and shimmered with its own internal light. She made out indistinct shapes far within its lambent depths, shapes which her brain was unable to decode.

"Kreller?" she said.

"The cause of the anomaly," he murmured.

"Yes, but *what* is it?"

He turned to her. "I don't know," he admitted. "I have never seen anything quite like it."

"Where's Harper and the Ajantan ship?"

"Approaching Kallasta," he said.

"So... we follow them down, right?"

He looked at her. "Just so."

She nodded, and decided she needed another beer.

CHAPTER TWELVE

"DEN, WE'VE JUST phased out and entered into orbit around Kallasta."

Judi's soft voice woke him from a deep sleep. He dressed and stepped into the corridor. As he was passing Zeela's cabin, he paused and listened. She was singing what sounded like a heart-felt lament in her own language. Her voice rose, lilting, and Harper admitted that it was beautiful. He hurried to the flight-deck.

He lay back in his sling and stared through the viewscreen. A blue world rolled silently below.

"*Judi*, tell Zeela that we're almost home."

Two minutes later Zeela hurried onto the flight-deck and slipped into the co-pilot's sling. She leaned forward and stared. "Kallasta..." she said. He detected wistfulness, almost sadness, in her tone.

Journey's end, he thought.

"Where do you want me to land?"

She was silent for a while, then said, "I'm not sure. My parents came from a small town called Jerez, on the equator. I don't recall if there was a spaceport nearby."

From the little she'd told him about her homeworld, he'd gained the impression that it wasn't an industrial planet. "Do you know if it had *any* spaceports?"

Some of the backwater worlds were so under-populated and rarely visited that maintaining a spaceport was hardly viable. She shook her head. "I'm sorry. I can't recall. When we left Kallasta I was only five."

He told *Judi* to establish radio contact with the planetary authorities. "We'll get directions to Jerez," he told her, "and come down as close as we're able. Do you have relatives still on the planet?"

"I think so. I remember aunts and uncles... They'll still be living near Jerez, I think."

"And they'll take you in?"

"I think so. If not, or if we can't find them... Well, I can look after myself." She avoided his eyes.

Seconds later, still staring through the viewscreen at the pale blue, banded world, she asked, "Will you stay a while? It's a beautiful place."

"That would be nice. With luck we've given the bounty hunters the slip, and there's nothing to fear from the Ajantans now."

He considered Janaker and the Vetch, and the uncanny way they'd managed to trace him and Zeela across the Reach... He wondered what the chances were of their being able to trace him through the void to Kallasta.

Judi said, "Den, I have failed to establish radio contact with the planetary authorities. Kallasta does not appear to have a spaceport, or if it does it is not responding."

"Strange. If the planetary authorities aren't reachable via radio, what about—"

Judi interrupted, "There is no detectable radio traffic at all, Den."

He asked Zeela, "But Kallasta is technologically advanced?"

"Agricultural, mainly. But yes, it did have technology."

"So I wonder why no one's responding? Keep trying, *Judi.*"

"Affirmative."

Zeela looked at him. "What do you think the problem is, Den?"

"I don't know. Even low-tech worlds have radio facilities."

Judi said, "I've conducted a scan of the continent directly below. I was looking for areas of population density, cities, towns..."

"And?"

"I detected several small townships, now deserted. There is no sign of extant human population."

"On the *entire* continent?"

"Affirmative."

"And how many townships were there down there?"

"Not many. It was a sparsely populated continent. But even so I would expect there to be still some signs of life."

"Me too."

Zeela said plaintively, "What happened down there?"

"When your parents left... what, thirteen years ago?... was it part of some mass exodus?"

She pulled a face. "I really don't know. I'm sorry. I remember that we left aboard a smallish ship, that's all."

"*Judi*, do you have any cached information on Kallasta?"

A second later *Judi* replied, "Negative, other than routine scientific data collected by the original survey team centuries ago."

"Okay..." Harper considered the options. "Zeela, can you recall any geographical features close to Jerez that might single it out from other equatorial towns? We might as well try to come down there."

Her brow furrowed as she tried to recall the town from her childhood visits. "It was inland, beside a river, where I went with my mother and father on picnics."

"That might describe a hundred towns," he said. He instructed *Judi* to keep looking for any signs of habitation, then sat back. "We'll land wherever we find life," he said.

She nodded, a worried look on her face.

Minutes later *Judi* said, "I have located signs of life, Den."

Harper was about to ask for more information when *Judi* went on, "Alert! I detect a pursuing ship."

Harper cursed. How the hell had Janaker and the Vetch caught up so soon?

"Details," he snapped.

"An Ajantan vessel."

"But..." He felt a wave of despair wash through him. "But we destroyed the Ajantan ship..."

"This is a larger vessel. I surmise that it was following the first ship, but was keeping its distance. They request a radio link."

"Do it," he said. "But like last time, do not provide a visual link."

The viewscreen flickered, and a second later he was staring at a familiar scene: a darkened bridge, with three amphibian figures perched on high seats in the foreground.

Deja vu, he thought.

The Ajantan on the right opened its shark-like mouth and spoke in a sibilant hiss. Seconds later the translation rolled along the foot of the viewscreen. "An ultimatum, human: give yourselves up or face the consequences."

In an aside to *Judi*, he asked, "How far away are they?"

"One million kilometres and closing."

"So within missile range..." *Our last remaining missile*, he thought.

"Affirmative."

"Transmit this," he said. "We do not recognise the judicial authority of the Ajantans."

His reply caused a hurried consultation amongst the trio, and the Ajantan spoke again. "You are responsible for the death of thirty-six innocent Ajantans, and the destruction of a prime class starship."

Harper leaned forward and snapped, "Innocent? We fired in self-defence. It was your ship that launched the first missile. We were merely protecting ourselves."

Again the trio conferred. "If you do not consent to arrest, we will be forced to take offensive action."

Harper looked at Zeela. "We have one missile remaining..." To *Judi* he said, "Evasive action?"

"Problematic. Their ship is potentially faster than ours."

"Great. What about our shields, are they up to withstanding...?"

"Negative."

He took a breath. "What do you advise?"

"Our best option is to fire upon the Ajantan ship, and then attempt landfall. Their ship is large, and I suggest less manoeuvrable in planetary atmosphere than ourselves. If the missile fails to destroy their ship, I will land, drop you in the rainforest, and then make for another area in order to draw the Ajantan ship."

"Not a scenario I'd normally opt for, but if you're sure we can't outrun them–"

"We cannot."

"In that case do it. Fire!"

"Affirmative," *Judi* said. "Hold on tight. We are about to take evasive action."

Harper smiled at Zeela. "I think she means that any second now we're going to make one hell of a dive."

He glanced at the viewscreen. Their final missile was streaking away through the upper atmosphere. As he watched, the pursuing ship fired an intercept missile and they collided in a quick, actinic fireball.

A split-second later the flight-deck canted at a near perpendicular angle and Harper lurched forward in his sling. Beside him Zeela shouted out and gripped the sling's frame as they plummeted, her face contorted in alarm. The surface of the planet rushed to meet them. Something exploded behind them and the ship jumped sickeningly.

"*Judi?*"

"The Ajantans are firing."

"Damage?"

"Dorsal shield breached. Rear landing stanchion inoperable..."

Which meant that, even if they evaded the Ajantan ship, the subsequent landing would be more than a little bumpy.

Another explosion detonated, this time to starboard. The ship tipped, side-swiping, righted itself and screamed towards the planet's surface. The viewscreen showed ripped clouds and a rapidly approaching rainforest.

"Damage?" he yelled.

"Rear sensors compromised. Port shield breached."

A missile, now, on target, would blow them apart...

They rattled, Harper's head batted back and forth. He expected the *coup de grace* at any second. The maindrive screamed, pressed to the limit of its tolerance. The rainforest expanded at an alarming rate.

Just when he thought impact inevitable, *Judi* levelled out and screamed a matter of metres above the tree canopy.

"Hold tight," *Judi* warned. "We're descending... three, two, one. Now!"

Descending? Harper thought, then realised what *Judi* meant.

They dropped, and the viewscreen showed a chaos of shredded foliage and tree trunks as *Judi* ploughed through the forest at mach five.

"Prepare to disembark," the ship said.

"We can't possibly jump," Harper yelled.

"I will slow down and lose altitude. Go."

He nodded to Zeela and they unstrapped themselves from their slings and staggered across the crazily tilted flight-deck.

"I will come down as close to the inhabited township as possible," *Judi* said.

They slowed, and as they did so Harper became aware of the multiple, thumping impacts as *Judi* skittled a thousand trees. The effect, he thought as he grabbed Zeela's hand and sprinted along the corridor towards the exit, was like being in the sound-box of an instrument struck by a manic percussionist.

The ship yawed, throwing them against the wall. "Damage report?" he cried.

"Port auxiliary engine dysfunctional."

They came to the hatch and Harper yelled at Zeela, "Hold on!"

She grabbed a hand-hold as the hatch slid open and the ramp descended, instantly shearing off as it impacted with a passing tree. They clung on and peered out. They were below the forest canopy now, but still fifty metres above the ground.

"*Judi*," he called, "we need to lose height."

"Understood."

The ship dipped nose down, throwing them forward. Harper almost fell from the open hatch. Zeela screamed and Harper clung to the frame in desperation. Across from him, Zeela was doing the same. He peered down. The ground flashed by a matter of metres from the ship's underbelly.

"We need to slow down!"

He heard the engine growl. Tree trunks strobed past the opening with decreasing frequency.

He called out, "The Ajantan ship?"

"Inserting itself into a pursuing orbit," *Judi* replied.

"How far away?"

"Approximately four minutes, but closing."

He should be grateful for small mercies.

Judi slowed further. They were only three metres above the ground. He looked across at Zeela and nodded.

He thought of something. "*Judi*," he called. "The town? Which direction?"

"In relation to our current trajectory, ten o'clock, and seven kilometres distant."

"I suggest radio incommunicado from now on. I don't want to risk the Ajantans homing in on my signal."

"Understood."

"I'll be in touch... eventually," he said.

He looked down. The ship was moving at a little above walking pace now, firing its retro-jets to compensate for its forward momentum. He looked across at Zeela and said, "Jump!"

She didn't hesitate. She bent her legs, looked down, and launched herself. Harper followed, bracing himself for the impact. He hit the rainforest floor and rolled, thrashing through ferns and fetching up in the embrace of a waxy, crimson bloom the size of a bed sheet. He lay on his back, staring into the air. The ship, horribly lop-sided thanks to its misfiring port auxiliary, ploughed on through the tree-tops, gaining speed and vanishing as he watched.

He looked around. Zeela was picking herself up and batting her way through the undergrowth.

She knelt before him. "You okay?"

He struggled from the sticky leaves and stood up. "Fine."

They ducked reflexively as the roar of a ship's engine passed overhead. Pressing his hands to his ears, he looked up. The Ajantan ship, its piscine bulk like a fish out of water, sailed high overhead.

Seconds later it passed from sight, the sound of its engines diminishing gradually. Harper allowed himself to feel a moment of hope.

Zeela grinned at him. "Welcome to Kallasta, Den."

He laughed. "It's great to be here." He looked around. "Now, which way did *Judi* say the town was?"

Zeela pointed through the sun-dappled undergrowth. He picked up his pistol, slipped it into his belt, and set off after her.

The soil of the rainforest was sandy, and the undergrowth sparse. There was no riotous, ground-hugging vegetation here, no barbed tendrils to dog his footsteps. Great searchlights of sunlight slanted through rents in the canopy, filled with dust motes, spores and floating insects. The calls of unseen creatures created a constant background sound-track.

He caught up with Zeela and asked, "Predatory animals?"

"None that I can recall. At least, my mother and father let me play in the rainforest when we were on holiday."

He nodded, but nevertheless kept a wary eye out.

They walked side by side, ducking under drooping branches and lianas. Zeela was quiet.

"I've been thinking," he said when they'd been walking in silence for fifteen minutes, "about when we get to the town."

She glanced at him. "Yes?"

"It's likely to be the first place the Ajantans look for us. We'd be wise to hole up in the rainforest, hide until they give up and go home."

"Do you think that likely?"

He smiled. For her sake he was putting an optimistic gloss on the situation. "I'm pretty confident that we can dodge their search parties."

"And if they do go," she said, "you might even come to like it here so much you'd want to stay."

He didn't know whether to be annoyed at her flippant remark, so replied in a tone just as casual, "Well, the temperature here is certainly clement."

"I'm worried by what *Judi* reported, about all the uninhabited towns."

"I know. It doesn't make sense. I thought at first that we'd have heard about a mass exodus from a planet on the Reach... But then Kallasta is a backwater. It was never really colonised in the true sense of the word – on a mass, industrial scale with hundreds of thousands of immigrants settling the planet. You said your parents were part of a cult of pacifists."

She glared at him. "I never used the word 'cult'."

"Forgive me. A 'group' of pacifists, then. I take it that the other settlers were of like mind?"

She nodded. "I'm pretty sure, yes. They selected Kallasta because it was so far away from any other inhabited planet, and wasn't ripe for colonisation. It has no deposits of heavy metal, or anything else that the big mining companies would want to get their hands on." She shrugged. "It's just an agricultural world."

"That's probably why we didn't hear about the exodus – because, on the scale of these things, it wasn't that big an operation, a few thousand souls. But... I wonder why they left?"

She shook her head. "Growing up here, I recall a paradise world. Sunshine, abundant fresh food, no predatory animals or native aliens."

They fell silent and walked on.

To their left, through the gaps in the canopy, Harper made out a distant range of snow-capped mountains. He scanned the sky for any sign of the Ajantan ship, then listened out for the sound of its engines. All was peaceful, and the only sound was the throb and screech of the local fauna.

The land inclined gradually, and after thirty minutes of climbing they came to a ridge. Zeela stepped forward and peered through the vegetation. Harper came to her side and looked down. They were standing on a rising shoulder of land that looked out over a plain, with a shimmering blue lake in the distance. Beside the lake was a small settlement, a collection of huts and pre-fabs set out on the margin of the rainforest.

Zeela smiled at him. "The town," she said.

He stared into the skies above the lake. There was no sign of the Ajantan ship. With luck, *Judi* had led it around the other side of the planet.

He turned his attention to the town. "I can't see any movement."

"Well, *Judi* did say it was inhabited."

The streets between the buildings were quiet, deserted. There was no sign of traffic, nor of pedestrians. He would have imagined some indication of life in even so small a community; it was midday – the sun was directly overhead – but even so the heat was not oppressive.

She looked at him. "What should we do?"

"Let's give it a while. Sit tight and make sure the Ajantan ship doesn't show itself. After a few hours... maybe then we should make our way down there, with caution."

She looked beyond him and smiled with sudden delight. She plucked a long red fruit from a bush and passed it to him. She took a fruit for herself and showed him how to eat it.

"I remember these from when I was little! They're called dhubars." She squatted on the edge of the ridge, facing the distant town, and raised the fruit to her mouth. "Bite into it only so far. The long seed in the middle is really bitter, but the flesh is delicious."

She dug her teeth into the red flesh and juice dribbled over her chin.

He sat next to her and took a bite of the dhubar. It was sweet, with a vanilla foretaste and an aftertaste of berries. Its juice was cold and refreshing. "Well, we certainly won't starve while we're here."

She picked two more dhubars, and a round green fruit like an apple growing nearby. He was about to bite into the apple-like fruit when Zeela looked up and said, "What's that?"

She was staring out across the lake to the distant mountains, and Harper followed her gaze. He made out two tiny airborne shapes moving through a gap in the mountain range on the horizon, mere specks at this distance but growing ever larger as they watched. At first he thought it was *Judi*, followed by the Ajantan vessel.

They moved at speed, eating up the distance between the mountains and the lakeside settlement, and it soon became obvious that they were neither the Ajantan ship nor his own.

"What *are* they?" Zeela asked.

The craft came in over the lake and approached the settlement. They were huge and bloated, and resembled less space-going vessels than something biological – grey-green whales made air-worthy and powered by some mysterious means. Harper made out no features on the tegument, either organic, in the form of fins and flukes, or manufactured like hatches or viewscreens.

"They look... horrible," Zeela whispered to herself.

They came to the settlement and slowed, hung in the air like great ungainly dirigibles, then settled to the ground. Only when they landed side by side next to a long-house did their true dimensions become apparent; they were perhaps two hundred metres long, and as they sank to the ground and their great weight settled, they bulged sideways as if constructed from some adipose matter.

Constructed? Grown more like, Harper thought.

He turned to Zeela. "What are they? Do you recall anything...?"

She cut him short. "No. There was nothing like this here when I was a child."

Something moved at the front end of the flying things. As they watched, a single thick, tube-like pseudopod obtruded from each craft, for all the world like the antennae of a slug.

Zeela exclaimed as something was ejected from the tube, and then another and another.

Dozens of big, featureless humanoid creatures slipped feet-first from the ovipositor, landed with nimble agility and moved off a little way to allow for the ejection of the next.

Zeela gripped his arm. "What are they, Den?"

He shook his head. He found his voice at last. "I've no idea. Aliens, obviously. I've never seen anything like them."

The creatures were perhaps three metres tall, and reminded Harper of anatomical diagrams of the human subcutaneous layer, empurpled and varicose. They moved with a fluid, boneless ease, their domed heads featureless apart from big, staring black eyes.

He counted more than a dozen of the creatures before the ovipositors were retracted.

The creatures moved away from the vessels and loped across the clearing towards the long-house.

They stood side by side, very still, and did nothing but stare at the building.

Zeela's grip tightened on his arm.

A wide door, like a barn door, opened in the end of the long-house and slowly, one by one, small, dark-skinned humans emerged. They stood in a frightened knot in the entrance, moving reluctantly forward only when others pressed at their backs. Harper counted almost a hundred colonists – Zeela's fellow Kallastanians – as they left the long-house and stood in a cowering group before the giant, embryonic creatures.

Nothing happened for what seemed like an age. Harper could sense the tension even at this distance. At last one of the aliens stepped forward and advanced on the humans. It stood before them, staring, and the colonists seemed to shrink back under its gaze.

The creature stretched out an arm, pointed, and another two empurpled giants stepped forwards and approached the human selected by their mate.

The young woman fell to her knees, and her fellow colonists suddenly backed away from her as if she were infected. The alien pair stood over the woman, each taking an arm, and pulled her to her feet. She struggled, wriggling like a child in their grip, as she was carried away from the long-house, through the cordon of aliens, towards the closest whale-like vessel.

Harper watched, incredulous, as a vertical slit opened in the flesh of the vessel and the creatures forced the young woman, still struggling, into the fleshy crevice; seconds later the lips sealed behind her.

A further five humans were selected, carried protesting from their fellows, and forced into the bodies of the bloated vessels, two more into the first and three into the second.

When the last human was ingested, the empurpled humanoids moved away from the long-house and approached the vessels. The ovipositor emerged and, one by one, the creatures were sucked up in quick succession.

Minutes later the biological craft eased themselves into the air – slowly, as if burdened by their extra human cargo – turned lazily and moved off across the lake, gaining altitude as they did so and heading towards the distant mountain range.

Harper murmured, "Perhaps, Zeela, we've witnessed the reason why the towns of Kallasta are deserted?"

"What are they doing to my people?" she said in a tiny voice.

Harper watched the vessels recede into the distance, and within minutes they were mere dots on the horizon. Was this what Zeela's parents had fled, all those years ago, and why life on Ajanta in thrall to the reptilian aliens had seemed preferable to *this*?

Seconds later he heard what he thought was a footfall in the rainforest at their backs.

Startled, he turned and caught the fleeting glimpse of a figure before it reached out and pressed something wet and foul-smelling to his mouth and nose. Beside him, Zeela gave an abbreviated scream.

His vision blurred, and he felt as if he were sinking under the influence of some powerful anaesthetic.

His first, fleeting thought when he'd heard the sound behind him was that the Ajantans had somehow tracked them down. But their assailants were human – or at least the quick figure who accosted him had been.

So how the hell had Janaker and the Vetch managed to locate him, yet again?

HE GROANED AND opened his eyes. He expected to find himself in the hold of the bounty hunters' ship. But, when he blinked in the sunlight and his eyes accustomed themselves to the glare, he found that he was lying on his back on the sandy floor of a crude timber hut, a shaft of sunlight slanting through a gap in the timbers and blinding him. He rolled to one side to escape the beam and fetched up against Zeela.

He sat up with difficulty and found that his hands and feet were bound.

Zeela moaned and rolled over. She blinked up at him. "Den? What happened? The Ajantans?" she asked in panic.

"Not the Ajantans. Not the bounty hunters, either."

She struggled into a sitting position, her hands tied behind her back. "Who, then?"

"Your fellow Kallastanians," he said. "Some homecoming greeting, Zeela."

She looked at him. "Well, it's better than being captured by the Ajantans or the bounty hunters, isn't it? Or..." she went on, "those *things* we saw..."

He agreed. "But they could have gone about saying hello with a little less force. Whatever they used to sedate us has given me one hell of a sore head."

He heard the sounds of footsteps outside the hut, and then a voice.

Zeela tipped her head, listening. She whispered, "They're saying that we're awake."

Seconds later the flimsy wooden door was dragged open, admitting a dazzling block of sunlight. A small figure appeared on the threshold, silhouetted against the light.

The woman spoke again to someone behind her, and a man and a woman slipped into the hut, hauled Harper and Zeela to their feet and bundled them outside. Their legs were bound with a length of rope which allowed them to take short steps as they were led along a deserted street to the long-house.

They passed inside, to find themselves faced by a massed audience of Kallastanians seated cross-legged in rows: the people who, earlier, had seen their fellows abducted by the aliens.

Hands pressed down on Harper's shoulders, and he sat down on the floor. He glanced at Zeela beside him. She looked frightened as she gazed about her with wide eyes.

The woman who had first appeared in the doorway now seated herself before Harper and Zeela, flanked by the man and woman. The woman was old, her black face weathered and wrinkled. The couple were younger, the woman bearing a striking resemblance to Zeela: thin face, high cheek bones and full lips.

The old woman spoke, and Zeela replied in Anglais, "My friend does not understand our language. Please speak in Anglais."

The woman bowed her head, then looked from Zeela to Harper. "I said, please accept our apologies. We do not usually apprehend strangers with violence."

The young man leaned forward and snapped, "We should not apologise to... to these... whatever they are. We don't know that they're not vakan."

"Vakan?" Zeela said. "What are the vakan?"

The aliens? Harper wondered.

The young man laughed bitterly. "She feigns ignorance!"

The old woman glared at him, and turned to Harper and Zeela. In a soft voice she said, "Who are you, and where do you come from?"

"I am Zeela Antarivo. Around thirteen years ago, by standard reckoning, my mother and father left Kallasta with me. I have dreamed ever since of returning. My friend is Den Harper, a star trader, and it is thanks to him that I am here."

Behind the trio a murmur passed through the gathered villagers. Someone spoke up from the back of the longhouse.

Zeela whispered to Harper, "They say they recall my father, Val Antarivo, a farmer." To the old woman she said, "They are correct, my father farmed land in a small village. My mother's name was Zara, and she was a wood-worker."

The young man said, "Why should we believe her?" The was venom in his words, and mistrust in his dark eyes. "The vakan have all this information. These two are spies, sent to work out who they will take next!"

The old woman turned to the man and, with what sounded like infinite patience, said, "But why would they do that? The vakan are all powerful. They do not *need* to send spies amongst us. They come and take who they wish without resorting to emissaries."

It occurred to Harper that if only his hands were untied, and he could don his ferronnière, he might learn what was happening here.

"And anyway," the young woman spoke up for the first time, "the vakan came amongst us just a day ago and took our people."

Harper glanced at Zeela and raised his eyebrows. So they had been unconscious for a day.

The young man said, "Obviously the vakan are breaking with tradition and want more of us!"

Harper said, "Please believe us. We have nothing to do with the vakan." He paused, then said, "A day ago, did you see or hear two starships pass overhead, or close by?"

The old woman inclined her head. "Yes, one after the other. The leading ship was damaged. They passed into the west, around the world and out of sight. Their appearance caused great commotion." She smiled. "We thought that perhaps they had come to rescue us, at last."

"We came from the leading ship," Harper said. "We were being pursued by... by our enemies. We fear for our lives."

The old woman asked, "Your enemies? The vakan?"

The young man said, "We know the vakan do not have ships of metal! Their star-boats are like themselves, organic, biological, grown."

Harper said, "No, not the vakan. We know of no race called the vakan, and I can assure you that we were not sent by them."

"They lie!" said the young man. "We know they can change their appearance, can assume any form they wish. And so they have – and they are here before us."

"Silence!" the old woman commanded, and Harper was gratified to see the young man hang his head mutely.

Zeela said, "Yesterday, from the ridge, we looked down on the township and saw two vessels arrive. Then we saw strange creatures emerge and take six of your people." She shook her head. "We were as horrified at what happened as you were."

The old woman said, "The vakan are monsters, terrible beings from our worst nightmares. They come from beyond the mountains, where they have their lair."

"They take you..." Harper said. "But why?"

"Every Kallastan month, which is almost two standard months, the vakan send their monsters to take six of my people back to the mountains, and we never see them again."

"And how long has this been going on?"

"The vakan first appeared perhaps twenty years ago. They came from the mountains, from a great hole in a valley between Fishtail Peak. At first they did nothing, just watched us. Even so, many of my people were frightened. You saw how... how *alien* these creatures were. A year after their arrival, individual humans went missing. Many people fled off-world, blaming the vakan. As the years passed, so the vakan ranged far and wide across the equatorial regions of our planet, taking who they wished. We are a simple, peace-loving people. We do not believe in violence, and we do not fight back. My people, those who fled this world, vowed to inform the authorities of what was happening here... but we could only guess, as the years passed and help was not forthcoming, that the authorities of the Reach had other matters to consider rather than the plight of a few thousand pacifists on a backwater colony world."

"The Reach has no real centralised authority, political or judicial," Harper said. "I have no doubt that the pleas of those who fled Kallasta fell on deaf – or apathetic – ears."

The old woman smiled sadly. "I surmised as much."

"But the vakan... they have said nothing about why they take your people?"

The old woman looked from Zeela to Harper. "They do not communicate in any verbal way. 'Vakan' is not what they call themselves. The word vakan comes from old Kallastanian, a term meaning 'monster'. The vakan come in many forms. We have seen smaller, spindly creatures like gargoyles, and things like great toads. Some say that they can change shape at will, but this is only rumour." The old woman gestured. "No, we do not know why they take our people, but there are rumours."

"They are experimented upon," the young man said, "dissected, their brains removed, their organs laid out so that the vakan can see how we work!"

"This is speculation," the old woman said calmly. "No one knows. No one has dared approach the mountain lair of the vakan."

Harper looked at the young man, who was weeping now. "But I will make the trek there, if it is the last thing I do." He stared at Harper. "Yesterday the vakan took my brother."

Harper said, "I am sorry. Truly sorry. We saw what happened and we were horrified." He paused, then went on, "I came here to bring my friend Zeela home. I can see now that Kallasta is no place for peaceable human beings. I would like to help you... but first I must explain my situation."

"You can help us?" the old woman asked.

A susurrus of comment passed through the gathering behind her.

"There is a chance that, yes, I might be able to do something. But first I must explain how we came to be here."

For the next fifteen minutes he detailed his meeting with Zeela and their flight from Ajanta, their trek across the Reach pursued by the Ajantans. He thought it best not to mention the fact that he was telepathic, and was being pursued by bounty hunters. He described their descent to Kallasta, fired upon by the Ajantans, and the damaged state of his ship.

"The situation is that we are in hiding from the Ajantans. My ship led them away from here. It is my hope to lie low, hide ourselves away, so that perhaps the aliens will give up their search and leave Kallasta." He shrugged. "That is my hope, at any rate. If we were allowed to remain in the rainforest... in time I could contact my ship, and when the Ajantans leave, then I see no reason why we cannot take you and your people away from here."

"All of us? We number almost a hundred souls. Your ship is big enough?"

"And you said it was damaged," the young man said.

"It is big enough to accommodate everyone here," Harper said. "And as for its state of repair... It can fly, though I suspect its progress will be slow." He looked from the old woman to the young man. "But how many other colonists remain here on Kallasta?"

The old woman shook her head. "We don't know the exact numbers. There are scattered bands, like ours, all across the equatorial region. We have not had contact with them for years."

Zeela said, "If you would trust us, release us, then as my friend says we will hide ourselves in the rainforest and then, when the time is right, do our best to help you get away from here."

The three bent and conferred in hushed tones.

Their deliberations were interrupted, seconds later, by the roar of a starship's engines. Harper ducked instinctively; the ship sounded as if it were coming down directly on top of the long-house. It passed overhead and he heard the diminuendo of its engines: it was coming in to land.

Zeela looked at him. "*Judi*?"

He shook his head. "It's the Ajantan ship," he told her.

A Kallastanian jumped up and approached the door. He opened it a slit, peered out, then hurried back to the group. "A great ship has landed across the clearing," he reported to the old woman, "and a dozen... creatures are approaching."

"The Ajantans," Harper said, "coming for us. Cut us free!"

The old woman snapped an order, and the young man hesitated for a split-second, looking from Zeela to Harper. At last he came to a decision, jumped to his feet and pulled a knife from his belt. He slashed the rope that bound Zeela's ankles and wrists, then moved to Harper and cut the rope.

"Come with me," he ordered. "There is a rear exit. We'll use the cover of the long-house to move around the lake."

Harper turned to the old woman. "The Ajantans should not harm you. Tell them that you saw us, and sent us back into the forest to the south."

He followed Zeela and the young man to the rear of the long-house, watched all the way by the stunned gathering. They came to a small door and the young man pulled it open. They slipped through into the sunlight. "Quickly. This way."

He crossed an open area between the long-house and the next building beside the lake, and Harper trusted they would not be observed from the ship. He sprinted after the Kallastanian, Zeela at his side. He looked over his shoulder. All that could be seen of the Ajantan ship was the bulge of its upper superstructure above the ridge of the long-house.

They passed into the cover of the building and paused, panting. He looked ahead. A string of buildings along the shore of the lake would provide excellent cover. If they moved from house to house around the lake they would soon come to the fringe of the rainforest. From there they could slip into its cover.

The young man was watching him, and pulled something from within his shirt. Harper saw that it was the pistol which Bjorn had given him.

He looked into the young man's eyes, his stomach turning. Had it come to this: a flight of light years across the Reach, pursued by aliens and bounty hunters alike, only to be shot dead by one of Zeela's own people?

The man smiled, then passed Harper the pistol. "I was wrong," he said. "You are not vakan. You might be needing this."

Harper inclined his head in thanks and took the pistol.

"This way." The Kallastanian took off again, leading the way to the next building along the shore.

They crouched in the cover of the timber shack. Harper leaned around the corner and peered across the clearing. The Ajantan ship resembled a huge, squat creature sitting malignantly before the comparatively tiny long-house.

He made out three small Ajantans, armed with incendiary weapons, moving past the long-house and around the lake. They came to the first of the wooden buildings and peered inside. Finding them empty, they moved on.

Zeela said, "But how did they find us?"

"They haven't," he said. "They've merely homed in on the only inhabited township in the region – or that's my best guess."

He considered what to do next. They could dart towards the next building, using this one as cover, but they were still perhaps half a kilometre from the forest. Concealment in the buildings themselves was out of the question.

"Come on," he said, taking Zeela's hand and running for the next building, the Kallastanian following. They moved around the dilapidated, sun-scorched hut and sprinted for the next in line.

Zeela shrieked as she saw something up ahead

and dragged Harper back around the corner. All three flattened themselves against the timber wall.

"What?" Harper gasped, his heart thumping in fright.

"I... I saw three Ajantans, coming from the opposite direction."

"How far away?"

"About fifty metres, less. They were just beyond the next building."

The Ajantans had caught the township in a pincer movement, leaving nothing to chance.

They stood against the timber wall, pinned in the sunlight, facing the building they had just fled. He judged that the Ajantans coming from the direction of the clearing would be upon them in a minute or less. He looked along the wall, saw the recess of a door and pulled Zeela towards it. He passed into the shadow of the bare room, the young man bringing up the rear.

"And now?" the Kallastanian asked.

Harper moved to an empty window frame at the rear of the building, pressed himself to the wall and peered out. He saw the trio of aliens move towards the neighbouring building; one remained outside, vigilant, while its fellows passed into the hut.

The young Kallastanian said, "What are we going to do?"

Harper looked around the room. There was nowhere to hide. He could always take out one of the advancing aliens, but that would leave the others – and they would be alerted to hostile presence.

The young man moved past Harper, saying. "There is only one thing to do. I'm going out there. I'll claim that I saw you earlier in the forest. I'll say that I can show them where you went, and try to lead them away."

Harper gripped his arm. "You'd be endangering yourself."

The young man held his gaze. "I'm in danger anyway, in here with you."

Harper passed him the pistol. "Take this, in case..."

The Kallastanian hesitated, clearly torn by a lifetime's inculcation against violence, but finally took the weapon and slipped it out of sight beneath his shirt. He climbed into the window opening and lowered himself to the ground outside.

Cautiously he stepped forward, into the line of sight of the approaching Ajantans, and raised his arms.

Harper pulled away from the opening, scanned the wall and found a slit in the timber. Zeela squatted next to him, pressing her fists into her eyes. "I can't watch," she whispered.

He knelt and put his face to the wood, squinting through the gap at the encounter outside.

The Kallastanian and the three aliens – soon joined by the second trio – stood five metres away. The aliens circled the human warily, weapons levelled – the young man the hub of a moving wheel with the Ajantans' weapons as the spokes. He was speaking quietly to them, nodding towards the forest two hundred metres away.

Harper willed the aliens to believe him, to take off into the forest...

The Ajantans deliberated, passing comments back and forth in their own fluting language. At last they came to a decision and prodded the human forward with their weapons. He moved off towards the forest; four aliens trotted ahead, while two brought up the rear with the incendiary weapons trained on the young man's back.

Harper allowed himself a surge of hope: he would give them time to disappear into the forest, then move on around the lake and take refuge in the forest further away.

Then one of the aliens called out in its own language, and the group came to a halt. The alien spoke to its fellows, and two of them looked up at the hut the young man had emerged from.

Harper's stomach turned.

The Ajantan pair approached the hut, their weapons levelled.

Behind them, the Kallastanian said, "No, I told you! I saw them in the forest!"

The alien pair advanced regardless.

"Den...?" Zeela looked up at him, her expression pleading.

The Kallastanian shouted, "They're not in there! I told you – I saw them in the forest."

The Ajantans ignored him and approached the hut.

The young man acted, then. He reached into his shirt, pulled out the pistol, and fired at the advancing pair. One of the aliens fell, but the Ajantan closest to the Kallastanian raised its rifle and sent forth a roiling gout of flame. The human screamed as he was consumed in a blinding ball of fire.

Harper closed his eyes and Zeela sobbed, "What? Den, what happened?"

He told her.

When he looked again, the remaining aliens were conferring. Harper heard fluting calls, and seconds later they were joined by a further four Ajantans. The original trio indicated the hut from which the young man had emerged.

Slowly, weapons levelled, the Ajantans left the margin of the jungle and approached the building. Four moved around the hut while the first pair stood their ground and raised their trumpet-muzzled weapons.

He reached out and pulled Zeela to him. He heard a roar and the rear wall of the hut was consumed in flame. Through the window he saw one of the aliens step forward and call out, its words lost in the sound of the conflagration at their backs.

Then the alien raised its rifle and fired again. Flame belched through the empty window and filled the room with its actinic heat. Another blast accounted for the flimsy timber wall. Harper backed from the raging flames, despair like physical pain in his chest. The rafters above his head were alight now, threatening to bring the room down on top of them.

Zeela clutched him. Through the window he saw the Ajantan pair step forward, raise their weapons and call out in their own language.

The façade fell outwards and the flaming ceiling sagged towards Harper and Zeela. The Ajantans gestured with their weapons, excited now that they had their prey in sight, their fluting calls vying with the roar of the flames.

Harper held Zeela to him and said, "I'm sorry," as he eased her forward, over the blazing remnant of the wall, and out into the sunlight. They were surrounded by the ugly, squat creatures, who gestured feverishly with their weapons. Harper and Zeela raised their hands above their heads.

The creatures barely reached Harper's ribcage, and in a one-to-one fight he would tear them limb from limb... He quashed the revenge fantasy and tried to focus his thoughts on reality.

Beside him Zeela was taking deep breaths. Part of him wanted to meet her gaze, reassure her... but he was unable to do so. He felt guilty; he had done his best to rescue Zeela from the Ajantans, had brought her to what he hoped would be sanctuary...

The aliens were dancing around them now, occasionally leaping forward to prod at them with their weapons. Harper made out a repeated, sibilant phrase, and he realised they were chanting, "The girl! The girl!"

They were prodded forward, and they stumbled in the sand as they made their way around the lake towards the clearing and the waiting Ajantan starship.

A dozen Ajantans emerged from the ship and crossed the clearing towards their triumphant fellows. If only he had a weapon, then he would go down fighting; anything would be better than this graceless capitulation.

He saw movement ahead and to the left. The Kallastanians were peering from the open door of the long-house, watching silently as Harper and Zeela were led towards the waiting starship.

He saw the old woman. Their eyes locked and he smiled at her. She raised a hand, her expression one of sadness and impotence.

Zeela whispered to him, "I don't want to go, Den. Not back to Ajanta. Not to... to what I know they will do to me."

"Zeela..."

"I'd rather die *here*, on the soil of my home. You go if you want to, but... Den, I'm sorry. I'm going to make a run for it..."

"No. Zeela..."

"I'm going. I... I can't let them take me back to Ajanta, Den. I can't!"

He stared at her, saw the tears tracking down her cheeks. She smiled, sadly, then looked around and tensed herself for flight towards the forest.

"Zeela..." he pleaded. He reached out and gripped her arm.

He saw a glint of something swift and golden above the rainforest, a second before he heard the sound.

Zeela moved, tugging herself from his grip.

She tensed, preparing herself to run, when a split second later the Ajantan starship exploded in a fountain of flame as if all hell itself had erupted, radiating cascading debris of hot metal and flame. Harper reached out, grasped Zeela and pulled her to the ground as the watching Kallastanians cried out in alarm and took refuge in the long-house.

All around, the Ajantans were falling, sliced by lancing laser beams that screamed down from the sky.

Harper looked up and saw a sleek golden ship swooping over the clearing, laser fire raining down from a nacelle slung beneath its nose-cone. As he watched, laser beams targeted the aliens one by one in quick, fraction-of-a-second bursts. The Ajantans barely had time to cry out as they were sliced as they ran. It was wholesale butchery, with severed limbs and body parts sliding to the ground all around. Harper had never witnessed such slaughter, and in less than a minute, he calculated, there was not one green alien left standing or in one piece.

The Ajantan ship burned, secondary explosions detonating deep within its shattered shell. He made out dancing, flame-engulfed figures in the ship's interior. He climbed slowly to his feet and pulled Zeela up after him.

The golden ship landed with a quick genuflection of its ramrod stanchions, and seconds later a ramp extended from its belly and – as Harper had expected – two figures marched down the ramp. They strode across the battlefield towards where he and Zeela stood amidst the rendered flesh and spilled blood of their erstwhile captors.

Sharl Janaker and the Vetch stopped before them, and the woman smiled. She carried a small pistol in her right hand, not yet raised.

"So, Harper, we meet at last."

He tried to stare her down. "If you think," he said, "that I am grateful for your intervention..."

"Spare me your futile words, Harper." Now she did raise her pistol. "Contact your ship and order it to get here, quick."

"My ship?"

"You heard the woman," the Vetch growled. "Contact your ship, now, and order it to open its hatch when it gets here!"

He was about to ask why they wanted the ship – but wasn't that obvious? They were rapacious mercenaries, and would gain as much in salvage fees for the ship as they would in hauling his corpse back to the Expansion authorities.

He looked from the Vetch to the woman. "Go to hell."

Janaker smiled. "If you contact your ship, Harper, then I might let you and the girl live. If not..."

"I say we kill them now!" the Vetch said, raising its weapon and aiming at Zeela.

"Harper," Janaker said, "let's do this the easy way, hm? Call your ship."

"If you refuse," the Vetch said, "then the girl will die."

Alone, he might have defied them. But Zeela, at his side, said pleadingly, "Den..."

He activated his wrist-com, got through to *Judi*, and ordered her to lock onto his current co-ordinates and make her way here immediately.

Janaker smiled. "There, that wasn't so difficult, was it, Harper?"

Then she raised her pistol and shot him.

CHAPTER THIRTEEN

"You've killed him!" the girl screamed.

Janaker holstered her pistol and watched the girl drop to her knees and stroke Harper's face. There was something touching about the sight, and at the same time unsettling. She told herself that it had nothing to do with envy.

She strode to the girl, knelt and gripped her upper arm. The kid was tiny, a child; even kneeling, Janaker was taller than her.

"Listen to me." She shook the girl until she ceased sobbing. "He isn't dead. I've merely stunned him."

"He isn't...?" The girl shook her head. "But he told me you wanted him dead, or that you'd take him back to the Expansion and they'd execute him there. That's what you'll do!" She struggled, but was unable to free herself. "You'll take him back to the Expansion and *they'll* kill him!"

Janaker stood, bringing the girl with her, and walked her away from where Harper lay. "I promise you that they will not kill him," she said. "It's a long story, but they want to hire Harper for his telepathic ability. That's why I was sent out here after him. Not to kill him, but to take him back."

Kreller approached and snapped, "Tell the girl to join the others in the long-house."

She turned to him. "Go to hell, Kreller. I'll take her there when I'm through explaining."

The Vetch muttered something and turned away, yelling at a knot of straggling Kallastanians to go back to the long-house. The natives looked stunned as they picked their way through the carnage of slain aliens and the scattered starship debris.

Janaker reached out and stroked a strand of hair from the girl's tear-streaked cheek. "If we wanted Harper dead," she said softly, "we would have let the Ajantans kill him and take you. I don't know what Harper told you about the type of people following him, but I assure you that I am not... inhumane."

She stared around her at the fragmented alien body parts, and shook her head sadly. "As for this... I regret the deaths of so many, but..."

The girl interrupted her. "I rejoice at their deaths! The Ajantans are monsters."

"They contacted us before we reached Kallasta, and said that they owned you."

The girl smiled bitterly. "They thought they did – just as they think they own every other human on Ajanta. But Harper saved me from certain death, and the frogs didn't like that." She turned and spat at the halved corpse of the closest alien. "I have nothing but hatred for their kind!"

Janaker eased the girl towards the long-house. "Do as Kreller says, for now. Join your people in the long-house."

"I don't want to leave Den!" the girl wailed. "He promised that he'd take us with him, all my people."

She nodded. "Very well. My ship would not accommodate so many, but when his ship returns..."

"You'll take us away from here, away from the vakan?"

"The vakan?"

"Terrible creatures that come from the mountains for my people..."

She was talking about the Weird... Janaker considered the anomaly in the planet's gravity well, the opaque 'lake' in the mountain valley. On the way down, Kreller had told her that he thought it a portal of the Weird.

She recalled the images Commander Gorley had shown her, and was gripped by a cold dread.

She said, "I promise that we'll take you away from here."

They arrived at the long-house and Janaker eased the girl through the door. "What are you going to do with Den?" she asked.

"I'll take him to my ship, make sure he's okay. Don't worry. You're safe now."

The girl watched her with big eyes. Janaker smiled reassuringly, then turned and walked back to where Harper lay amid the chaotic battlefield scene.

Kreller joined her, staring down at the telepath. "So this is the human who has dragged us so far across the Reach."

Janaker grunted. "Doesn't look like a conscienceless killer, does he?"

"Appearances," Kreller said, "can be deceptive." He reached out a boot and poked the telepath's body. "Remove his shield," he said. "Human telepaths wear things called a ferronnière which…"

"Spare me, Kreller. I read the dossier Gorley gave us." She knelt and touched Harper's head, feeling for the device. He wasn't wearing it, so she searched his cotton jacket and found the silver band in an inner pocket.

Kreller pointed. "Stand over there, out of range."

She stood and backed off, watching the Vetch as he approached the supine telepath and knelt. He closed his eyes, concentrated.

What irony, she thought, if after all the effort they had expended in chasing Harper light years across the Reach he turned out to be infected and they had to kill him…

A minute later Kreller grunted and stood up.

"Well?"

"He's clean."

Janaker found herself releasing a relieved breath. She gestured to the long-house. "You should scan the girl, and the other Kallastanians."

Kreller grunted. "In my own time," he said. He turned away and stared into the sky above the rainforest.

Janaker lifted the telepath's limp body, slung him over her shoulder, and crossed the clearing to her ship. She strapped Harper into the co-pilot's seat, ensuring he was secure, then checked his pulse. She reckoned he'd be unconscious for at least another hour.

She gazed out through the viewscreen. Aside from the dead aliens and the burnt-out remains of their starship, the scene appeared idyllic, paradisiacal. She looked across the lake to the hazy, distant mountains, and wondered what horrors lurked there.

Kreller was standing in the middle of the clearing, staring out over the surrounding tree-tops. He seemed intent on something, and seconds later she knew what. She heard the sound of a starship's engine, and a minute later Harper's ship came into view, limping lopsidedly over the rainforest.

The ship landed, easing itself down on its ramrod haunches. When the dust of its descent had settled, a hatch in its flank slid open.

She saw Kreller raise his wrist-com, and a second later hers buzzed.

"Janaker," Kreller said, "get yourself over here."

SHE LEFT HER ship, the blazing sunlight prickling her skin, and crossed to where the Vetch stood before Harper's starship. Its ramp had been sheared off, leaving a margin of jagged metal.

"You said you'd explain..." she began.

"Be quiet," he snapped, "and you'll get your explanation."

He strode off, stepped over the torn remains of the ramp, and disappeared inside.

You bastard, she thought, and followed him.

Harper's ship was much older than hers, and over the years he'd outfitted it to his own peculiar tastes. It was unusual to find rugs and tapestries adorning the functional interior of a starship, but Harper had made his ship like a home – which, she supposed on reflection, it was. Or had been.

They strode along a lateral corridor hung with artwork depicting a dozen worlds, then dropped to a lower deck. The Vetch seemed to know exactly where he was heading.

A minute later they stood outside a sliding door marked: Hold 2.

Kreller raised a big hand and touched the panel, almost lovingly.

"This hold hasn't been opened for well over a decade," he said. "No one has been able to gain access. Even by force."

She looked at the Vetch. "How do you know this?"

"Because what is in there once belonged to my people."

"What *is* in there, Kreller?"

He ignored her. He reached out, pressed his palm against a precise spot high in the centre of the hold door, and laughed when the panel moved, slid slowly aside.

"I thought you said no one..." she began.

"The opening mechanism is keyed to the genetic code of the Vetch," he said, "for security. Only we can gain access, operate what is within. It closed itself down, sealed itself in here when it was stolen."

"By Harper?"

"No, not Harper. By another, more foolish human."

The door slid fully open and a golden glow poured out, filling the corridor and dazzling Janaker. She raised a hand to shield her eyes and laughed uneasily. "What the hell...?"

Kreller stepped into the effulgent golden chamber, and she followed him hesitantly.

The hold was empty but for a central, hexagonal pedestal which held a dozen metre-long crystals; they throbbed with light, giving off a hum at the very threshold of audibility. From the pedestal flowed a pulsing light-show, which slid down and spread across the floor, walls and ceiling of the hold – a nexus of golden light that pulsed like a photonic heart.

"What is it?" she asked in a whisper.

"A Vetchian weapons system," Kreller said, "the most sophisticated ever devised. Nothing as powerful has ever existed in the universe. This," he went on, striding towards the crystals like a devotee towards some holy icon, "will be the means by which we overcome the Weird."

CHAPTER FOURTEEN

HARPER OPENED HIS eyes and was surprised to find that he was still alive. He sat up – or rather tried to. He was strapped into a couch on the flight-deck of an unfamiliar ship. The bounty hunters' ship, of course. Through the triangular viewscreen he could see the clearing, with the blazing Ajantan ship in the foreground surrounded by dozens of dead aliens. Beyond was the long-house and, beside it, his ship. The hatch was open.

He struggled, but the clamps on his wrists and ankles held him fast.

"You're wasting your time trying to get free, Harper."

Janaker moved into sight and leaned against the console below the viewscreen. She was holding a carton of beer and taking the occasional sip. She was bigger than he recalled her from Tarrasay, both taller and broader, and more muscular. She wore a jerkin with the sleeves cut away to reveal impressive biceps.

He looked around. "Where's Zeela?"

"With her people..." She indicated the long-house over her shoulder. "And don't worry. We didn't harm her."

She stood over him, her gaze unreadable. "I must admit, Harper, you're not what I was expecting."

He glared at her. "And what the hell were you expecting, Janaker? A violent thug, or a raving madman driven psychotic by his mind-reading ability?"

"Commander Gorley painted a picture of a ruthless killer who would stop at nothing to maintain his freedom."

He had to laugh at that. "'A ruthless killer'? Coming from an Expansion Commander? Now I've heard it all."

To his surprise, she smiled at that. "And the man I find, after chasing him halfway across the Reach, turns out to be – if the evidence of his ship's library is to be believed – cultured and educated, if self-educated..."

"I'm delighted you've had your prejudices overturned," he said. He strained against the straps that held him fast. "What do you want with me? Why didn't you just kill me and take my corpse back to the bastards...?" Because, of course, the Expansion authorities wanted the pleasure of doing that themselves, executing him as a warning to other potential errant telepaths.

"Because they want you alive, Harper."

"I bet they do."

She smiled and drank her beer. "It's not like that. They don't want to kill you – even though that's what they did to absconding telepaths in the past."

"So what's changed? Don't tell me the authorities have gone soft. What can I expect when you take me back, solitary confinement for the rest of my life?"

"Not at all. You can expect a place aboard a starship, with a highly trained crew, and you'll be paid a very competitive salary."

She was speaking in riddles. "What do you mean? I'll be back on the treadmill, reading minds for the authorities again?"

"In a manner of speaking, yes."

"Why the hell do you think I fled to the Reach? I detested what I did back then, and if you think I'd willingly go back to it..."

She was watching him closely, her lips pursed. "You might go willingly, when I explain what you'll be doing."

"I very much doubt that. Do you know what it's like, reading criminal minds, day after day? And it makes it worse that the people I worked for were cruel, ruthless, authoritarian bastards."

"The devil you know..." she said with a shrug.

He shook his head. "What's that supposed to mean?"

She pushed herself away from the console, sat down on a couch beside his and swivelled to face him. "Look, Harper, for your information I'm not a big fan of the Expansion authorities, either. I didn't choose to race across the Reach after you – a slimy bastard called Commander Gorley gave me little choice in the matter. That's beside the point. I just want you to know where I stand. The fact is, sometimes enemies must come together to fight a greater enemy."

He grunted an unamused laugh. "And there's a greater enemy than the Expansion fascists?"

She held his gaze, then nodded. "Oh, yes, Harper. There's a much greater enemy."

The way she said this, with a gravitas he could tell was genuine, stopped the protest that he'd been about to voice. He said, "Would you mind telling me what's going on?"

She leaned back in her couch, still staring at him, and said, "The Expansion, and the Reach – in fact all human space – is being invaded."

He stared at her. "The Vetch? They've resumed hostilities?" But why, then, had she teamed up with a Vetch sidekick?

Janaker was shaking her head, smiling. "Good God, no, Harper. The Vetch are pussycats compared to this enemy. In fact, Vetch space is under threat too."

"Then who?"

"They are known as the Weird – or, in the language of the people on Kallasta, the vakan."

He sat forward, straining against the clamps. "We saw them – and later the colonists told us about the vakan."

"The Weird first manifested themselves in the region of space beyond Vetch territory known as the Devil's Nebula. They enslaved a human colony there. I was told that what they did to these people was... horrendous. They also took individuals to their own realm, to... to study them."

Harper said, "Which is what they are doing here. But... their own *realm*?"

"The Weird are not from normal space. They inhabit a strata of reality beyond void-space. Gorley described it as another dimension."

"They *first* manifested themselves in a region beyond Vetch space, and now they are here..."

"And, apparently, at one or two other locations in human inhabited space. They can... they have the ability to open portals between their dimension and our space, and send their... *creatures*... through them."

"We saw a vakan ship land in the clearing yesterday," he told her, "though it wasn't like any ship I've ever seen. Things emerged from it, formless, humanoid creatures."

"I've read Gorley's account of his experiences in the Devil's Nebula. He said they're called the Sleer. But the Weird come in many weird – if you'll excuse the pun – and grotesque forms."

He shrugged, the gesture restricted by the clamps. "I can't see why the Expansion is that worried, Janaker. The Weird might be able to overcome a relatively rural, unsophisticated people like the Kallastanians, but against the military might of the Expansion... A couple of well-armed marine units would blow them out of existence in seconds. Surely they..."

Something in her stare stopped him in his tracks. She shook her head. "You underestimate the type of enemy the Weird is, Harper. They don't posses technology as we know it. Individual Weird are units in a much vaster... hive-mind, if you like. They can take considerable losses and still their portals churn out more and more grotesque monsters, thousand after thousand after thousand. And so far their portals have proved indestructible. Two or three have opened in Expansion space over the course of the past six months, and Gorley sent in a crack strike force. Nothing, repeat nothing, could destroy the interface between Weird space and our reality. And with the Weird having the ability to open portals at will across the Expansion..."

Harper considered her words, nodding. At last he said, "Which is all very well, but I fail to see how my ability fits into the picture."

Janaker pointed at him. "What I've described so far, Harper – the portals, the monsters they send through – that's not the greatest threat."

"It's not?"

"If it were, then the battle would be bad enough, and hard enough to win." She paused, staring at him with her intense, dark eyes. "But, you see, the Weird are cleverer than that. They have also infiltrated themselves into the Expansion, and into Vetch space, into both command structures."

He recalled what the young man had said about the vakan being able to change their forms, assume other guises, and began describing this to Janaker.

She stopped him, then said, "Not like that, Harper. They have a far more sinister, insidious way of going about the infiltration than that."

"Go on."

"Around a century ago they entered this realm when they opened the portal in the Devil's Nebula. Apparently they took over a space-going alien race there and built a fleet of starships – the precise number is not known – and sent them into Vetch and human space. These ships came to rest on colony worlds, but the strange thing about them was that they seemed to be empty, devoid of life."

Her words stirred the memory of the alien starship on Teplican...

Janaker went on, "They *weren't* devoid of life, of course. They were devoid of *visible* life. But in fact they were crewed for the duration of the flight by creatures which, on landing, broke into constituent parts... and these parasites lay dormant until suitable humans came along."

"How long," he asked, his throat dry, "could they lie dormant?"

"A long time. We think that humans are still being infected. The Weird parasites can dwell in the human cortex for years, decades, and then, when they judge that the time is right, assume control and take over the individual. As yet we don't know whether or not infected humans can pass on these Weird parasites. The authorities have their best scientists working on the problem."

She stopped when she saw his expression, and read it correctly. She nodded. "The ship on Teplican," she said, "was a Weird ship."

"So... the scientists there," he began... Di Mannetti, Ti Xian and the others.

Zeela and himself?

He said, "Would I know if I... if a parasite had...?"

She shook her head. "Of course not."

He stared at her. "I was on Teplican, if only briefly," he said. "I myself might be infected..."

She smiled at him. "We know you are not infected," she said.

"You do?"

"My ugly partner in crime, Helsh Kreller, the Vetch, is telepathic. While you were unconscious, he ensured that you were uninfected."

He leaned forward as far as he was able. "And Zeela?"

She said, "We returned her to her people. Kreller had more... important matters to attend to, at the time. He will scan the gathered Kallastanians later, before we leave this world."

"And if he does find infected individuals?"

"Our orders are unequivocal, Harper. We must eliminate the infected. You have to realise the necessity of this."

A thought occurred to him. "If your tame Vetch is telepathic, then how was it that he failed to read Zeela in the café on Tarrasay? He would have read that she was with me, through her read my identity."

"Like yourself, Kreller doesn't have his enhancer enabled all the time – and no doubt for the same reason. He says the mind-noise is too much. But you can be assured once we'd let you slip through our fingers on Tarrasay, he was scanning from then on."

"Which is how you came to find us with such ease on Vassatta..." Harper said.

"Precisely. Your friends' decoys didn't fool Kreller for a second."

He stared at her, going over everything she had told him, then said, "Of course, I have only your word about all this. How do I know that your story of the Weird, the parasites, is not some fabrication?"

She laughed derisively. "To what end, Harper?"

"Exactly. I've been trying to work that out." And, for the life of him, he could not see what the bounty hunter might gain from making up such a fabulous story.

"Everything I've told you is the truth. And, if anything, I've understated the full horror of the Weird. I have seen photographs of the creatures, and the human individuals they've... worked on." She paused, then went on, "It is imperative, Harper, that I return you to the Expansion, so that you can begin training and start work rooting out those officials, and others, infected with the Weird parasites."

"There is one way I would be able to tell if you're speaking the truth."

She flung back her head in a full-throated laugh. "And if you think I'll let you into my head, Harper, you're wrong." She stopped, suddenly, and stared at him.

"Having second thoughts? It wouldn't take long. A matter of seconds, to verify your story – in that time I wouldn't go deep, read all your secrets, your guilt and remorse..."

"Quit it, Harper. I wouldn't allow you inside my head for a billion units. But..." she went on, "if Kreller was unshielded, could you...?"

He watched her, sensing that there was something else going on here. He guessed, then, that her relationship with the Vetch had underlying currents.

She said, "How much can telepaths read of an alien mind? Helsh claims that mental comprehension is limited, though some emotions, thoughts can be deciphered."

Harper shrugged. "That's true, to a certain extent. It differs from individual to individual, and from race to race." He paused, then took the plunge. "What do you want me to find out?"

She stood quickly, strode to the viewscreen and stared out.

"Look," she said, pointing at *Judi*.

"What does he want with it?" he asked.

She turned to him, resuming her perch on the console. "What do you know about your ship, Harper?"

He shrugged, uneasy when it came to discussing *Judi* with a stranger. "Enough," he said.

"Like, who it belonged to before you... appropriated it?"

"A commander of the Expansion navy. It was his private vessel."

"And before that?"

"Pass."

She smiled at him. "It belonged to a thief, a human from the world of Capadoccia. Not your regular thief, either. He had ambitions. His territory was the hinterland – the no man's land – between Expansion space and Vetch territory. He prospected, and stole from, the planets in that disputed region. To cut a long story short, he raided a Vetch experimental weapons technology lab on a sequestered asteroid and came away with... for want of a better expression, a super-weapon. Worse, he destroyed the facility in his wake and killed over fifty top Vetch scientists. In so doing he managed to set back the weapons program some fifty years. What the Vetch scientists were working on was ultra-secret, and every scientist working on the project perished... All understanding of the weapon was lost in the raid and the subsequent slaughter.

"We don't know how he did it, and the Vetch, quite understandably, aren't about to enlighten us. Anyway, he stored the weapons system aboard his ship and high-tailed it out of Vetch territory, thinking he'd snatched the goose that laid the golden eggs."

"Only?"

She nodded. "Only the weapon was self-aware, the latest Vetch AI technology. It had certain inbuilt safety mechanisms. So it closed itself down and sealed itself in behind an impermeable barrier."

He nodded slowly. "Hold two. No wonder I've never been able to get in there."

"The thief, or prospector, found himself in a bar on Maddison one evening, and started bragging...

but he happened to brag to the wrong person. It's never wise to tell a commander in the Expansion marine corps that you posses a super-weapon... albeit one that you can't access. The commander arranged for the thief to be... dealt with, let's say, and appropriated the ship."

My ship, Harper thought. "So why didn't the Expansion authorities take it apart?"

"Because the commander had morals as loose as the person he stole the ship from. He kept the knowledge of the weapon to himself, and, on the quiet, employed engineers to attempt to get to the bottom of the enigma. This was on the planet of Hermiston, which is where you come in."

Harper smiled, reliving the memories. "That's where I came across the ship just after..." He stopped, then went on, "At a time of my life when I couldn't go on doing what I'd been doing. Commander Rodriguez trusted me, which was a mistake, and it wasn't that difficult to take command of his ship while he was off-planet and escape to the Reach."

"But, all the while, the Vetch wanted their property back. They sent agents out, under the guise of ambassadors and peace envoys, and attempted to track down the ship. Kreller was one of these 'envoys'. He traced Commander Rodriguez and... shall we say, *persuaded* him to tell his side of the story. When Kreller discovered that you'd taken the ship and fled to the Reach, he pulled strings and had himself seconded to my brief – to find you and your ship."

Harper considered Janaker and her story. "So... what is it you want me to find out from him?"

Janaker ran a big hand through a hank of jet black hair. "There's an understanding between the Expansion authorities and the Vetch," she said. "We're to work together against the threat of the Weird, as it's a threat to both our races. To this end the agreement was that the super-weapon, when it was discovered, would be brought from the Reach, investigated and developed – and mass produced – by both Vetch and human scientists."

"Ah..." Harper said. "But you don't trust Kreller as far as you could throw him?"

"That's one way of saying it, yes. I fear that the Vetch, once they get their paws on the weapon, will decide to renege on the deal and take back what they see as rightfully theirs – which would have unfortunate consequences, of course, for Expansion security. Quite apart from undermining our efforts to defeat the Weird."

"So you want me to get inside Kreller's head, see just what it is the Vetch are planning?"

"That's about the size of it."

"You do realise that he'll be shielded, especially now that I'm around?"

"Of course. However..." She turned to the ship and pointed. "Look..."

Harper strained against the clamps. "It might help if you'd release me from this damned thing."

She regarded him. "Very well, Harper. But remember, I'm armed."

"I'd be a fool to try anything now, wouldn't I?"

She paused in the process of deactivating the clamps. "So you agree to come back to Expansion space, of your own free will, and work with the authorities against the Weird?"

He'd gone over the pros and cons, while she'd been speaking, and realised that there was only one course of action a sane individual might take, given the circumstance. A part of him bridled at the very idea, even so. He nodded. "I agree."

She released him and he stood slowly, rubbing his chafed wrists. He moved to the viewscreen and stared out.

Janaker indicated *Judi* and said. "See that, close to the dorsal fin?"

A golden glow emanated from the ship's carapace, an effulgent nexus which, as he watched, expanded and gradually covered all of the ship's stern.

"What is it?"

"Kreller calls it a command nexus. For want of a better word, it's a living, externalised *brain* which, for the duration of flight, the pilot will be paired, or bonded, with."

"I see. So for the period of the flight back to the Expansion, Kreller will be... incapacitated?"

She smiled. "When he's in the command sling and bonded, I'll be able to remove his shield and you can do your stuff. Only, there's something you should know – Kreller's plan isn't to go directly back to Expansion territory."

"Then where?"

She pivoted on her heel and pointed out across the lake, to the distant mountain range. "Now that Kreller has the weapon," she said, "he wants to use it."

Harper understood. "Against the lair of the vakan, the Weird?"

She inclined her head. "Against the Weird portal in the mountains, yes."

Harper's heart pounded. "And... I take it that the Weird won't idly sit by and allow this attack?"

"That, Harper, remains to be seen. I don't know what the defensive capabilities of the Weird here might be, but I think we're soon going to find out."

The golden nexus had steadily crept around *Judi*'s body now, engulfing her in its dazzling glow. From its former dull grey, excoriated condition, her carapace appeared pristine, lambent.

He said, "But my ship was damaged."

Janaker smiled. "It was, until Kreller started work on it, with the aid of the nexus."

Her wrist-com buzzed. She took the call, spoke briefly into her com, and nodded. She cut the connection and looked at Harper.

"That was Kreller. He's ready to take off."

Harper touched his jacket pocket, feeling for his ferronnière. It wasn't there. Janaker smiled, reached into her jacket and pulled out the loop.

They left the ship and crossed the clearing towards his transformed ship. He thought of Zeela, imprisoned within the long-house with her fellow Kallastanians. He saw a dozen faces at the slit windows and the door, staring out.

They came to *Judi* and climbed into the hatch over the ragged metal. He was glad to see that the interior was as it always had been; the golden metamorphosis was only skin deep. He looked around at the familiar fixtures and fittings, as they made their way to the flight-deck, with the bitter knowledge that soon the ship would no longer be his.

Soon, he would be working for the Expansion, hard though that was to stomach.

Always assuming, of course, that he survived the imminent encounter with the Weird.

Experimentally, he raised his wrist-com to his lips and said, "*Judi*? Are you reading?"

Silence greeted the question. He wondered if *Judi*, as he had known her, was no more.

They came to the flight-deck to find the giant Kreller striding its length, as if impatient to be airborne. He looked from Harper to Janaker. "You brought him. Good. Be seated, human. I want you to witness the might and power of Vetchian technology."

Harper smiled as he took a padded seat at the back of the flight-deck. "It will be a privilege, Kreller."

The Vetch spoke in his own, guttural tongue – and *Judi* responded. The maindrive fired and, slowly, they rose into the air, turned forty-five degrees and moved out over the lake.

Only as they ascended towards the distant mountain range did the Vetch slip his bulk into the pilot's sling.

It was a sling, Harper saw, much transformed. He made out extra leads and jacks, and an extension of the golden nexus that covered the outer layer of the ship had intruded and worked its way across the fabric of the sling.

Kreller had evidently not yet melded with the operating system. He turned to where Harper was seated and said, "Janaker has told you about the... transformation of your ship? The system is simple in concept, though complex in application. Put simply, the nexus with which the ship is coated is a conductor – though that does not adequately describe the function of the matrix. It connects the ship to the basal strata of the void on a quantum level, and thus facilitates the transmission of... energy. Think of it, simply, as a lightning conductor. Though the power we will conduct is of an order a million times more powerful than any explosion generated by human – or Vetchian – weapons."

Harper nodded. "I'm impressed."

The Vetch regarded him with huge, bloody eyes. "You will be when the Weird's portal is annihilated, human."

Janaker asked, "When are we due to reach the portal?"

The Vetch consulted his instrument panel. "Seven minutes and counting."

Harper glanced across at the woman, who kept her gaze on the scene through the screen.

They had passed over the lake and were approaching the folded foothills. Ahead, the mountain range rose, grey and forbidding, its peaks covered with snow and streamers of cloud.

He recalled what Janaker had said about the resistance of the other Weird portals to regular marine bombardment. If they succeeded here, then there was hope that the spread of the alien menace might be curtailed.

All that would remain, then, was the small matter of tracking down and eradicating all those hapless individuals who were playing host to Weird mind-parasites.

Harper leaned close to Janaker and murmured, "I thought you said he'd be melding with the system?"

She nodded tightly. "He will, if he's to direct the weapons."

He sat back, sweating.

And if he did read in the Vetch's mind that his race had no intentions of sharing their weapons with humanity? Then, presumably, somewhere on the flight back the alien would attempt to deviate off course, towards Vetch territory... and what plans might he have for the fate of the accompanying humans?

They were sailing close to a vast slab of rock that was the mountain's northern face. It passed in monumental silence, the peak seeming to move slowly as if in a dream. Ahead, Harper made out the green upland valleys of the interior; they could only be a matter of three or four minutes from the portal.

Harper heard a long sigh and turned his attention to the Vetch.

The alien had sunk back into the sling, and from the headrest the dazzling golden nexus crept across the Vetch's unkempt mane. Kreller made a sound more like a gasp and his body spasmed as if in ecstasy.

Janaker glanced at Harper. He nodded, apprehension clenching the muscles of his stomach.

She sprang from her seat, crossed the flight-deck in three strides, and slid a hand under the Vetch's leather jerkin. Seconds later she held up a small silver oval device the size of a flattened egg. She retreated to her seat beside Harper, sweat coating her broad face.

In the sling, Kreller twitched as he melded with the ship.

With trembling fingers Harper reached into his jacket and withdrew his ferronnière. He looped it around his head, then paused and turned to Janaker. A thought occurred...

"What?" she asked, her eyes wide.

He smiled at her. "You must take me for a complete fool, Janaker."

"Harper, what the hell...?"

"How do I know that you're telling the truth, about any of this, the Weird, the 'super-weapon'...?"

"Harper, I thought you'd agreed..." She glanced through the viewscreen, desperately. "Look, are you going to...?"

He said, "I want to read you. I'll be quick, a matter of seconds. Remove your shield, and Kreller's, and put them both out of range."

"Harper!" Her eyes bored into him, hate filled.

"Do it."

"Fuck you!" she spat, then stood abruptly, reached into her jerkin and pulled out her shield. She strode across the deck, placed her shield and the Vetch's in a recess and returned, standing over him.

"Okay," she said, "get this over with, Harper."

He closed his eyes and scanned.

He skimmed through the fiery nova of Janaker's mind, encountering fragments of thoughts, memories; he read her dislike of the Vetch, and her horror at what Commander Gorley had told her about the Weird. He saw the images of the Weird that Gorley had shown her before she set off on the mission: hideous bloated creatures similar to those he'd seen in the clearing, and stick-thin homunculi.

He read enough, in seconds, to know that everything she had told him about the threat of the Weird was true.

He opened his eyes, nodded, and Janaker strode to the recess and snatched up her shield. Instantly the flare of her mind abated.

He passed on, mentally approaching the alien territory of the Vetch's mind with trepidation. He knew he would have to immerse himself in the maelstrom of Kreller's mind more fully than he would in the mind of a human: in the latter, the territory was familiar, the landmarks, as it were, known to him from many past encounters. Now he was in an alien land, where the geography was inimical, threatening in its incomprehensible originality. There were, however, pointers he could grasp, signs that were common to all sentient organisms: the visual images that populated the Vetch's sensorium. By latching onto these he could navigate his way through Kreller's psyche, and even ascribe emotions to certain recalled images.

Instantly he was blasted by an encounter Kreller had had with a human commando many years ago, and the resultant rush of feeling Harper read then was hatred. He saw Kreller mating, and felt the corresponding alien sensation of love or affection. He even caught fleeting images of Janaker in the alien's mind, and realised that her dislike of him was reciprocated.

He searched for images of his transformed ship, and any indications of the Vetch's future plans for it...

He recoiled suddenly. At first he thought that the Vetch had set up some sort of mental defence to repulse anyone, any telepath, who came looking for clues as to the Vetch's intentions regarding the super-weapon. He mentally backed off, rebounded, and then dived back in – knowing that he had found something, some indication that all was not as it seemed.

Something pulsed in the core of Kreller's mind – not a defence mechanism set up to repel an intruder, Harper realised now, but something... *other*. He probed, curious but at the same time wary. He realised, suddenly, that the thing was growing, expanding, taking up more and more room in the alien's mind, in fact *becoming* the alien.

He tried to break into this other mind, but his probes slipped around its edges. Then, as it grew and he probed again, a cascade of bizarre images burst upon him and he screamed in mental anguish.

He felt the Vetch fight back – not against him, Harper, but against the mental invader, the parasite, as it grew inexorably within him. He read a stray, terrified recollection in Kreller's mind: he saw images of a crashed alien starship which Kreller had investigated years ago...

Kreller was infected. The Weird parasite – alien beyond Harper's comprehension – was little by little assuming control of his mind and body. He probed again, repulsed by the Weird parasite's nascent mind, but catching Kreller's diminishing fear... Harper knew, in that second, what the parasite wanted – because Kreller suddenly, terrifyingly, understood, and that understanding manifested itself in a visual image. The Weird wanted the transformed ship, the super-weapon, and far from instructing the ship to attack the Weird portal it was relaying orders for it to pass through the interface and enter the dimension of the Weird.

Harper screamed, verbally this time, and withdrew his mind from the terrible Vetch/Weird amalgam that Kreller had become. Through the viewscreen he saw mountain peaks flash by, saw the land below come ever closer as the ship angled down towards the valley where the Weird had their portal.

"Harper?" Janaker stared at him.

"Kreller's infected! He's taking the ship through the portal... Give me your pistol!" The only hope, he knew, was to kill Kreller where he lay, twitching as he was being taken over by the parasite in his head.

Janaker said, "A Weird parasite? You're sure?"

"I read it!" he screamed in frustration. "Give me your pistol!"

She hesitated, staring at him. "How do I know...?"

"He's infected, damn you! He's taking us through the portal!"

She unholstered her pistol, still hesitant, and Harper grabbed it from her.

He stood over the Vetch, aiming at the alien's chest so as not to damage the golden nexus that encompassed Kreller's head.

He knew, once the Vetch was dead and removed from the sling, that he would have to take its place, meld with his transformed ship and re-issue orders – not to fly into the portal, but to unleash the super-weapon and destroy the Weird interface. *If* he could achieve control, that was.

Harper fired once, twice, the pulses drilling bloody holes into the massive chest. Kreller cried out in pain, spasming. Harper gestured to Janaker, and together they hauled the Vetch from the sling.

He took the alien's place, feeling the familiar, welcoming sensation of the sling adapting to his contours, almost embracing him. What was wholly unfamiliar, however, was the heat that quickly encapsulated his head, that filled him with its golden glow.

In his mind he heard *Judi*'s familiar, maternal contralto, and he almost wept as she said, "Den... What has happened? A miracle. I feel... empowered. But – the thing that was in control, alien beyond my understanding..."

He thought: *Gone now, Judi.*

Through the viewscreen he saw that they were still arrowing towards the valley at the centre of which, reduced by the distance but growing ever larger, was a great lake of opalescent light, a flat disc perhaps a hundred metres wide. He thought he discerned images beyond the milky membrane, monstrous shapes, but that might have been a trick of his subconscious providing visible nightmares to accompany his fears.

As the ship tipped, he saw Janaker slide past him and fetch up against the console, brace herself against its housing and stare out in fear at the imminent impact.

He felt himself meld with the vessel, become one with it; he felt as if he could flex his muscles and the ship would respond, as if he could direct a thought and a corresponding program would obey his command.

He thought: *Judi, ignore all previous instructions and pull out of the dive.*

"Affirmative."

The opaque portal grew larger, and around its perimeter he made out bizarre shapes – the bloated flying vessels he had seen earlier, the embryonic humanoid figures that had issued from it, and great adipose protoplasmic horrors that dragged themselves across the ground on gelatinous pseudopods.

The ship screamed towards the portal, and just when Harper thought that impact was inevitable the scene beyond the viewscreen changed: blue sky and mountain peaks filled the screen as they accelerated away, and he flung back his head and yelled with heartfelt relief.

"That," Janaker said shakily, "was way, way too close."

"And now," Harper said, "we go in again."

She stared at him. "Are you mad?"

"I might be at that," he said, "or supremely rational."

Judi, he thought, *am I able to command the weapons system as I can command your flight?*

"Affirmative."

In which case bank and approach the portal again, but this time don't go in so close, and ready the system to fire.

"Understood."

Judi rose and made a long, graceful curve through the air. He saw lofty peaks sail by as they turned, swooped, and seconds later the nestled green valley came into view again.

"Harper?" Janaker said.

He told her what he had instructed *Judi* to do. "Hold on tight."

She braced herself against the console and stared out.

They dived, at a shallower gradient this time, coming in over a series of low peaks and approaching the portal from the south. Far below, a dozen bloated flying vessels rose into the air and turned to face the approaching ship.

One of them fired something, and then another and another.

What looked like globules of silver-grey metal hurtled towards ship.

What are they? Harper asked.

"Whatever their constituents," *Judi* replied, "they will prove ineffective."

Seconds later, as two dozen projectiles arced towards them, as many golden needles bristled from *Judi's* nose-cone and lanced towards the valley. They struck the ballistic missiles and exploded in dazzling starbursts.

Harper sensed *Judi* almost chuckle as she reported, "Acid, Den. Potentially dangerous if it were to breach our defences."

They accelerated towards the portal, and more acid projectiles hosed up towards them, and *Judi* responded in kind.

Judi, Harper thought, *at your leisure, take aim at the portal and fire*.

"Affirmative."

He saw Janaker grip the edge of the console, white-knuckled.

Seconds later the ship bucked as a great golden column of light lanced from the nose-cone, temporarily blinding him. He blinked, and as his vision adjusted he watched the bolt of energy fall on the valley and strike the portal. They peeled away, and he instructed *Judi* to patch images of the resultant destruction through the viewscreen. A scene of serrated mountain summits and blue sky flickered, to be replaced with a view of the valley: he saw a pall of steam, slowly rising, and when it lifted he expected to see... what? A crater where the portal had been, a gaping, fiery hole like the entrance to hell?

He strained forward in the sling, peering through the viewscreen.

The steam evaporated, and in its place was the opaque oval of the portal, seemingly undamaged.

His stomach turned sickeningly.

Judi, he thought, *turn and approach and fire again*.

They made a second approach run, and when *Judi* fired he sensed that the pulse lasted a little longer this time. The beam of blinding light plummeted, struck the portal and created another mushrooming roil of superheated steam. *Judi* peeled away, and Harper stared at the viewscreen and the portal now in their wake.

He cursed and gripped the sling's frame.

Yet again the portal was pristine, pearly in the light of the afternoon sun.

And then, as he watched, a series of vessels emerged from the light – not the bloated, semi-organic ships this time but craft seemingly manufactured of plate metal and plastiglass.

The leading ship fired a dazzling blue laser lance, and seconds later *Judi* rocked.

Judi? Report damage.

"Negligible," she responded. "I am effecting immediate repairs."

Very well. Let's get out of here. Make for the lake. Land close to the long-house and prepare for a swift phase out on my orders.

"Understood."

They accelerated and left the valley in their wake.

Janaker stared at him. "You know what this means, Harper? If even the finest Vetch weapon can't touch the Weird's portal..."

He nodded, not wanting to consider the consequences.

The viewscreen showed the scene to the rear of the ship. A dozen and more Weird vessels were trailing them from the valley.

Judi, take offensive action.

Golden beams lanced out, struck the leading ship.

He saw an explosion, and when the smoke cleared he saw that the beam had struck a shield. The ship ploughed on, inexorable.

He ordered *Judi* to split the viewscreen between fore and aft, and in the right of the screen he made out the welcome sight of the placid lake and the collection of huts along its shore.

When we land, Judi, how long will we have before the Weird ships come within firing range?

A second later she responded. "Approximately three and a half minutes."

Would that give them time to get the colonists aboard the ship before they phased out?

Janaker paced the flight-deck. "We'll be cutting it fine, Harper."

He stared at her. "We can't leave them here!"

"I never suggested that, did I?" she snapped. "But you do realise, don't you, that potentially some of them might be infected?"

Of course he realised, and her words brought to mind Teplican and the alien ship, and Zeela... He pushed the thought away. "My priority now is to save the colonists," he said. "We can deal with that possibility later."

They came in low over the lake and settled in a maelstrom of sand.

Harper leapt from the sling and sprinted from the flight-deck. He jumped down the ramp into dazzling sunlight and ran across the clearing towards the long-house. The rickety timber door shuddered open and a knot of timorous colonists peered out.

He yelled, "Aboard the ship! Hurry!"

He looked out across the lake. In the distance, kilometres away but closing, was the fleet of Weird ships. He stood staring in fear, an island around which a river of Kallastanians flowed.

Someone ran to him, her face streaked with tears – and his heart leapt at the sight of her.

She halted suddenly before him, unsure how to greet him. She murmured, "Den... I, I thought you'd left me here."

He reached out, pulled her towards him. "As if," he said, "I'd ever do that."

The first acid bolt from the leading Weird ship fell short, hit the lake like a bouncing bomb and ploughed into the long-house at their backs. A hail of fragmented kindling peppered the fleeing colonists.

He gripped Zeela's arm and half-dragged her towards *Judi*. Behind them, the timbers of the long-house ignited and raged with flame.

They came to the old woman, struggling to climb into the ship. She caught his gaze with wise eyes and said, "Such violence."

He took her arm and assisted her the rest of the way. He began to say something, thought better of it, and turned to urge on the stragglers. The Weird ships were approaching at speed across the lake, and the leading vessel fired again. A bolus of acid ploughed into the blazing remains of the long-house, and a second hit the sand between the wreckage and the ship and bounced, missing *Judi* by a matter of metres.

Harper crossed the clearing, scooped up a child and grabbed the arm of its mother. They were the very last, and he almost dragged them across to the ship and in through the hatch. He climbed aboard after them and pushed through the milling crowd as the hatch sighed shut. Into his wrist-com he shouted, "*Judi*! Phase out now!"

"Affirmative. Ten seconds and counting..."

Zeela found him and they hurried to the flight-deck. Janaker was speaking urgently into her wrist-com. As Harper appeared, the bounty hunter said, "I'm instructing my ship to attack the Weird. It might gain us a few seconds."

Zeela stared at the Vetch's body, sprawled out on the deck. "What happened, Den?"

"I'll explain later."

He moved to the viewscreen and peered out. Janaker's ship powered up, a golden wasp turning on its axis and darting out over the lake. A ball of acid shot from the leading ship and hit the ground metres from *Judi*'s nose-cone. *Judi* responded with spokes of golden fire, and the Weird ship took a strike amidships and listed.

Seconds later Janaker's ship was blown from the sky before it had a chance to fire on the enemy.

Harper willed *Judi* to phase out. He felt a small, hot hand in his, and smiled down at Zeela's desperate expression.

Three Weird ships advanced over the ruins of the long-house, spitting acid as they came... and seconds later the idyllic lakeside scene, marred by violence, vanished and was replaced by the soothing grey immensity of the void.

HARPER AND JANAKER dragged Kreller's corpse from the flight-deck and stored it, at her insistence, in the cool-room. She said that she was going to talk to the colonists, tell them of the threat of the Weird and the fact that they were heading for Expansion territory. Harper considered what the colonists were leaving; after the Weird, he thought, anything would be preferable... even life in the Expansion.

It was something he too would have to get used to, and fast.

He returned to the flight-deck. Zeela was standing by the viewscreen, staring out. She turned when she heard him. "What now, Den? What's happening?"

He told her about the Weird, and the threat they posed, and the Weird parasites, and how he would work with the Expansion authorities to track down those infected.

She was silent for a time, leaning against the console and gazing down at her hands. At last she looked up and said quietly, "And me?"

He took a long breath and gestured to the seats at the rear of the flight-deck. He sat down on a lounger, and she came and sat beside him.

"Remember, on Vassatta... how you asked me to read your mind, to enter your head, so that I could read what you felt about me?"

She dropped her gaze, murmured, "How could I forget?"

"I had my reasons for not wanting to do that, Zeela. Good reasons."

"You feel nothing for me."

"It's not that at all," he said.

"Well, what was it?" She stared at him, defiant.

"Something happened a long time ago, something which affected me. Something which I never really managed to...."

She stared at him, her expression pleading with him to tell her.

He owed her this, he thought. To do what he was about to do was against everything his old self had counselled, and he knew it would be hard.

"Very well," he began. "Back in the Expansion... I'd been working as a telepath for five years, reading minds I'd rather not have read, immersing myself in the neurosis and psychosis of criminals and spies and sick, sick people."

Life had been hell back then. He had no friends, no family. No one trusted a telepath, and he rarely met his fellow telepaths – and on the rare occasions that he did, he found that they were as wary of him as was everyone else out there. He hated his job, disliked the organisation he worked for, and dared not look too far into the future for fear of losing his sanity.

"So," Zeela said, "you fled to the Reach."

He shook his head. "Not right then," he said. "First, I met a woman."

Her name was Sabine Legrange; she was tall and dark and beautiful, and he fell head over heels. It was his very first experience of love, of intimacy, and it transformed his life. Suddenly existence had purpose; there was no longer the endless prospect of corrupt minds to read for ever and ever – there was Sabine to love, and the miracle of the fact that she loved him. He had a future, and for the first time in his life he was happy.

Sabine worked in an administration department for the Expansion, handling sensitive government material on the world of Hennessy, which was where Harper had been trained for the past five years and where he was based. Because of her position with the government, she was shielded. A few months into their relationship, she offered to discard her shield briefly so that he could read her mind – get to know her fully.

Zeela was shaking her head as she said, "I understand now. You read her, and found something in there... found that she didn't really love you. And now... that's why you're so reluctant to read me, right?"

He shook his head. "Wrong, Zeela. I didn't take up her offer. I loved her, and I believed she loved me. As far as I was concerned, nothing could make our relationship any more perfect than it was. I didn't *need* to read her mind..." Perhaps, he thought now, he had been subconsciously afraid of finding something in Sabine's mind that might have corrupted the perfection of his love for her.

"Then what?" Zeela asked.

He touched her lips to silence her.

Sabine had a lot of free time from her job, and they travelled the Expansion together when he was sent on missions to read suspect minds on far-flung colony worlds. With Sabine at his side, with the love she showed him, he could take the stultifying routine of reading criminal minds, of immersing himself in the psyches of people he would rather not have even *spoken* to. Sabine made his working life bearable, and his free time a thing of wonder.

"What happened?" Zeela murmured.

They had been on the newly founded colony outpost of Zindell, out by Vetch territory, and he'd read the mind of a colonial official suspected of passing military secrets to the Vetch. It turned out that she was innocent, and he and Sabine stayed on a week, holidaying in the equatorial atolls.

"One night we met a government official in a bar, someone I recognised from college, though only vaguely."

The following day, the man contacted Harper and arranged to meet him – alone, he stipulated.

Suspicious, he met the man in the same bar... and it was there, in paradise, that his world, his future, came crashing down.

"The man told me that Sabine was a Minder – a government agent, in other words, whose brief it was to shadow telepaths, as an added security measure. She had Minded a colleague of his several years ago, until the colleague tumbled her, after which she'd vanished from the scene.

"But..." Zeela began, "but she said that you could read her..."

Harper smiled, bitterly. "Of course. She was playing my bluff. She knew me, knew I'd decline."

"What happened?"

He'd returned to the hotel, confronted Sabine, asked her if it was true – that she was a paid government Minder tasked to shadow him and ensure that he was loyal to the Expansion.

She denied it, of course. She put up a brilliant show of disbelief that he'd take the word of a stranger over her avowals of innocence; then she was outraged at his accusations, and then pleaded with him not to leave her.

They rowed bitterly, and he demanded that she remove her shield, let him read the truth.

He still recalled the hatred in her eyes as he'd asked this, and she had replied that she refused to accede to the demands of someone who did not *trust* her.

"We lasted as long as it took to return to Hennessy.

I was half deranged with doubt, veering from hatred of her to self-hatred. When we landed, Sabine just... disappeared without a further word."

He requested a transfer, and a week later was posted away from Hennessy.

But the rot had set in. Sabine had been his future, and now that was denied to him. Her love had been no more than a sham, every aspect of their relationship a cruel charade. She had used him, the Expansion was using him. It was then that he decided that he had to get away, and three months later the opportunity arose to steal a starship and flee to the Reach.

He was silent for a time, staring across the flight-deck at the marble grey void.

Zeela said, "But... but that's no reason to... to mistrust *everyone*, Den. And anyway..." She shrugged. "Has it ever occurred to you that you might have been wrong? That she was telling the truth?"

He stared at her. "Of course it had! I tried to persuade myself of that, even when I'd fled to the Reach. But, you see, later I found out that what my colleague had told me was indeed correct. Sabine was a Minder. More – she was a highly trained government operative."

She was shaking her head. "But how...? How did you find out?"

"Because," he said, and the words came with difficulty, "because a year after I fled the Expansion and set myself up on the Reach, I found out that they had sent someone after me, a bounty hunter... I faced a choice, flee for the rest of my life, or confront and kill the hunter. And I chose the latter, I drew the bounty hunter into a trap, and confronted... her."

She stared at him, wide-eyed.

"It was over in seconds. I had one chance to shoot my pursuer, but in the second before I pulled the trigger I saw that they'd sent Sabine after me."

And he had fired, filled with anger and rage, and killed her with one clean shot... and in the years after the event he had gone over and over the encounter and tried to relive the exact rush of emotions he'd experienced then.

Anger, and betrayal, and love... and then the desperate desire to survive.

"And since then," Zeela said, "you've remained alone, aloof, entire unto yourself..."

He smiled. "That's a rather poetic way of putting it."

"It's a line from a song I used to sing, back on Ajanta."

He said, "Is it any wonder, Zeela, that I was reluctant to let you in?"

She smiled, and shook her head, and stared down at her hands.

He wanted to weep; a vast pit of despair seemed to excavate itself in his chest. He had to tell her, of course. He had to...

She looked up at him. "Den, Den... Please believe me, you have nothing to fear from me..."

He stared at her, her upturned face, the tears welling in her eyes.

"Zeela," he began, "when we were on Teplican, we faced a very real danger..." And he silenced her murmurs of incomprehension and explained to her about the alien ship, and the parasites, and what Janaker had told him about the infected.

She listened to him in silence, her eyes wide.

"So..." she said at last, "I might be infected?"

"The chances are that you're not." He told her about Kreller's reading him, finding him free of the parasite.

"Zeela... before I found out about the parasite... please believe me when I say that a part of me, the part that knew that running away from what had happened all those years ago was wrong... that part of me wanted to read you."

"And now," she murmured, "now you *must* read me."

He reached out and stroked her cheek.

Her eyes were massive as she stared at him. "And... and if you do find that I'm infected?"

He shook his head, and could no longer stop his tears.

She took his hand and smiled at him. "I understand, Den. I understand that you must do it. Read me, and... and don't be afraid of what you might find in there, okay?"

He stared at her, trying to interpret her words as he drew his ferronnière from his jacket and slipped it around his head.

She sat back on the couch, took a deep breath, and closed her eyes. "Just do it," she said.

Harper activated his ferronnière and probed.

CHAPTER FIFTEEN

JANAKER FOUND IT hard to believe that just two weeks had passed since she had left her ship at the spaceport, taken the monorail to the government headquarters, and received her orders from Commander Gorley. So much had happened in that time; she had killed a hell of a lot of aliens... and brought the errant telepath back to the Expansion.

Now it was starting all over again. She was due a fortnight off, and then she would be sent on her next mission. This time, she hoped, not accompanied by an irascible telepathic Vetch.

She took he exterior upchute to Gorley's penthouse office and, as usual, was kept waiting.

She wondered why Gorley wanted to see her now. She'd made a long written report of her mission, detailing the chase and eventual capture of Den Harper. She wasn't due to embark on the next mission for another two weeks, and Gorley had set a date for the meeting prior to her departure to go over the details.

Twenty minutes later Gorley deigned to see her, and she strode into his office and stood over his desk.

Gorley sat back in his seat, steepled his fingers before his chest, and smiled up at her.

"Sit down, Janaker. A drink?"

She sat down, wondering at his sudden hospitality. "I'm fine."

Gorley gestured at his desk-screen, presumably at the report she'd sent him. "Excellent work, Janaker... The telepath, *and* his ship."

She glared at him. "It would have helped matters if I'd been told about the ship before we set off."

He spread his hands. "One of the provisos the Vetch stipulated when sharing the information about the ship with us was that as few people as possible should be told. In the event, things worked out well. You located Harper, and he proved his worth by detecting the parasite in Helsh Kreller."

She relived the frantic seconds as they hurtled towards the Weird portal. "It was touch and go, Gorley. If it hadn't been for Harper's last ditch efforts..." The mere thought of it brought her out in a hot sweat.

"And you had the foresight to put the Vetch's corpse on ice so that his people could perform an autopsy, and so back up your report. All in all, Janaker, excellent work."

"Pity that the fucking super-weapon didn't turn out to be so super after all."

He frowned. "Our scientists are working on ways to... improve its efficacy," he said. "But that in no way devalues the success of your mission."

"Is that why you dragged me all the way here, Gorley, to pat me on the head?"

"Just as sarcastic and bitter as usual, Janaker. I'm glad to see that your little sojourn to the Reach hasn't done anything to change you."

She smiled at him, mock-sweetly, "As if."

He leaned forward, "What I'd like to know," he said, "is how you found Harper?"

"Do you mean literally," she asked, "or on a personal level?"

"The latter," he said, "I have your report of the capture, after all. I'm curious... What is Harper *like*?"

She sat back in the chair and stared at the commander. "According to what you told me, he was an evil killer, a ruthless criminal made cynical from years of reading human minds."

"I sense a 'but' coming."

"But you were wrong. He wasn't like that at all. I found him quiet, reserved, but oddly sophisticated, cultured even. And compassionate."

Gorley widened his eyes in evident surprise. "Compassionate? You're talking about someone who cold-bloodedly killed the bounty hunter sent after him."

"We talked about that on the way back. He didn't kill the woman in cold blood. He was fighting for his life. It was self-defence."

Gorley looked as if he were about to say something, but stopped himself. He gestured. "So how did his... compassion manifest itself?"

"In a number of ways. He saved a girl from the aliens I mentioned in the report, the Ajantans. And later, when he scanned the Kallastanians we brought back... I watched him scan them one by one. It was obviously a painful experience, fearing what he might find, and then when he did find two individuals who were infected..." She shrugged. "I could see the pain this caused him." She hesitated, then asked, "Those two...?"

"They were separated from the other refugees on landing at the port here," he said, "and dealt with."

She nodded, "Humanely, I hope?"

He smiled his razor-thin smile. "Of course. They weren't told of their condition, merely given a meal, a drink which contained a painless poison. The remaining refugees are to be relocated, together, on an agricultural world in this sector."

Janaker nodded. "Harper knew the pair were infected, and asked if they might be spared, quarantined somehow. But I think he knew what you... the authorities... would say to that." She shrugged. "His part in the process caused him... pain, let's say. He's far from the cold-blooded killer you assume him to be. Also," she went on, "he told me that he intended to set aside a portion of his monthly salary in order to pay for the treatment of a friend of his, an engineer affected by a form of alien parasitism. The cure will be expensive, but Harper is determined to help his friend. That's the kind of person he is, Gorley."

"I'm looking forward to meeting this... paragon," he said.

She felt she had to defend the telepath. "Considering his upbringing, his conditioning, and everything he went through after having the cut and reading corrupt minds... I'm amazed that he has turned out to be the kind of person he has. I put that down to his experiences on the Reach," she finished.

"He was one among thousands of individuals who are tested psi-positive and have the operation every year. They serve loyally without absconding and then killing our operatives."

She smiled, sarcastic. "He told me about who you sent after him," she said. "And the phrase 'mental cruelty' comes to mind."

Gorley leaned forward, enraged. "You know nothing about the situation, Janaker! She was sent because she was the obvious person to do the job. She knew him, knew how he thought, could second-guess his reactions."

And got herself shot as a result, she thought.

She sat back. "Is that why you brought me here, to ask about Harper?"

Gorley appeared to calm down by degrees. He looked from his desk-screen to her, and then said, "That, and to give you a little information about your forthcoming mission. I want you to meet your next partner, get to know the individual."

She groaned inwardly. "Not another Vetch?"

He smiled. "I'll spare you that, Janaker. No, I think you'll find your next partner more... amenable, let's say."

He turned the screen to her, and she stared with surprise at the revealed image. A small, blonde woman smiled out at her, her hair pulled back, a ferronnière bisecting her high forehead.

Well, she thought, this certainly beats being paired with an alien as ugly as the back-end of a dog...

"Aimee Deschamps," Gorley said. "A telepath, fresh out of training school. This will be her first mission. You're to go to the world of Nova La Paz, where we have our suspicions about a number of high-up officials. If you work well together, your partnership will be made permanent."

Janaker nodded. "She looks young."

"Twenty-two," he said, "and inexperienced, which is where you come in. I'll introduce you tomorrow, and give you the details of the case. After that, you can get to know each other a little."

Just a little, she thought? Not if she had anything to do with it...

Gorley glanced at his wrist-com. "Now, if you'll excuse me, I'm due to meet Harper in a little under an hour and introduce him to his new team."

Dismissed, she rose from her chair and strode from the office. As she took the downchute down to the street, she smiled at her reflection in the glass wall and contemplated the immediate future. Things, she decided, were looking up.

She found the closest bar, hitched herself onto a bar-stool, and ordered a beer.

THINGS HAD CHANGED little in the years Harper had been away from the Expansion. After the ramshackle appearance of societies in the Reach, Hennessy's World appeared ultra-modern, the buildings soaring and sleek, the transport systems – the monorail that serviced the spaceport, and the inner city slideways – fast and efficient.

And all of it, he thought, under threat from the encroachment of the Weird.

He stood in the sunlight at the edge of the spaceport, an armed guard standing a discreet distance away. Even though he'd been tagged earlier that day – a subcutaneous tracker pumped into his left bicep – they obviously thought it wise to keep him under surveillance here at the port.

A big golden ship, as sleek as some massive bird of prey, stood fifty metres away. The guard had led him from the terminal building, across the apron towards the vessel, and Harper guessed that this was the ship that would be home for the foreseeable future.

He would miss *Judi*. On their return to the Expansion, it had been appropriated by the military and – with the aid of Vetch engineers and scientists – stripped of the weapons system so that bigger, more advanced versions might be developed. He had said a silent goodbye to *Judi*, but not before downloading the content of her smartcore to an array of data-pins, which he'd compressed and uploaded into his wrist-com.

A sleek black roadster approached in a long arc from the terminal building. It slowed and settled to the tarmac and three figures climbed out. One was an Expansion official in the severe black uniform of a commander, while the other two – a tall man and a shorter woman – were garbed in typical spacer uniforms.

The guard cleared his throat and gestured Harper forward.

The commander was small, rodent-like, and introduced himself as Commander Gorley. "Welcome back to the Expansion, Harper," he said, with heavy irony. He remained with his hands firmly clasped behind his back.

"I wish I could say that it's good to be back," Harper responded, looking not at the commander but at the beautiful starship.

"You'll be working, for the next six months at least, with Captain Carew and Co-pilot Takiomar," Gorley said. "You'll be replacing the telepath they worked with, who was shot dead in the line of duty on Bayley's World."

"Welcome to the team," Carew said, taking Harper's hand. He was a tall, severe looking man in his forties, hatchet-faced and deathly pale, who smiled sincerely as they shook hands. His co-pilot was a small woman with slanting eyes, long black hair and dark skin which reminded Harper of Zeela.

"In a little under a week you'll be heading for Lucifer's World at the very edge of the Expansion," Gorley told him. "We have intelligence that suggests the Weird plan to open another portal there, with the help of infected local officials. We'll meet tomorrow with my security team and go over the details. Before then, Captain Carew will show you around the *Hawk*."

Carew and Takiomar moved towards the ramp, but Gorley stopped Harper by gripping his upper arm. The commander gestured for the spacers to climb into the ship, then turned to Harper.

There was a look of barely concealed loathing on the face of the Expansion man, and his next words explained why. "The operative you murdered on Rhapsody..."

"It was self-defence, Gorley–"

"Don't worry, Harper," Gorley interrupted, "I'm not going to have you executed for your crime, just yet. For the time being you are too valuable to the Expansion. But let me assure you that, once this affair is over and the Weird are defeated, I will personally ensure that you pay for what you did."

Harper stared down at the commander. "Sabine Legrange tried to kill me, Gorley. I was fighting for my life. What do you think I should have done, lay down my pistol and let her drag me back here to be executed? Or let her shoot me on the spot? If anyone is responsible for her death, it's the bastards who sent her after me."

Gorley smiled. "She was doing her duty in attempting to bring a miscreant – and enemy of the state – to justice. You murdered her, Harper, and I will not allow your crime to go unpunished. Bear that in mind over the course of the next year or two. I'll be watching you."

Harper said, "I got away once, Gorley, and I'll do it again. If you want me dead, then you should do it now. Go on... As I walk up the ramp, draw your pistol and shoot me in the back." He smiled at Gorley, then finished, "It was what Sabine would have done, given the chance."

The Expansion man stared at him, hatred in his eyes. "Sabine was a fine woman, Harper."

"She was a ruthless Expansion killer," Harper said.

"She was," Gorley said, "my daughter."

Harper looked into the small man's face. His expression was rigid, wiped of all visible emotion. He was glad, then, that he was unable to read the commander's mind.

He said, "I loved your daughter, Commander Gorley. You cannot begin to imagine my pain..."

Gorley said, "Oh, but I think I can, Harper."

He opened his mouth to respond, and found himself saying, "I'm sorry..." and at the same time hating himself for doing so.

And with that he turned quickly and strode towards the golden ship, feeling as if a target was imprinted between his shoulder blades. Unbidden, as he stepped onto the ramp and began the short climb, images of Sabine came to him – but Sabine during the time they had been lovers: Sabine in his arms, smiling at him and declaring her love, Sabine naked as they made love, Sabine stroking his hair as they sat and watched the sun go down.

He closed his eyes, reached the top of the ramp, and paused. He stood there for ten seconds, allowing Gorley ample opportunity to carry out the extra-judicial execution. Then he turned and stared down at the Expansion man. Gorley turned quickly and hurried towards the waiting roadster. Harper entered the ship.

Carew gave him a short conducted tour, and thirty minutes later they stood on the flight-deck with Lania Takiomar and drank ice cold beers as they stared out across the port.

"I've heard all about you, Harper, and so that we get off on the right footing I want you to know that we – Lania and myself – are no lackeys of the Expansion. Before we were coerced into the fight against the Weird, we ran a ship hauling contraband across the Expansion."

Lania smiled as she sipped her beer. "Among other things," she murmured.

"I applaud what you did in getting away from the Expansion," Carew went on. "I'm sure you'll be happy aboard my ship." He raised his glass. "To the success of our mission on Lucifer's World," he declared.

Harper and Lania raised their bottles and drank to that.

He stared through the viewscreen and briefly considered the tortuous events that had brought him to this point. Then he dismissed the past, as best he could, and thought about the future and what the next few months might hold in store.

EPILOGUE

HARPER CLIMBED FROM the cab and stood before the dome that sat on the headland overlooking the falls. The sun was going down, its last rays illuminating the spume of the waterfall. Nightbirds wove through the star-filled night, their crystalline song filling the air.

He took the path around the dome and leaned against the rail, staring down at the turbulent water. For all its modernity, for all that it was the hub of the hated Expansion, Hennessy's World was idyllic.

Who would have thought, a mere week ago, that he would be back here so soon, and contemplating working for the Expansion once again? He considered Gorley's threat, and far from feeling apprehension at the commander's malign promise, considered it yet another obstacle to be overcome. He was sure, when the time came for him to face the assassin, he would rise to the challenge.

For the past few days he and his new team had been briefed about their mission on Lucifer's World. Half a dozen officials on the planet had been suspected of being infected. It would be Harper's job to read them, identify those harbouring the Weird parasites, and leave the rest up to the accompanying security team.

After that, he would return to Hennessy's World for debriefing and a month of rest and recuperation.

He had rented the dome for a year, with the option to renew the lease after that time. It would be pleasant to come home to his possessions, which he'd had transferred from *Judi* that week. The Expansion was paying him a generous wage, and the work should not be *too* onerous.

He entered the dome and stared around at his tapestries, his shelved books and music needles.

The sound of singing brought a smile to his lips.

"Zeela?"

She appeared in the doorway to the bedroom and smiled across at him. She wore a short yellow dress, its body-hugging material contrasting with the mocha of her skin.

"You're home early!" she said.

"My last evening here before we phase out in the morning," he said. "How could I be late?"

They ate at a restaurant overlooking the falls, the occasion touched with sadness.

"I'll miss you, Den," Zeela said as they drank and stared out at the massed core stars above the waterfall.

He told her that he would miss her, too.

He took her hand and said that he'd be back in a month or less, and that in the interim she'd have her singing to occupy her time and attention. She'd successfully auditioned for a slot at a nightclub in the city, and would start work there next week. Harper's only regret was that he would not be here to watch her first performance.

As they walked back home around the headland, Zeela said, "And if you find that the Weird are trying to open a portal on Lucifer's World...?"

"Then it will have been well named," he laughed.

She punched him. "Seriously!"

"Then the combined human-Vetch navy will be called on to bombard whatever might issue from the portal," he said. "That's all they can do, given the failure of the so-called 'super-weapon' to destroy the portal on Kallasta."

"But by that time you'll be well away from there, won't you?"

He squeezed her hand and assured her that he would.

They arrived back at the dome and leaned against the rail, staring out at the stars above the thundering waterfall.

"I'm so happy, Den, and yet the threat of the Weird is so real..."

He pressed a finger to her lips. "Don't let the Weird spoil what we have," he whispered, "or they will have won the battle already."

He took her hand and led her into the dome.

ERIC BROWN

Eric Brown began writing when he was fifteen, while living in Australia, and sold his first short story to *Interzone* in 1986. He has won the British Science Fiction Award twice for his short stories, has published over forty books, and his work has been translated into sixteen languages.

His latest books include the SF novels *The Serene Invasion*, *Satan's Reach*, and the crime novel *Murder by the Book*. He writes a regular science fiction review column for the *Guardian* newspaper and lives near Dunbar, East Lothian.

His website can be found at
www.ericbrown.co.uk

'Eric Brown spins a terrific yarn.'
SFX on Guardians of the Phoenix

Eric
Brown

WEIRD SPACE
THE DEVIL'S NEBULA

UK ISBN: 978-1-78108-022-1 • US ISBN: 978-1-78108-023-8 • £7.99/$7.99

Ed Carew and his small ragtag crew are smugglers and ne'er-do-wells, thumbing their noses at the Expansion, the vast human hegemony extending across thousands of worlds... until the day they are caught, and offered a choice between working for the Expansion and an ignominious death. They must trespass across the domain of humanity's neighbours, the Vetch – the inscrutable alien race with whom humanity has warred, at terrible cost of life, and only recently arrived at an uneasy peace – and into uncharted space beyond, among the strange worlds of the Devil's Nebula, looking for long-lost settlers.

NO MAN'S WORLD

BLACK HAND GANG

PAT KELLEHER

UK ISBN: 978-1-906735-35-7 • US ISBN: 978-1-906735-84-5 • £7.99/$9.99

On November 1st, 1916, nine-hundred men of the 13th Battalion of The Pennine Fusiliers vanished without trace from the battlefield, only to find themselves stranded on an alien planet. There they must learn to survive in a frightening and hostile environment, forced to rely on dwindling supplies of ammo and rations as the natives of this strange new world begin to take an interest. However, the aliens amongst them are only the first of their worries, as a sinister and arcane threat begins to take hold from within their own ranks!

 WWW.ABADDONBOOKS.COM

Follow us on Twitter! www.twitter.com/abaddonbooks

UK ISBN: 978-1-907992-15-5 • US ISBN: 978-1-907992-16-2 • £7.99/$9.99

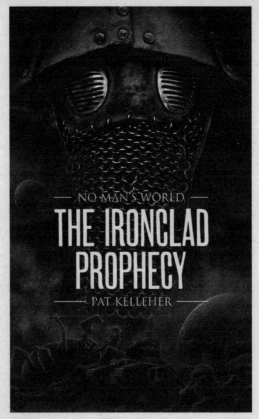

— NO MAN'S WORLD —

THE IRONCLAD PROPHECY

— PAT KELLEHER —

Three months after the Pennine Fusiliers vanished from the Somme and found themselves stranded on an alien world, Corporal 'Only' Atkins and his Black Hang Gang are sent to track down the HMLS Ivanhoe, the Battalion's tank, currently exploring the wilderness and days overdue. The encampment is coming under attack by the alien Khungarrii, and the tank may be their only hope for a decisive victory. Fighting for their lives against the mounting horrors of No Man's World, Atkins and his men - and their alien prisoner - uncover an abandoned edifice, and a terrible secret. They must bring their discovery, and the tank, back to the base, but their only hope for survival - and a way home - lie in the psychotropic fuel-addicted crew of the Ivanhoe... and its increasingly insane commander!

WWW.ABADDONBOOKS.COM

Follow us on Twitter! www.twitter.com/abaddonbooks

UK ISBN: 978-1-78108-024-5 • US ISBN: 978-1-78108-025-2 • £7.99/$9.99

'Meticulous historical detail, with a pulse-pounding pulp plot.'
RED ROOK REVIEW ON BLACK HAND GANG

— NO MAN'S WORLD —

THE ALLEYMAN

— PAT KELLEHER —

Four months after the Pennine Fusiliers vanished from the Somme, they are still stranded on the alien world. As Lieutenant Everson tries to discover the true intentions of their alien prisoner, he finds he must quell the unrest within his own ranks while helping foment insurrection among the alien Khungarrii. Beyond the trenches, Lance Corporal Atkins and his Black Hand Gang are reunited with the ironclad tank, Ivanhoe, and its crew. On the trail of Jeffries, the diabolist they hold responsible for their predicament, they are forced to face the obscene horrors that lie within the massive Croatoan Crater. Above it all, Lieutenant Tulliver of the Royal Flying Corps soars free of the confines of alien gravity, where the true scale of the planet's mystery is revealed. However, to uncover the truth, he must join forces with an unexpected ally.

 WWW.ABADDONBOOKS.COM

Follow us on Twitter! www.twitter.com/abaddonbooks

FEATURING ORIGINAL STORIES BY

James Lovegrove // Paul Cornell // Nancy Kress
Allen Steele // Adrian Tchaikovsky // Robert Reed
Norman Spinrad • // Nick Harkaway // Kay Kenyon
AND MANY MORE

EDITED BY
IAN WHATES

SOLARIS
RISING 2

THE NEW SOLARIS BOOK OF
SCIENCE FICTION

'One of the best SF anthologies published this year,
there's almost nothing here that isn't good or outstanding.'
Gardner Dozois, *Locus* on *Solaris Rising*

UK ISBN: 978-1-78108-087-0 • US ISBN: 978-1-78108-088-7 • £7.99/$8.99

Solaris Rising 2 showcases the finest new science fiction from both celebrated authors and the most exciting of emerging writers. Following in the footsteps of the critically-acclaimed first volume, editor Ian Whates has once again gathered together a plethora of thrilling and daring talent. Within you will find unexplored frontiers as well as many of the central themes of the genre – alien worlds, time travel, artificial intelligence – made entirely new in the telling. The authors here prove once again why SF continues to be the most innovative, satisfying, and downright exciting genre of all.

 WWW.SOLARISBOOKS.COM

Follow us on Twitter! www.twitter.com/solarisbooks

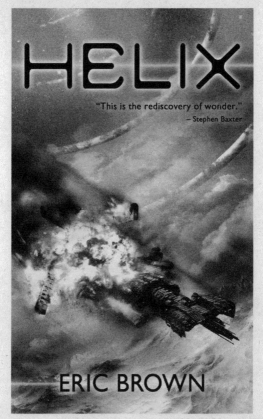

HELIX

"This is the rediscovery of wonder."
— Stephen Baxter

ERIC BROWN

ISBN: 978-1-84416-472-1 • £7.99/$7.99

Five hundred years from its launch, the colony vessel Lovelock is deep into its sub-lightspeed journey, carrying four thousand humans in search of a habitable planet.When a series of explosions tear the ship apart, it, it is forced to land on the nearest possible location: a polar section of the Helix – a vast, spiral construct of worlds, wound about a G-type sun. While most of the colonists remain in coldsleep, the surviving crew members of the Lovelock must proceed upspiral in search of a habitable section. On their expedition they encounter extraordinary landscapes and alien races, meet with conflict and assistance, and attempt to solve the epic mystery that surrounds the origin of the Helix.